PRAISE FOR
EMBRACING THE DEMON

"What a rush! This sexy, intense page-turner swept me away!"
—*Carolyn Crane,* USA Today *bestselling author*

"*Embracing The Demon* is fun, sexy urban fantasy that will appeal to readers looking for a strong female lead. Dale Highland is kickass and snarky, the plot is dark and twisty, and the action sequences are top-notch."
—*Rysa Walker, author of the* Delphi Trilogy

"*Embracing The Demon* is a thrilling, sexy, dangerous ride of a book. Count me as Team Dale, one hundred percent."
—*Nik Korpon, author of* Queen of the Struggle

"*Embracing the Demon* felt both darker and somehow more transcendent than Dale's introductory story. The plot's focus on one group against a perceived "other" resonates in the current political climate, yet is universal enough to feel timeless. The final paragraphs left my heart in my stomach, but I also need to know how Dale will face the latest revelation. Can she continue to embrace her humanity while facing the challenge of protecting the demons who look to her as Amara's successor?"
—*Jodi Scaife, Fanbase Press*

A DALE HIGHLAND NOVEL

EMBRACING THE DEMON

A CALIFORNIA COLDBLOOD BOOK
RARE BIRD BOOKS
LOS ANGELES, CALIF.

A DALE HIGHLAND NOVEL

EMBRACING THE DEMON

BETH WOODWARD

THIS IS A GENUINE CALIFORNIA COLDBLOOD BOOK

A California Coldblood Book | Rare Bird Books

453 South Spring Street, Suite 302

Los Angeles, CA 90013

rarebirdbooks.com

californiacoldblood.com

Set in Minion

Cover design by Leonard Philbrick

Credits: D-Keine, Evdokimov Maxim, rabbit75_dep

Printed in the United States

Distributed by Publishers Group West

Publisher's Cataloging-in-Publication data

Names: Woodward, Beth, author.

Title: Embracing the Demon / by Beth Woodward.

Series: Dale Highland Series

Description: Los Angeles, CA :

California Coldblood, An Imprint of Rare Bird Books, 2018.

Identifiers: ISBN 978-1945572845

Subjects: LCSH Demons—Fiction. | Fantasy—Fiction. | Paranormal fiction. | Paranormal romance. | BISAC

FICTION / Fantasy / Paranormal. | FICTION / Fantasy / Romantic. | FICTION / Fantasy / Urban.

Classification: LCC PS3623.O6832 E43 2018 | DDC 813.6—dc23

DEDICATION

To Jason

Have I told you today how much I love you?

PROLOGUE
John

I WASN'T DEAD, BUT THAT WAS just a technicality.

I lay on the rocks beneath Zamorski House. I couldn't move. It took all the energy I had just to draw air into my lungs. When I closed my eyes, I could still see her, her face crumpling in shock and pain at my betrayal. She was long gone now; she'd been carried off the roof by one of Amara's people. One of *her* people. But it didn't matter. That image of her face would haunt me as long as I lived. Which wouldn't be much longer.

It started to rain.

I wanted to laugh, because it was just my luck: I'd survive the fall off the roof, only to drown in a few inches of rainwater because I couldn't move. I managed to turn my head to the side, coughing and sputtering. But it was enough to keep my nose and mouth cleared.

I don't know how long I was there. It could have been minutes. It could have been hours. But I heard footsteps approach from the forest. I heard a woman calling my name. "Dale?" I whispered.

But even in the dim light, I could tell that the woman wasn't Dale. She was taller and thinner, blond to Dale's auburn-haired. I recognized her immediately; she'd been wearing the same face the last time I'd seen her, when she dropped one of my closest friends from the sky.

"You killed Isaac," I hissed.

"I did my job," Rebekah said coldly. "Gabriel is dead?" I didn't reply, but she took my silence as confirmation. "Good." Then she picked me up and began to run.

"Let me go!" I shouted at her with everything I had left. "I don't want you to save me." What I didn't know was whether I didn't want *her* to save me…or whether I didn't want to be saved at all.

"I can't!" She stopped then, right in the middle of the forest, in an area that was probably still crawling with Amara's people. She brushed my cheek. "You're our leader now."

———————◇———————

SHE TOOK ME TO A hidden compound that served as a secret base for the Thrones, a militant guild of angels that run the show in the supernatural world. They believe in keeping the bloodlines pure—angels with angels, demons with demons, humans with humans—but if Rebekah was to be believed, I was now their leader.

Me. A part-blood angel.

The compound stood on the edge of the Allegheny National Forest. Once upon a time, it had been the Honeymoon Hideaway Resort, a luxury destination for couples akin to the resorts in the Poconos and the Catskills, but closer to home if you lived in western Pennsylvania or Ohio. But the resort had fallen upon hard times and closed down back in the 1990s. The Thrones bought the property some years later, the old resort abandoned and decayed. (It was the height of human arrogance: to build something and then leave it to rot—as if they had an unending supply of world to conquer.) We restored the property, taking it back to the way it had looked in its 1960s heyday, with its wood paneling and plush carpets. It served no purpose but to give the place an ambiance that most humans would probably call "retro," but I knew the angels who designed it didn't see it the same way. When you're facing immortality, it can be comforting to come to a place that makes you feel as if the world hasn't changed quite so much around you. For me, though, it wouldn't have mattered if they'd mimicked the 1960s or the 1760s; the world had shifted too much, too many times, for me to ever feel like I had a foothold.

The medical bay was set up in what had once been an indoor miniature golf course. They'd taken out the putting greens but left the obstacles behind, including stacked dice the size of a nightstand and a fiberglass bear that looked more like a mutated dog. The orange-and-green carpeting and the overpowering aroma of rubbing alcohol gave the place a dizzying, surreal quality, and I found myself closing my eyes to stop the room from spinning. The patient beds were lined up along the walls, three on each side. Only two were occupied: mine, and the bed two down from mine.

The medic took an X-ray, reset my dislocated back, and then shrugged his shoulders and told me to wait. The supernatural approach to health care has always been, "If you don't die, you'll get better." Medicine isn't exactly a lucrative career for a species that lives forever, and I was almost certain that this particular practitioner hadn't even made it through a first-aid class at the local YMCA. Still, there was some truth to it. Either I would heal, or I wouldn't. Either I would walk again, or I wouldn't. And as far as I knew, there wasn't a whole hell of a lot they could do about it either way.

I waited.

I learned the rhythm of the ward. The florescent lights buzzed from six in the morning until midnight, when they were turned off for the night, making it difficult to get much real sleep. They served breakfast precisely at seven, lunch at noon, and dinner at six. The medic who worked the daytime shift watched soap operas in the room adjacent to the ward, and the medic who worked the overnight shift watched cooking shows. I did not watch anything, because there was no television in the patient area.

One of the medics was kind enough to give me some books to read. Romance novels. They reminded me of her—of Dale.

Dale Highland. A cunning half demon I'd been tasked to kill. She'd been my greatest quarry, evading me from city to city as she left a trail of bodies in her wake. I thought she was a monster, but when we met, I discovered a fractured soul on the run from her own past.

Dale was *good*. She'd probably deny it, but Dale was one of the best, kindest people I'd ever known, despite the body count she'd amassed. She was an incredibly powerful half demon subject to supernatural blackouts she called Rages. Under certain stressful circumstances, Dale would lose consciousness and control, slaying whatever threatened her—or her friends. That meant Dale's victims were always the worst of the worst.

Rapists. Abusers.

I'd thought Dale was a monster. It turned out she only killed them.

But that didn't matter to Dale. She only thought about the people she killed when her Rages manifested. I guess being raised by humans endows you with a peculiar kind of moral compass—murder is murder, no matter the victim.

But I hadn't been raised by humans, and I'd killed too many in my life to be bothered by the deaths of a few rapists or abusers. I saw the people she saved, the ones she protected.

I thumbed open a romance novel and thought about the bookstore where she worked. I'd bought dozens of these lurid penny dreadfuls just to have a little more time to talk to her. At the time, I'd told myself that it was to gain intelligence on Amara and to assess the threat level Dale presented, but it wasn't. I sought her out because, even then, she intrigued me.

The other patient was a man named Elijah. I tried to speak to him, but he wouldn't talk to me—or maybe he couldn't. The medics spoke of him in hushed tones. They didn't know what was wrong.

And then one night he started screaming. "It burns! Get them out!"

I expected the medic to come running, but he didn't. I craned my head toward the side room and saw that it was empty. Damn. "It's all right, Elijah," I said to him in the most comforting voice I could.

"I can feel them! They're in my skin!"

"He'll be back soon. Everything is going to be just fine."

Minutes crawled into hours, and his screams faded into sobs.

BETH WOODWARD

Then he spoke again. "They're getting to my brain. Burrowing. I can't do this anymore. I need to make it stop…"

His tone frightened me—the desperation, the finality. I didn't have much time. More importantly, *he* didn't have much time.

The feeling in my legs had started to return, but slowly; I could still barely twitch my toes. I pushed myself as close to the edge of the bed as I could and then rolled to the floor, using my body weight for momentum. The cast on my back restricted my movements, but I crawled over to Bartholomew's bed, dragging my useless legs behind me, ignoring the rug burns that scraped my palms and elbows.

The bed was probably only twenty-five feet away, but it might as well have been a million. As I reached the side of his bed, Bartholomew's cries grew louder, more frantic. "It's okay…I'm coming!" I called through panting breaths.

"I can't!"

"Just…wait."

I grabbed the metal frame of his bed and used it to hoist myself up, grasping and pulling until I was in a roughly upright position.

But I was too late.

It was a pen, a stupid pen that someone had left on Elijah's bedside table without thinking twice. He'd taken it and stabbed himself through his eye, digging it in until it couldn't go any deeper. Blood dripped down his face onto the white pillowcase below. His body was still twitching, but I knew he was gone. I no longer felt the telltale buzz in my skin that told me another supernatural was nearby. To my power, a dead angel was nothing more than meat.

Finally, the medic returned from his break. He saw me first. "John, what are you doing? You know you're not supposed to be—" He froze when he saw Elijah's body. "Oh God. Oh shit. I need to…I should…call someone." He ran into the side room, leaving me clinging to Elijah's bed.

I didn't know if I had the energy to get back to my own bed, and it felt wrong to leave Elijah here alone, so I kept holding on to his bed, staring at his body. The blood didn't bother me; I'd been the Thrones' pet assassin for too many years for it to register. What unsettled me was the look on Bartholomew's face.

He had died smiling.

CHAPTER ONE
Dale

YOU KNOW IT'S GOING TO be a bad day when a dozen people try to kill you before breakfast.

I was living in Nawdown, Kentucky, near the Indiana border. It wasn't so much of a "town" as just a convenient place to stop off of I-71, sandwiched in the no-man's-land between Louisville and Cincinnati. I worked at Griddles n' Grits, a twenty-four-hour diner that served nothing but breakfast food. Didn't matter if you walked in at noon or two a.m., you were getting pancakes. Or waffles. Or eggs. And everything with a side of grits. If you wanted anything resembling lunch or dinner, you were stuck going down to Gino's Authentic Italian Pizzeria down the street (which was run by a guy named Travis, who had never been to Italy and had never met anyone named Gino, but whatever). Since Gino's only opened at 11:00 a.m. and closed by 9:00 p.m., we got all the early-morning and late-night traffic off the highway.

I worked the overnight shift, eight at night until four in the morning, when the early crew came in to set up for the breakfast rush. We had a few regulars, mostly big rig drivers who ate quickly and then showered at the truck stop next door. But occasionally, I'd get someone who sat at their booths for hours, nursing their bottomless cups of coffee without a word, and then would leave me a twenty-dollar tip right at the end of my shift. I think they were lonely. I understood.

Griddles n' Grits hadn't been redecorated since the 1980s, and it showed in the wood-paneled walls and the vinyl-covered chairs patched with duct tape. The ghosts of old cigarettes seemed to haunt the places, even though it had technically been nonsmoking for years—though I suspected Sally, the owner, cheated when we weren't looking.

It was early December. Christmas music played over the speakers, and Sally had decided the best way to get into the holiday spirit was to string lights all over the diner. For eight hours, I had to squint at my order pad because, shockingly enough, twinkle lights weren't great to read by. As usual, my relief was fifteen minutes late. My shoulder-length brown hair was falling out of its ponytail, the pads of my fake glasses were digging into my nose, and I had a tension headache. I wanted nothing more than to go home and go to sleep.

Tyler, one of the line cooks who also worked the overnight shift, met me at the door. "Can I drive you home?"

"That's all right. But thank you."

He frowned at me. "It's twenty degrees outside, with a wind chill of twelve, and you don't have a car. I don't want to come in tonight and find out that you've frozen to death on the side of the road because you refused to get into my car. I also have an extra pair of gloves, if you want them. I noticed you didn't have any tonight."

"Anne, honey, come here for a minute. I think you've got something on your coat," Sally called to me. It took me just a second too long to respond. Anne had only been my name for three months, after all.

I went behind the counter, and Sally proceeded to brush some invisible lint off my coat. She was about fifty, with bottle-blond hair and lipstick in every shade of the rainbow. She lowered her voice. "I know it's not really my place to give you advice, but honey...take that boy home and fuck his brains out!"

"Sally!"

"Shush!" She glanced around to see if anyone had heard me—as if I were the one just talking about hot and crazy sex in the middle of a family restaurant. "He's cute, and he's obviously crazy about you."

"He's being nice. He knows I don't have a car."

"He's flirting with you." I frowned, and Sally gave me a sympathetic look. "He seems like a decent enough guy, anyway. He wouldn't pressure you into doing anything you don't want to do. And you know if you don't use them, your lady parts will just shrivel up down there. I'm not kidding. I've seen it happen."

I glanced at Tyler. He *was* cute, with brown hair that seemed to perpetually flop into his eyes and a permanent smile on his face. He'd only been working at Griddles n' Grits for two weeks, and I didn't know much about him except that he seemed to laugh all the time. Every time I walked into the kitchen, he and the other cooks would be chuckling at some joke I hadn't heard. There was a lightness to him that I envied. I liked him, in spite of myself. My life had taught me that it wasn't a good idea to like people.

"He's just so *young*," I said to Sally. He couldn't have been more than twenty-two. I was twenty-nine going on a hundred.

"He's old enough to know where to stick it. That's the important thing. Besides, the younger ones are easier to train."

"He does have gloves." My coat was a thrift store find, but I hadn't had the time or money to buy gloves or a hat. I'd had some when I'd lived in Minneapolis, before I'd moved here, but I had to leave rather…suddenly. Certain sacrifices had to be made.

I rolled my eyes and walked back up to Tyler. I took the gloves he offered and we headed out the door together. We walked through the gravel parking lot to a red Volkswagon Jetta. Tyler opened the door for me. "Thank you for taking me home," I told him as he got into the driver's side.

"You're welcome." He turned on the engine and set the heat to full blast. "Of course, you do know that if we get stranded out here in the cold with no food, all this chivalry goes straight to hell. It'll be full-on Donner Party shit then. I do not deal with hunger well."

I couldn't help it. I laughed. It sounded dry and rusty. "I'll consider myself warned."

"Good. Just so we're on the same page."

I shook my head, still chuckling. "All right, Sir Galahad, so what's your story? What are you doing in Nawdown, Kentucky?"

"Ah, well, you know. The usual. I graduated from the University of Michigan in May. I couldn't find a job back home in Kalamazoo, and after four years of school, I wasn't sure I was ready to stuff myself into a desk job, anyway. So I thought, 'Why the hell do gap years just have to be for rich people and Europeans? I'm going to go on the road and find myself.' Like that guy in *Into the Wild*, you know?"

"Did you actually watch that movie? It didn't turn out too well for him."

"Yes, I have seen *Into the Wild*…and I read the book. His problem wasn't so much the 'finding himself' part as it was 'freezing to death in the Alaskan wilderness.' And you'll be relieved to know, I have no intention of going to Alaska. If I'm going to leave the continental United States, I'll go to Hawaii. I could totally make my living as a cabana boy, don't you think?"

He batted his eyes at me. I snorted. "Good luck with that. But you still haven't explained how you ended up in Nawdown."

"Ah, yes. Well you see, Inga and I were making our way south…"

"Inga?"

"Yes." He stroked the steering wheel. "Inga. My girl."

My head was spinning. "Isn't Inga a Swedish name?"

"Shhh!" He put his finger to my lips. "We don't talk about that. Inga's a little sensitive over the fact that she's not…" he lowered his voice to a whisper, "…a Volvo. Anyway, so we were on our way to Nashville when Inga broke down. Who knew a twenty-year-old car with two hundred and fifty thousand miles would just *die* like that?"

"Shocking!" I was starting to get caught up in his enthusiasm.

"I know. But the good news is, Inga is all fixed and better than ever." As if to demonstrate, he put the car into gear and pulled onto the road, revving the engine once we got onto the dark street. "The bad news is, I'm pretty much broke now."

BETH WOODWARD

"So you ended up stuck in Nawdown."

"I don't know if 'stuck' is the right word. I mean...I *did* finally get the prettiest girl in Griddles n' Grits to let me drive her home, so that's something." He reached over and took my hand, never removing his eyes from the road. "I'd say Nawdown's looking pretty good right now."

Two minutes later, we pulled into my driveway. I had rented the basement apartment of a modest Cape Cod-style home that had passed the "seen better days" stage twenty years ago. The biggest advantages were that it had its own entrance, so I rarely saw the people who lived in the upper half of the house, and that it was only a fifteen-minute walk from Griddles n' Grits. Tyler parked on the street and, before I could say anything, ran around the car to open my door again. When we got to the entrance of my apartment, I hesitated. "Would you like to come in? I have hot chocolate."

A big grin broke across his face. "That sounds great."

The ad for my apartment had called it a "luxurious, spacious finished basement." It was neither luxurious nor spacious, and its claims on being "finished" were iffy at best. The floor was still cement, uncovered beams lined the ceiling, and bare light bulbs illuminated the space. When I'd pointed this out to the owner as I toured the place, she'd called it "industrial chic"—which told me only that she'd been watching too much HGTV. But whatever. It was cheap, and that was what mattered most.

Tyler sat down on the futon, and I stepped over him into my "kitchenette"—a four-foot-wide space with a sink, a refrigerator that looked like it had been designed for Barbie dolls, and a microwave. A hot plate and an electric kettle rounded out my appliances, which meant that my food intake was pretty much limited to ramen noodles and Bagel Bites. Industrial chic, indeed. Some days, I would have given my right lung for a pasta cooker.

I hit the button on the electric kettle. Then, I opened a cabinet and took out two packets of instant hot chocolate mix. As I shut it, it fell off one of its hinges. I jammed it back into place, hoping Tyler hadn't noticed.

By the time I got back to the futon with our mugs, Tyler had made himself comfortable, wrapping one of my blankets around himself. "Is it always this cold in here?" he asked.

"It's only been this bad since the temperature dropped. It was actually pretty nice in the fall." As long as your definition of "nice" is somewhere between "Unibomber cabin" and "*Law and Order* crime scene."

Tyler took a sip of his hot chocolate and then set the mug on the end table, next to my oversized alarm clock. "So what about you, Anne-with-an-E? I've asked about you at work, but no one seems to know anything about you. What's your story?"

I was about to give him my standard answer—and then stopped. "Is that an *Anne of Green Gables* reference I just heard?"

"No, never…maybe…well, definitely. I have three younger sisters, and I babysat a lot. I might have read it once or twice…or maybe I have entire chapters memorized. Just don't tell anyone. I'll totally lose my man card." I chuckled, and he nudged my chin up toward him. "If you're about to say something like, 'I don't really like to talk about it' or 'it's not all that interesting,' please don't. I'm not trying to pry, I'm really not. I just want to know more about the beautiful girl I'm sharing hot chocolate with."

He stroked my cheek, and I turned my head and leaned in to the sensation. It had been *so long* since I'd let anyone in, so long since I'd felt… anything. I was lonely. I'd been lonely for most of the last twelve years. But for one brief shining moment in New York, I hadn't been. And maybe for one more night, here in Nawdown, Kentucky, I didn't have to be. "There was a guy."

"Ahhh." Tyler leaned back, ready to listen. To his credit, he didn't look any less interested when I didn't bother pretending that I was still a virgin, that there had never been anyone before him, blah blah blah.

"I was…really crazy about him. I'm kind of ashamed to admit how much." By the time I'd met John, I'd already been on the run for ten years. It had been the first time I'd really connected with someone since I'd been in high school, and the first time I'd fallen in love with a guy since…ever.

BETH WOODWARD

The fact that he was drop-dead gorgeous, with blond hair and eyes that reminded me of a lion, didn't hurt.

"You should never be ashamed of caring about someone," Tyler said.

"Maybe...I don't know. It just all happened so fast, and I really felt like he understood me, you know?"

John understood me, because he was just like me: half angel to my half demon. He was the one who'd told me I was a supernatural, the one who'd brought me into that world. For the first time, so many things in my life made sense: my inability to fit in, my Aunt Barbara's disdain of me, even the Rages—violent blackouts I'd been having since I was a teenager. He'd trained me and helped me tap into my powers. Everything I knew about being a demon was because of him.

"Lemmie guess," Tyler interjected gently when I stopped speaking. "He turned out not to be the kind of guy you thought he was."

I nodded, tears filling my eyes. "He did some really horrible things to my family." My mother, Amara, had been the leader of the demon world for thousands of years. John killed her. He'd killed my mother to satisfy a three-hundred-year-old vendetta. It had all been a ruse: his protectiveness, his helpfulness, even his feelings toward me. Every last bit of it had been to get close enough to my mother to kill her. "After what he did, I just...I couldn't stay. So I left. It's been about a year and a half now. And then three months ago, I came to Nawdown. And now I'm here."

"And now you're here." Tyler reached out and squeezed my hand. "And I'm glad."

The air between us became charged. I stood up, my mug of chocolate still in my hands. "You know what really sucks? For the first time, I felt like I belonged somewhere. I had friends, people I really cared about." That, too, had been a first. I'd worked to keep people at arm's length during my years on the run. But Nik Cohen, my roommate and my first real friend since high school, had a way of making people like her. And with Nik came Chaz, a comic book artist who'd been her BFF since time immemorial. I'd had lovers during my time on the run, no one particularly special or important, just guys who could scratch the itch with varying degrees of proficiency. But I'd never really had *friends*. Nik and Chaz showed me how much I missed that. Some days, I resented John more for making me lose them than for what he did to me personally.

Tyler stood up. He took my still half-full mug in his hands and set it down on the end table. "Well, maybe you could belong here for a while." He tucked a strand of hair behind my ear. "With me."

Then he kissed me.

His mouth was warm and tasted like chocolate, and he waited for a signal from me to deepen the kiss. When I gave it to him—by brushing my tongue against his lips—he didn't hesitated to open up and let me in.

He removed the mug from my hands and set it on the table. Then, he pulled me down onto the futon and kissed me some more. His cock pressed up against me, and I arched into it. He groaned and whipped off his shirt. I did the same.

He kissed his way down my chest, lingering at my nipple. I shivered. "Cold?" he asked. Before I could answer, he wrapped the blanket around my shoulders and pulled my body closer to his. "I'll keep you warm."

I closed my eyes and kissed him some more.

He wriggled out of his jeans, but hesitated when he got to the waistband of mine. "Is this…is this all right?" he asked.

In response, I reached into the drawer of my end table, pulled out a condom, and dropped in onto his chest. He flipped us around, so that he was on top and I was on the bottom. He rolled on the condom and thrust into me.

I moaned, reveling in the sensation of Tyler's body pressing into mine. If I couldn't help but think about the last time I'd done this—hard and frantic and desperate, in the backseat of a stolen car, with a man who was about to betray me—and if I couldn't stop a couple of tears from rolling down my face, well…that was only natural, right? Broken hearts don't heal overnight. And I hadn't realized how lonely I was until I wasn't alone anymore.

When it was over, Tyler retreated into the bathroom to take care of the condom, and I put my clothes back on. I smelled like bacon grease

BETH WOODWARD

and ashes, and suddenly I felt nauseated. When Tyler came out of the bathroom, I couldn't look him in the eye. "You should probably go now," I told him. "I'm covering the swing shift for Celeste this afternoon, so I should probably get some sleep."

He frowned. "Anne, did I—"

I put my hand up to stop him before he said the words. "You didn't do anything wrong. I'm just…kind of stuck in my head right now."

"Ah," he said. He voice was still surprisingly, achingly gentle. "Is this a 'it's not you, it's me' sort of thing?"

I gave him the best smile I could manage—which probably looked more like a constipated grimace. "I'll walk you out."

We walked out to Tyler's car, the sound of a lone cricket chirping through the night. Tyler's windows were covered in frost. He turned on the engine to de-fog them, and then leaned against the Jetta. "I know you're kind of blowing me off right now, but I wanted to tell you that I had a really good time."

"Tyler, I'm not—" But then I stopped. Because something was decidedly *not right* here, and I couldn't quite put my finger on it.

"Anne, are you all right?"

"I don't know. I think something's wrong."

He put his arms around me in a gesture that was probably supposed to be reassuring. "Anne, I know you're kind of freaking out right now, but you don't have to worry about anything. What happened here is just between you, me, and the crickets."

Crickets. In December. In subfreezing temperatures. The lone chirp had been joined by a chorus of others. "I need you to go back inside."

"Anne, what's go—"

I didn't have time to argue with him, so I reached out and grabbed his mind with my powers. "I need you to go back inside. There's an alarm clock on the end table, right above the condom drawer. Grab it, and then press the 'AM Radio' button over and over again until the clock reads 'five oh five.' Got it?"

I could tell he wanted to fight me, feel his resistance pushing against my mind. But his will was nothing against mine—and more than anything, I wanted to get him away from whatever was about to happen. His eyes glazed over, and he ran back into the apartment without another word.

The chorus of crickets grew louder. I stepped away from the car, scanning the area. Then, I heard a whizzing noise, and something pricked my neck. I reached for it and pulled what appeared to be a small, cylindrical dart with a pom-pom attached to the end.

And then the world faded around me.

I fell to my knees, fighting to remain conscious. It felt like someone was covering my eyes and ears, though I could see and hear just fine. The world had just shifted from three dimensions to two, and I couldn't get my equilibrium back. This was…not good. I struggled to stand up, my knees shaking with the effort.

Tyler ran to my side. "Anne, are you all right? What's happening?"

Shit. I'd told him to go inside, but I hadn't told him to *stay* inside. I opened my mouth to give him another command, and then I realized what was wrong. Even when I wasn't actively using my abilities, I could still touch the minds around me. I was so used to it that I scarcely even thought about it anymore. Tyler's mind had been flexible but solid, like one of those bouncy balls they used to sell in vending machines when I was a kid. But now I couldn't sense it at all. I pushed out with my abilities, trying to sense anyone or anything around me. I felt…nothing. My powers were gone. "Tyler, you need to run."

"What's going on?"

Shadows emerged from the tree line, maybe a dozen of them. They carried guns, all pointed straight at us. "Tyler, run!"

They fired. I ducked to the ground and rolled toward the nearest one, grabbing his ankle and yanking his feet out from under him. He tumbled to the ground, and I crushed his windpipe.

But the next two were on me already. I wrenched away from them, but not fast enough to avoid the bullet that lodged itself into my back, sending a wave of fire through my body. I knew instinctively that it was a fractal

BETH WOODWARD

bullet—a bullet designed to fragment and drift toward the heart or, barring that, poison a supernatural's body with liquid silver. I could feel it hitting my bloodstream already, making my limbs feel heavy.

One of my attackers stepped into the light, wearing black BDUs. I didn't know him, but I recognized his bearing: he looked like someone had made a *Jason Bourne and Green Beret* cocktail with a splash of *the Terminator* and a twist of *deep-seated bigotry.*

He was a Zeta, as in the Zeta Coalition. Imagine if the KKK targeted supernaturals—that's the Zetas, only better armed and better organized. And despite my best efforts to hide, they'd found me.

Shit.

Tyler screamed. He was in a ball on the ground, covered in blood, and two Zetas were beating him with their rifles.

I summoned all my anger and fear and protectiveness, and I felt a Rage growing inside me. I pushed myself to my feet. "Leave him alone! I'm the one you want." The Zetas attacking Tyler looked at me.

I took advantage of their distraction by lunging at the first one, knocking him off his feet. While he was down, I tore the rifle from his hands and shot him.

The other aimed his weapon at me, but I was faster. The bullet went through his head and came out the other side, leaving a trail of blood and ichor in its wake. I crouched in front of Tyler's shuddering form. "I'm so sorry. Just hold—"

I was struck from behind, the force cracking my skull. I tried to get up, but the blood loss and the silver had taken their toll. Bullets rained down upon me, explosions shattering the night. I fell.

I heard sirens in the distance. But it was too late for me. I was already dead.

CHAPTER TWO
Dale

I AWOKE TO A STEADY BEEPING noise. Everything hurt. I opened my eyes. I was in a hospital room, and the beeping noise was the sound of my own heartbeat on the monitor. I was covered in bandages, and wires came out of my body in every direction. An IV dripped fluids into my arm.

A nurse walked into the room. At least, I assumed she was a nurse by the name tag that said, "Mabel Vandenberg, LPN." But she didn't look like any nurse I'd ever seen. She was tall, probably close to six feet, with a solid frame. Her hair was perfectly styled into waves that fell to her shoulders, and her fingernails were painted the same bright red color as her lips. And instead of the comfy sneakers every nurse I'd ever seen wore, she had beige pumps on her feet. If it hadn't been for her scrubs with pictures of Tweety Bird all over them, she would have looked like she'd just stepped out of a World War II newsreel. I wanted to ask whether she had an aging portrait of herself hidden away somewhere, but I couldn't speak: there was a plastic tube stuck down my throat.

When Nurse Mabel saw me struggle, she stopped what she was doing. "Oh! You certainly don't need that, do you?" She came around to the top of the bed and grasped the tube. "I'm sorry, but this is going to hurt." Then she yanked the tube out. My gag reflex went haywire. I started dry heaving, and Nurse Mabel grabbed a trash can and held it in front of me in case I puked. I did not, thankfully. When I stopped heaving, Nurse Mabel set the trash can down. "How are you feeling?"

I felt like I'd been trampled by elephants while simultaneously swallowing broken glass. But since the alternative was "dead," I guessed I wasn't doing too badly. "All right."

"Let me tell you, Irene had a hell of a time keeping those human doctors from giving you the wrong doses of medication. If they'd had their way, you'd have been flying to the moon and back! Luckily, Irene can be very persuasive at times—and when she can't, Nurse Mabel doesn't mind a little bit of chart tweaking for the greater good..."

I felt dizzy, and I wasn't sure if it was the rapid-fire nature of Mabel's dialogue or the head injury I'd just received. I tried to sort it all: *I'm in a hospital. Nurse Mabel knows I'm not human. So does Irene. Who is Irene?*

But there was one question that stuck out above all the others. "Is Tyler okay?"

"Tyler? Was he the human who was brought in with you?" Her voice was crisp, businesslike, but when she saw my face, her tone softened. "No, I'm sorry. He didn't make it."

THE NEXT TIME I REGAINED consciousness, I heard Nurse Mabel's voice. "Covington called again. We need to get her back."

Another voice, one I didn't recognize. "I know that. But she's still fragile. I think the Zetas must have laced their ammo with silver."

"So irrigate her."

"I'm doing as much as I can. But the staff here is already beginning to ask questions, and my 'visiting doctor' cover is about as flimsy as a paper airplane."

"Then the best thing we can do is get her out of here."

"And we will. As soon as I can figure out the best way to get her out of the hospital without rousing suspicion and transport her eight hundred miles without killing her."

I opened my eyes. Nurse Mabel was arguing with a woman in a white coat. She was thin, almost too thin, with medium-brown skin and curly hair struggling to escape her ponytail. She looked like she was in her thirties, but she carried herself with the authority of someone much older. I'd learned a long time ago that appearances were deceiving in this world. When the woman in the white coat looked at me, she raised her eyebrows. "Oh. You're awake."

"Seems that way," I said.

"Do you know your name?"

"That is…a very complicated question."

The woman in the white coat looked like she was about to strangle me. "Fine. Do you know where you are?"

"I'm guessing I'm still in Kentucky, unless they moved me."

"Do you know why you're in the hospital?"

"Because a group of zealots tried to kill me." And then I remembered all at once. "They killed Tyler. He's dead because of me."

My heart rate spiked, and the woman checked my monitors. "That's good enough. Don't stress yourself. My name is Dr. Irene Kordova. You've already met Mabel. Covington sent us."

Fantastic. My rescue had finally arrived, but they were too late to actually *do* anything. I took a deep breath—or as deep as I could manage, anyway—and tried not to be bitter. If I'd expected Covington to be like Batman, always showing up right in the nick of time when bad things happen, that was on me.

Irene, oblivious to my distress, continued. "It's been about six hours since you were attacked. You sustained a head injury, but I don't think there's any permanent damage, and there's a lot of silver floating through your system right now. But you probably won't die. How are you feeling?"

"As long as I don't move or blink too hard, I'm fine."

BETH WOODWARD

A small, Asian woman came into the room, dressed in blue orderly scrubs, and shut the door behind her. I wasn't sure how she could be an orderly, considering she looked like she'd have trouble carrying a grocery bag. But what was more unusual was that she was armed to the teeth. I'd become very adept at spotting concealed weapons during my time with John—who wouldn't so much as go to the bathroom unarmed. This woman had at least two guns holstered to her hips, another near her right ankle, and two more tucked into a cross-body holster underneath her arms, all concealed by her baggy scrubs. She was hyper-alert, checking the room before she spoke. "Lot of cops out there."

Mabel looked thoughtful. "I guess that makes sense. She did kill five men before the Zetas brought her down. Even if they don't think she did it—which they probably don't, because humans are stupid like that—they'll want to know what she remembers."

Shit. Adrenaline surged through my system, and I managed to push myself into a sitting position. "I need to be gone before they can question me." Or take my fingerprints, or run a blood sample, or—God help me—test my DNA. I had no idea what the police departments of various localities had on record about me. What I did know was that for the last decade, I'd left a trail of dead bodies that would make Hannibal Lecter jealous.

"That's not the problem," the Asian woman said. "Problem is that they're really the damn Zetas."

Irene swore under her breath, while Mabel crept over to the door. When she opened it, she put her hand up in what looked like a "Halt!" gesture.

And everything outside the door froze—including the officer standing a few feet away. Mabel peered out. "There are more than twice as many as I saw when I came in the room."

"More have been coming to the floor for the last hour. I've seen Green Berets raiding terrorist strongholds packing less heat than these guys are."

"How the hell did the Zetas find her so fast?" Irene said.

Mabel slammed the door shut just as the "bubble" of frozen time she'd created burst, giving me that same ear-popping sensation of the cabin pressure re-normalizing in an airplane. She looked frightened. "Tina, maybe you should sneak out before they realize you're with us and bring the car around," she said to the Asian woman. "I can probably freeze—"

"Hell, no." Tina shifted her stance so that the guns at her hips were visible, though I think she was doing it more to prove a point than to intimidate.

Irene rolled her eyes. "We don't have time for this. We have to do this now. Mabel, grab her IV. She's still suffering from silver poisoning, and the last thing we need is for her to croak on the way back. Tina, help me transfer her onto a gurney."

The three women snapped into action. Mabel grabbed my IV bag and attached it to a stand with wheels on it, and Irene and Tina rolled out a stretcher that had been hidden behind a flimsy white room divider. Here I'd been thinking there was another patient over there.

They transferred me to the stretcher quickly but carefully. Even so, I felt like I was going to throw up all over them. Tina checked out the door again. "Coast is clear." They unlocked the wheels of the stretcher and pushed me out of the room.

We made it to the end of the hall when the Zetas swarmed us.

There were about ten of them, all still in their cop disguises. Tina had been right. They all carried assault rifles, and they wore full body armor and riot helmets. Not to mention that they had extra, large-caliber ammunition crisscrossing their bodies, like they were all on their way to audition for a production of Let's Kill Dale Highland: The Musical.

One of the Zeta/cops stepped out from the group. "Where are you taking this patient?"

Irene spoke in an authoritative voice. "I can't give out any information on our patients."

"This woman is a person of interest in the murder of Tyler Kellerman."

Of course I was. But Irene didn't even flinch. "That's not my concern. My job is to treat this patient to the best of my ability, which right now means getting her to the third floor for an MRI to determine the extent of her head trauma. You, sirs, are preventing me from doing my job, and I will file a complaint with the hospital board and your chief of police before you can say 'Miranda.'"

The Zeta/cop hesitated, and for a minute I thought he might let us through. Then, a nurse ran up behind them—a real one this time, with a hospital ID badge and actual sneakers on her feet. "Officers! These three women don't work for the hospital! I don't know where they're taking her!"

Oh, shit.

Mabel threw her hands in the air. The Zeta/cops in front of us froze.

We ran.

Thirty seconds later, my ears popped and the Zeta/cops unfroze. Irene turned around and waved her hands. Dozens of supply carts that had been lining the walls all overturned simultaneously, launching syringes and tongue depressors at the Zetas. Tina grabbed the guns she had hidden on her hips and fired at any of them who managed to make it through Irene's deluge, taking out three of them without missing a beat. We turned down another hallway, racing toward the elevator. "We need to move fast. That isn't going to hold them for long."

Alarms started to go off. Three more Zetas burst through the doorway of a stairwell behind us, taking aim at our heads. Irene waved her hands again, and the rifles flew into the air and broke in half.

That didn't stop them. They charged us. One of them grabbed something that looked like a grenade from his belt. "Watch out!" I shouted. Mabel turned around and froze the Zeta—but not before he'd pulled the pin on his grenade. Irene knocked the grenade back, while Mabel and Tina grabbed my stretcher and ran.

Several loud blasts went off in succession, flashing through the hallway and setting off the hospital sprinklers. "Is anyone hurt?" I asked. God, did the Zetas even *care* that there were other patients in the hospital—innocent patients who didn't know a damn thing about angels or demons or any of this?

Tina—who was the closest to my head—answered. "Just a flash bang. Nonlethal, just meant to disorient, so everyone's probably fine. Unless they were too close to the blast or got caught by shrapnel." Tina must have seen the look of horror on my face, because she followed up with, "But that's unlikely."

We made it to the elevators…only to find that several Zetas had beaten us there. At the same time, more of them emerged from the other hallways, surrounding us on all sides. "Shit," Irene said. "Mabel, can you freeze them?"

She shook her head. "Not all at once."

"All right, then we do the best we can."

The Zetas fired. Mabel froze as many of the bullets as she could, while Irene deflected the strays with her telekinesis. Tina, meanwhile, pulled out the guns she had hidden on her ankles and fired.

We might actually make it out. There was only one problem: no one had pushed the elevator call button. I reached behind me, but the button was just a few inches from the tips of my fingers. So I used what little strength I had to push myself to the very edge of the stretcher. I grazed the button with the tips of my fingers—just barely, but it was enough.

Tina had taken out six of the Zetas, but four more remained standing and firing at us. "I'm running out of steam," Mabel said. Sweat dripped down her face, and her hands shook badly.

"Just a little bit longer, baby," Tina replied. "Almost got it."

I don't know where the sudden surge of strength came from, but Mabel stood up straighter and froze the remaining four Zetas altogether. Tina stood up and shot them one by one, four perfect head shots. Since they were still frozen by Mabel's power, they didn't even bleed.

The elevator dinged.

Tina and Mabel pushed the stretcher inside, and Irene pushed the door close button frantically. When the doors finally closed, she slumped against the wall. Mabel closed her eyes and breathed in and out slowly; whether it was some kind of meditation technique or just to avoid passing out, I wasn't sure. Only Tina seemed unfazed as she reloaded her weapons. "Was that a Walther P22 you used on the Zetas?" I asked. She nodded. "Jo—I mean, my trainer tried to teach me to shoot with the same gun. I wasn't very good. I'm just surprised, though, because he told me that a twenty-

BETH WOODWARD

two-caliber didn't have enough power behind it to shoot through a stick of butter."

"He's right: a twenty-two shot doesn't have enough momentum behind it for a through-and-through. Wouldn't be my choice for a body shot. But if you shoot someone in the head, it'll bounce around in their brain and pulverize it." She slammed the magazine into the gun. "Looks like ground turkey after." Then she smiled, the first expression I'd actually seen on her face since she walked into my hospital room.

It was official: I was being rescued by psychopaths.

When we got outside, there was an ambulance parked in front of the building. Irene and Mabel loaded my stretcher into the back, while Tina got into the driver's seat. We'd barely made it out of the parking lot when two police cars got on our tail, sirens wailing. "Flip the siren on, Tina. We're going to need to make a speedy exit."

We sped up, and I heard the ambulance's siren wailing above me. The police cars followed. "Shit." Irene scanned the roadway from the back window. "With all the traffic, it's too dangerous to use telekinesis here."

"I could try freezing them," Mabel said. "Maybe if I focus on the cars rather than the people."

"Still too dangerous," Irene replied. "We'll just have to keep going. Tina, can you go any faster?"

"I'm trying!"

But every time we accelerated, the police cars kept pace. "Damn. We can't outrun them," Irene said. "They're just going to keep chasing us down until they can get a good shot at us."

"I might be able to do something," I said. I pulled myself off of the stretcher and dragged my body to the back window. Two Dodge Chargers were on our ass, lights flashing from their dashboards. *Just two*, I told myself. Two cars, two drivers. I could handle that.

I reached out with my mind, not knowing what would happen. I was just about to give up when I felt it—the telltale brush of minds against mine. I grabbed the two drivers. "Exit here. The people you want have gotten onto the highway." The two cars veered abruptly to the right, speeding up the ramp onto the interstate. "Tina, I don't know how long I can hold them, so move this piece of shit as fast as you can." Tina accelerated again, and the ambulance flew down the road.

I held the connection for another thirty seconds before it broke—probably not as long as I normally could have, but enough to get the police away from us. Tina switched the siren off and turned onto a side street, parking along the side behind a white van with "Pete's Plumbing" on the side. Tina hopped out of the front and ran to the van, while Irene and Mabel opened the back doors and positioned themselves on either end of the stretcher.

I hoisted myself back onto the stretcher—because I wasn't going much farther without it—and rested my body against the flimsy mattress. I felt like I'd just run a marathon.

Mabel said, "Hey Irene, is it normal for blood to be leaking out of her ears and eyes?"

"*What?*" Irene said. "Mabel, how could it be normal for blood to be leaking out of her ears and eyes?"

"I thought maybe it was a half demon thing."

"It's not an *anybody* thing. Here, help me."

They pushed me into the van, and then came the inevitable pricks of more needles.

"Don't let her die," Irene said. "Covington'll *kill* me."

Then I passed out.

CHAPTER THREE
Dale

I WOKE UP IN A RECTANGULAR room that looked like a cross between *One Flew Over the Cuckoo's Nest* and a Cold War-era nuclear fallout shelter, and smelled like it hadn't been used since then, either, all mildew and dust. The walls were made of cinder block and painted teal green—as if the cheery color could distract you from the fact that it felt like a prison. Metal grating covered the windows, giving the sunlight streaming in a waffle-like appearance. Old florescent lights buzzed from the ceiling. But the strangest part was the mural that covered the short wall closest to me. In it, a headless man rode on a horse through an old graveyard, carrying a pumpkin in his hand. It was probably an attempt to cheer the place up. It ended up being immensely creepy instead.

Someone had taken the casts off of me. An IV still dripped into my arm, but besides that there was no other medical equipment in the room.

The door opened, and Mabel walked into the room, wearing high-waisted pants and a fitted blue blouse. She'd pulled her brown hair back with a bandanna, giving the impression that she'd just stepped off of a

"Rosie the Riveter" poster. "Oh, good, you're awake. Irene didn't think you'd be up this soon."

I sat up. "Yeah, I'm just…admiring the artwork."

She grinned. "It's amazing, don't you think? Back when this place was a state hospital, this place used to be the children's ward. We're near Tarrytown, so I guess that's why they went with the Washington Irving theme. I think he was from around here somewhere."

"Tarrytown?" The name was familiar…too familiar. "We're in New York City?"

"Outside of the city, technically, but yes."

"Why the hell would Covington have brought me here?"

"Because this is where everything started," she said.

I had no idea what she meant, and, at the moment, it didn't really matter to me. Panic surged inside my chest. I had no idea whether John was in the city, or somewhere else altogether. But just thinking of him… "I can't be back here."

Mabel held her hands out in a soothing gesture. "Everything's going to be fine. I'll get you some food, maybe some chamomile tea…or a Valium, perhaps? The human version might not work in your system, but I'm sure Irene's got something calibrated to supernatural physiology…"

I put my hand up to stop her from speaking. "I just need to see Covington. Is he here?"

"Yes. But he's in a meeting right now."

I fought the urge to roll my eyes. "Can't you interrupt? I mean, I did just almost die and people are currently trying to kill me."

"There's a lot…" She bit her lip, as if reconsidering what she was about to say. "I'll see what I can do."

Mabel left the room, closing the door behind her. Based on Mabel's tone, I doubted she'd be able to get Covington away from his mysterious meeting, and the thought of being cooped up in that room any longer gave me the willies. The Headless Horseman? Did they really think that was going to make sick kids feel better? They might as well have painted the room with serial killers…or clowns.

BETH WOODWARD

Thankfully, someone had thought to leave me a change of clothes on the chair beside the bed—Mabel, I was guessing, since the sweatpants were several inches too long for me. A pair of flip-flops sat underneath the chair. Normally, I considered flip-flops an affront to decent footwear everywhere, but given the fact that the hospital smelled like it hadn't been cleaned since the Eisenhower administration, I decided I'd rather take my chances with crappy arch support than the floor.

When I opened the door, I heard voices coming from the other end of the building. I shuffled through the hallway as quietly as I could—which wasn't very, given that I still felt like I'd been run over by a midsize sedan and the fact that my flip-flops made suspicious crunching noises whenever they touched the floor.

When I got to the source of the noise, I found myself peering inside a large room. I peered in through the side of the entryway, hoping no one would see me. About two dozen people had gathered inside. Some sat in folding chairs, some stood, but almost all of them looked tired and uncomfortable. There was an observation room off to the side, about eight feet long with wired-glass windows, where nurses would have been able to keep an eye on unruly patients back in the day. One of the windows was almost completely broken, spider-web cracks shimmering from the remains at the edges. It looked as if someone had decided to give the safety glass a run for its money and hit it with a chair; I guess the chair won. I just wished I knew whether it was the hospital's *past* residents that had broken it, or its current ones.

Mabel stood on one side of the room, tapping her foot nervously on the floor. Tina, to my surprise, was not near Mabel. Instead, she had positioned herself near the back, weapons visible (four guns, holstered on her hips and ankles, and at least a dozen knives), on alert for any sort of violence. She stood like an MP. I thought about her Green Beret comment from the hospital and wondered if she'd been in the military at some point.

I thought Tina was playing door guard at first, but based on the angle of her stance and the direction of her stare, I realized she was more worried about what was going on *inside* the meeting than something *outside*.

In the front stood Covington.

Covington had been my mother's butler and doer-of-all-things. I'd met him eighteen months earlier when I'd found my mother. He was the one who'd gotten me a legal identity for the first time since high school—Dale Highland was there, whenever I wanted to pick her up again—and who had informed me before I left that everything in my mother's estate, down to the very last dust bunny, belonged to *me*. None of it had been enough to get me to stay.

Covington was one of the unlucky demons who would ultimately die of old age, a side effect of mixing with human DNA too many times. He looked like he was in his seventies, although from the way he talked I assumed he was much older than that. Every time I'd seen him, he'd been impeccable: his hair neatly combed, his clothes perfectly pressed, his skin just shaved.

Today, his skin was drawn and gray, showing the growth of a few days' worth of stubble. His suit looked like he'd slept in it, and there was a cowlick sticking straight up from the crown of his head. I think that was what got me: not the tension emanating from everyone in the room, not Tina's hyper-vigilant stance like she was waiting for a bomb to go off, but Covington's cowlick. A man who thought khakis and a polo was slumming it, was now doing his best Alfalfa impression.

What the hell was going on here?

Irene stood at the front of the room, talking to the group. "...so with the deaths this morning, we have 68 confirmed dead and another three hundred forty-three known infections. Of those, forty-two are currently under lockdown in this hospital, and two hundred twenty-six are in facilities in other parts of the world. The rest we haven't been able to contain."

A chorus of murmurs spread around the room. "You 'haven't been able to contain' them? Do you think that's good enough?" The speaker, a woman, seemed familiar, but I couldn't place her. She looked like the love child of Claudia Schiffer and Legolas—blond, thin, and gorgeous, with the kind of patrician features that reeked of the privilege that comes with walking into a room and knowing everyone will notice you. I disliked her immediately, and I wondered if I was so shallow that I just hated other women for the crime of being beautiful.

"No, we don't think it's good enough, but I don't know what other option we have," Irene replied. "I've opened up several clinics throughout the world, but many of the sick aren't close enough or can't travel. Their only options are to stay at home or go to a hospital and risk that their DNA get into human hands."

The blond sneered. "Well maybe you should try, you know, curing them." Nope, I didn't dislike her because she was beautiful. I disliked her because she was a bitch.

Covington jumped in. "That's exactly why we brought you here, Rebekah. The infection is spreading too rapidly for us to contain it, and none of the infected have survived so far. We know that the Zetas are behind the attack, but we have no idea how far-reaching the illness will become or how to begin curing it. Without more information, we are flying blind." Covington paused. "I'd like to reintroduce the idea of breaking into the Zetas' data haven, the Grave."

Murmurs broke out. A man stood up. "The Grave? We've already discussed this. That place is a glorified file cabinet, buried in the middle of nowhere. Why they guard it so jealously is a mystery. Infiltrating it is folly."

"The situation has changed," Covington said. "Amara's daughter is back."

Silence. Tense, uncomfortable silence. Finally, Rebekah spoke again. "Mr. Covington, with all due respect, I don't believe that Amara's daughter is the right person to help us with this endeavor. I've seen her, and I've seen what she can do. She may be powerful, but she's also uncontrolled—and control might be the *only* trait that matters if we break into the Grave." Shouts of agreement followed her statement, until she put her hand up and silenced them. "I agree we need to do more, but Amara's daughter is of no use to us."

It was her words that got me. I'd heard them before. A year and a half earlier, the Thrones—a group of powerful angels led by the now-dead Gabriel—had tracked me down at an amusement park where I'd been hiding out with John and our friend, Isaac. It was just one in a long line of games people had played of using me to get to my mother. Isaac—a part-blooded angel who'd been exiled from the Thrones for being "too human"—had refused to give me up. And the Thrones had dropped him from the sky.

And *this bitch* had been the one leading the charge.

I burst into the room. "You can't trust her!" I yelled. "She killed Isaac! She's a fucking Throne!"

Everyone turned and stared at me. In the front of the room, Irene glared at me, and in the back, Tina hovered her hands over the guns on her hips.

That's when I realized what a big mistake I'd made.

Every Throne I'd ever seen—with the exception of John—had worn an emblem somewhere on their body: the image of an angel holding a sword above his head, his face and wings engulfed in flames. Rebekah wore a pendant around her neck.

And at least half the people in the room wore identical ones.

I thought the room had been tense before. I was wrong. It had merely been one of those controlled burns, like the fire departments do at the beginning of summer to prevent larger wildfires. I'd just taken that controlled burn and dropped a shit-ton of nitroglycerin on it.

The room exploded.

"…the hell…"

"…is she really…"

"…she'll kill…"

"…thought she was…"

"…knew we couldn't trust…"

Covington tried to bring the room back to order, without much success. Finally, one voice emerged from among the rest, a dark-haired man sitting near the edge of the room. "Amara murdered my brother in 1898. She cut up his body and sent pieces of him to us through the mail."

"I'm sorry," I said, backing toward the door.

But others were already chiming in with their stories.

"She cut my mother's hands off!"

"Her people raided the stable where my breeder was living. My son was killed in the conflict."

As they shouted, the dark-haired man stepped toward me menacingly, his fists clenched so tightly the knuckles had turned white. "If Uriel can't be here, then neither should she."

He lunged at me, pulling a gun from the waistband of his pants. A shot blasted through the air. The dark-haired man fell instantly, a dime-sized hole in his forehead, a pool of blood spreading underneath him.

I looked at Tina, expecting her to be wielding the deadly weapon. But she had her gun lowered and was searching the room, trying to figure out where the shot had come from.

I felt him before I saw him. The whole room seemed to grow warmer as I heard his heavy footsteps behind me. The air smelled of butterscotch.

"She stays," John said.

CHAPTER FOUR
Dale

He wore a gray suit with a dark shirt and a blue tie. The suit was a coating of silk on his muscular frame that must've been custom tailored. His dark blond hair had been combed and gelled into submission. Normally, it stood up in random spikes around his head—not as a stylistic choice, but because he had the tendency to run his fingers through it nervously until it went in about fourteen different directions.

Until that moment, I hadn't been convinced he'd survived the fall off the roof of Amara's estate. I had nightmares about it almost every night: breaking through his shields with my power when I realized he'd used me and killed my mother and then John falling off the roof onto the rocks below. Every night in my dreams, I stared at his broken body, tears running down my face. I wasn't sure why I'd cried: because I had killed him, or because he had destroyed me.

But here was John, very much alive, looking like the fantasy of some billionaire boss about to have hot monkey sex with his secretary on the desk. He didn't look like the John I remembered, who'd spent most of our time together wearing blood-covered T-shirts. Which one was the real

John, I wondered, the suave businessman or the urban warrior? And then I noticed the pin on his lapel: a flaming angel that matched the ones on the others' pendants. John had declared his allegiance, and it wasn't to me.

"My apologies for the mess," he said. "Ephraim, Leah, please clean that up. Make sure you dispose of the body well. I don't want him coming back to haunt us one of these days." A man and a woman jumped out of their seats and scooped up the body, leaving just a puddle of blood behind. Guess they'd be getting that later.

John turned to the rest of the group. "Let's not forget why we're here. This illness is already devastating our community, and it's getting worse. The Zeta Coalition created it with the intent of wiping out supernaturals— angels *and* demons. And if we can't cooperate, they will succeed."

"She's the daughter of our worst enemy!" someone shouted.

"Amara is dead. And Dale is not Amara." He paused. "Covington is right. We need more information if we're going to survive this, and Dale is our best hope of gaining access to their records containment facility."

"What about taking an army and storming the compound, like we talked about a few weeks ago?" someone asked.

To my surprise, it was Tina who answered. "The compound is too heavily fortified, and its underground architecture would make it difficult to strong-arm. We've run the scenario many times, accounting for the different variables. The most likely outcome is that we'd end up trapped down there while the Zetas pick us off."

"There must be another way," a woman said.

"Maybe, but this is the *best* way," John replied. "We all know Dale can do things that no one else can. Her return may have been a coincidence, but we should use that to our advantage."

"I haven't *agreed* to anything yet," I managed to get out through gritted teeth.

John stared at me, a blank expression on his face, as if it wouldn't even *occur* to him why I might say no. We remained like that for an awkwardly long time, until he spoke. "Obviously, we have a few things to talk about.

EMBRACING THE DEMON   43

And I think Dale and I will need to discuss our…shared history before this conversation can go further. Would all of you mind leaving us for a while?"

"No," I said firmly. "Covington and Irene stay. Everyone else can go." Whatever was going on here, it was clear that those two were in charge of Team Demon right now. Plus, I couldn't stomach the idea of being alone with John right now.

When everyone except Covington and Irene had left, John turned and looked at me. "Hello, Dale. Is it still Dale? Or do you prefer something else now?"

His presence left me feeling dizzy, like someone was slowly sucking all the air out of the room. So I did the only thing I could manage. "What the hell, Covington?"

John raised his eyebrows. "You didn't tell her we were working together?"

"I didn't have a chance," he replied.

"You're working *together*? Are you kidding me?"

"Dale…" Covington's tone was stern.

"No. He killed my mother, Covington. He used me so he could kill my mother."

"I remember."

"Do you? Well, did you know that he fucked me, too?"

Covington was taken aback, whether by the vulgarity of my words or the content of them I don't know. John, for his part, kept his expression neutral. I turned to him. "I mean, I get it. Honestly. Hatfields and McCoys, Montagues and Capulets, angels and demons. Whatever. But what part of your supernatural grudge match involved making me care about you? Was it power? An ego trip? Or was it all a part of your stupid fucking vendetta because Mommy and Daddy can't tuck you in at night anymore? Well, guess what? Neither can mine. So I guess you have everything you want."

"You can't let your feelings about me prevent you from doing the right thing. The Zetas are trying to kill all of us."

I started to laugh. "Well, guess what? They'll probably manage to get me first. They've already tried twice."

All three of them stared at me. "This wasn't the first attack?" Covington said finally. "Why didn't you contact me then?"

"I thought it was a crime of opportunity. They have those supernatural detector things, and I just happened to be a supernatural in the wrong place at the wrong time." Not to mention the fact that going back to the supernatural world, being anywhere near John's radar again, had sounded about as appealing as performing a root canal on an alligator. "I was in Minneapolis. There were only three of them, and they jumped me on a dark street. I managed to get away, and I left the city."

"When was this?" John asked.

I didn't answer, so Covington repeated the question. "About three months ago. That's when I went to Kentucky. You think it's related to whatever you have going on here?"

John and Covington exchanged a look of silent communication.

I groaned. "See, that's it, that right there. Covington, I don't know what the hell has been happening for the last year and a half, but I can't imagine what would have prompted you to start an epic bromance with *the man who murdered my mother*, but it's gross. Seriously. If you start doing a secret handshake, I'm gone. I'll take my chances with the damn Zetas!"

"Dale..." John interjected.

I put my hand up to stop him. "No. I don't want to speak to you. As far as I'm concerned, you don't exist."

There was a long moment of silence. It was Covington who finally spoke again. "John, I think you should give Irene and myself some time with Dale to explain things."

John nodded. He walked to the door and hesitated, looking back at me. I thought he was going to say something, and I armed myself with every snarky retort I could think of. But instead, he left without another word.

I collapsed into one of the folding chairs. My head hurt. Hell, *everything* hurt. Covington sat down next to me. "John approached me about a year ago. He told me that he was the leader of the Thrones now, and that there had been an outbreak of a mysterious, deadly illness among the angels. I rebuffed him, said some unkind things, and he left."

"Obviously he didn't stay gone," I muttered.

"Not long after that, Dr. Kordova contacted me. She is a demon, and she's been specializing in the treatment of supernaturals for a very long time. She had seen the same illness John described. Purebloods and part-bloods alike could succumb, and there was no treatment."

"I was able to determine that the illness couldn't spread to or come from humans, and trace the origins of the outbreak to New York City, but I couldn't get any further than that without additional resources," Irene said.

"I contacted John again. By this time, they had captured a Zeta Coalition operative. The operative confessed that the Zetas had released the illness, but unfortunately, the operative…failed to provide any more information about the nature of the illness or how to treat it."

"That's putting it mildly," Irene interjected. "Those assholes tortured the hell out of him, and he broke like a cheap toy. Now all he does is rock back and forth, muttering about cuckoos."

Covington interrupted before her rant could go on any longer. "The Thrones have resources and organization that we lack. They made sure that Dr. Kordova had the funding and equipment to continue her research, and they purchased several sites around the world where we could house the sick in an environment where they'd be protected from humans. This illness is affecting demons and angels equally, and we can't do this in isolation."

I closed my eyes and sighed. "That's good for you," I said. "But you still haven't explained what any of this has to do with me."

Covington sat down next to me. "We're stuck. Without more information about the Zetas' plans or the illness's origins, Irene can't determine how to treat it."

"I'll continue to do research, but that could take years. Decades, even. These people don't have that kind of time," Irene said.

"Our intelligence indicates that the Zetas keep a records storage facility in Montana. Although it's remote, hundreds of miles from any other Zeta site, the employees there are under heavy surveillance. The first time I brought up the idea of raiding the facility a few weeks ago, I was voted down. The others felt it was too likely to fail. But that was before you came back. I think your power could make the difference between success or failure on this mission."

"I didn't come here to be a hero, Covington. I came here because I was *desperate*. I'm not part of this world anymore."

Irene rolled her eyes. Covington, however, seemed unfazed by my response. "There's something you need to see," he said.

———— o ————

COVINGTON, IRENE AND I WALKED down a dark, silent corridor. The smell of Simple Green cleaner permeated the air, which should have masked everything else, but it didn't. Vomit. Feces. Death. I felt like I couldn't breathe. "Covington…"

"Before you make any decisions, you need to see what we're facing."

I shook my head, but I didn't say anything else.

The doors had those little rectangular windows with wired glass, the kind you see in old elementary schools and every community center ever. But these doors had been modified so they were hermetically sealed. Not so much of a molecule of air could escape. Rows upon rows of hospital beds filled the rooms, with patients strapped down by their wrists and ankles. Mostly they were silent. Except the ones who were screaming. "From what we've observed, the disease progresses similarly to rabies in humans," Irene said. "Early symptoms are minor: a star-shaped rash that disappears within a week, possibly a low-grade fever. Most of the patients we've seen ignored those initial symptoms. Other symptoms appear two to four weeks later: headache, vomiting, excessive salivation, anxiety, confusion that later progresses to hallucinations. Once the disease reaches its final stages, the body becomes unable to regulate its biological processes. The infected either choke on their own saliva or blood or go into cardiac arrest, unless…"

Irene's voice trailed off. "Unless what?" I asked.

"Unless the hallucinations cause them to kill themselves first, which has happened in about twenty percent of the cases."

EMBRACING THE DEMON   47

I said nothing. I could now see some of the medical personnel through the window, taking the patients' vitals. They were covered from head to toe in what looked like radiation suits: white waterproof fabric, oversized hoods, plastic face masks. Any seams or gaps in the material were sealed shut with silver duct tape. "We don't know how the illness is transmitted," Irene said when she saw my face. "We have to take precautions."

"Precautions? Jesus, it looks like you're in the middle of an Ebola outbreak."

She shook her head. "Humans can recover from Ebola. With the right care and treatment, many of them will get well. So far, everyone infected with this illness has died. Everyone."

We continued walking until we emerged through the end of the corridor to the outside of the building. I sat down on a weathered bench in front of the door, taking deep breaths to clear the smell of sickness and death from my nose.

Covington tried to crouch down in front of me. When his joints made a loud cracking noise, he pushed himself up using the bench for support and sat down next to me instead. "This doesn't make sense to me," he said. "We're a race of the long-lived and the immortal. I turned one hundred seventeen on my last birthday, and I'm considered one of the unlucky ones. I am aging, slower than most humans, but still aging, and my time is almost up. But I've seen more and done more than most people ever will, and when I go, I'll be satisfied with a life well lived. But this…" He gestured toward the doors and the screaming, writhing infected behind them. "This isn't the way things are supposed to be. And you might be the only person who—"

"Don't," I said through gritted teeth. "The sick people, the plea for help…none of that changes the fact that you've betrayed my mother."

Covington's sharp intake of breath was the only thing that told me I'd scored a hit, but it was Irene who spoke. "It wasn't like that. I was the one who—"

Covington put his hand up to silence her. "I know you're hurt, and I'm sorry," he said to me. "The Thrones have contacts, facilities, and assets that we lack. But we have Irene, possibly the only doctor *in the world* dedicated

BETH WOODWARD

solely to the treatment and study of supernaturals. If we don't help each other, we'll all fail."

"I'm surprised the Thrones are even bothering with the sick," I muttered. "The Thrones exiled my friend Isaac when he was diagnosed with a brain tumor. He was too 'human' for them."

"Under John's leadership, the Thrones have become much more accepting of part-bloods." Irene folded her arms across her chest. "John challenges the old ideas about racial superiority. A lot of them hate him for it, but they obey him."

"Yeah, because he kills them if they don't! Hope you have a biohazard team to clean up that dead guy's blood puddle, because I don't think John's people are gonna come back for it."

Covington stood up, anger flashing in his eyes. "I served Amara faithfully for ninety years. She, more than anyone, understood that as a leader, sometimes you have to put your personal grievances aside—"

"I'm not Amara!" I shouted. "John killed Amara. But apparently *I'm* the bad guy for holding a grudge against the man who killed my mother. Well, guess what? This is not my fight. I didn't come back to save demonkind. I came back to *hide*. All I need is a safe place to stay until the Zetas get off my ass, and then I'll be out of your hair forever."

Both Covington and Irene fell silent. A gust of wind blew past, making me shiver, reminding me that it was December and I was wearing flip-flops. I hugged myself but said nothing.

Then, out of nowhere, Irene started to laugh. "Of course the princess doesn't want to help. What did you expect?"

"Excuse me? Who the hell do you think you are? You don't know anything about me."

"I think *I'm* the person who has been in the trenches, fighting this battle from day one. I was the first medical professional to document anything about this disease, and I was the one who alerted Covington. When Covington told me that the Thrones had contacted him about the same disease, I was the one who suggested we form an alliance. When human hospitals couldn't help our people, I set up clinics for them. When hundreds of our people get sick, I work into the night reviewing their blood work and X-rays and MRIs. And when they die, I autopsy their corpses and dispose of the bodies." Tears filled her eyes. "I watched my husband die because of this disease. He stabbed himself through the eye with a screwdriver when the hallucinations became too much. I hadn't been home for a week. I didn't even know he was sick." Her eyes filled with tears, but her voice was still livid. "So who do I think *I* am? I think I'm the person who gives a fuck. Which is more than I can say about you."

She stormed back inside, slamming the door behind her. Covington looked at me. "Dale…"

I shook my head. "I'm done."

CHAPTER FIVE
John

I RETURNED TO MY ROOM, IN another building across the hospital grounds. The other angels roomed on that side, as well, as far away from the demons as they could get without physically being in another building. Old grudges. Old wounds.

The other Thrones were housed in a dormitory-style room, twin beds lining the walls. When I walked in, everyone froze. All conversation stopped, their eyes following me. I ignored them, and crossed into the small room I'd claimed for my own, shutting the door behind me.

And breathed a sigh of relief.

My "room" was really just an old supply closet that had been coated with decades of dust and dead insects when I'd found it. It couldn't fit a bed, so I'd lined the floor with egg carton padding and threw a sleeping bag on top of it.

I knew it would be better to claim a bed outside, to sleep with my people, to build the cohesion and comradery we currently lacked, but I just...couldn't. I spent most of my waking hours pretending it didn't bother me that they looked at me like I was a stranger to them. Like I hadn't fought for them, fought *beside* them. Like I hadn't given up *everything* to create a better future for all of us.

I'd become a harsh leader, but I'd learned it was necessary. They'd been used to Gabriel's dictatorial rule, to my father's pretense to godhood. I was the first part-blood to lead the Thrones, the first to challenge the old guard.

Change takes time, I reminded myself. A year and a half is nothing when you have forever. But I couldn't fake it all the time. At least in here, crammed into my closet, I could take my masks off.

Dale would understand.

My back hurt. That was nothing new. For months after I'd fallen off the Zamorski House roof—long after I should have been completely healed—I'd been in enough pain that I'd resorted to taking human medications, even though they screwed with my system so much that I became nearly nonfunctional. Eventually, the pain subsided enough that I was able to wean myself off the meds, but it never went away entirely. I got so desperate that I went to see Irene Kordova, long before we'd started working together to combat the Zetas. She was a demon, but she was the only doctor I knew of who specialized in the treatment of supernaturals. I wasn't the first angel to seek her out.

"Everything seems to have healed just fine," she'd told me after she'd looked at my X-rays and MRI scans. "I'm not sure why you're still having pain. Could be arthritis, maybe. That's not something that supernaturals are known to get, but you never know exactly what you're going to get when you factor in the human DNA. But I didn't see any signs of inflammation."

"So it's psychosomatic?"

"Possibly." She tapped her pen against the side of the table. "It might help if you kept a log of when you were experiencing the pain, what you were doing, what you were thinking about, what you were eating, and so forth. Any details you could give me might be helpful."

I didn't need a log. I already knew. When I thought about Dale, my back hurt. I thought of Dale often.

As I was getting ready to leave the office, Kordova asked me to wait. "Is it true that Isaac Azizi is dead?"

"Yes." My back flared again when he remembered that day in the amusement park. I twisted until the bones in my spine cracked. "How did you know Isaac?"

"I can't discuss..." Kordova shook her head. "Well, I guess it doesn't matter now. I was treating him. I was trying to 'activate' more of his angelic DNA to override the cancer. I told him it was a long shot. The further away a supernatural gets from their pureblooded ancestor, the more complicated it gets. For Isaac to get the cancer in the first place, he must not have inherited the part of our DNA that causes quick healing and resistance to human afflictions. But I have this theory that you can splice..." She shuffled her feet and tucked a stray curl behind her ear. "Anyway, you don't want to hear about all that. Isaac said you were a good friend. I think he was lonely those last few years, after his family exiled him. So I just wanted to say that I'm sorry for your loss."

I wouldn't let her give me mercy. "It's my fault he's dead."

Kordova didn't even have the decency to look shocked. "Did you kill him, or have him killed?"

"No. But the people who did kill him were only there because of me." *And because of Dale.* But it wasn't Dale's fault. I knew how Gabriel operated, the kinds of games he played. I knew exactly how far Gabriel would go to get what he wanted—and what he'd always wanted was Amara. Everyone else had been expendable to him...even me. I should have known better. And now Isaac was dead.

But Kordova only shrugged. "If you didn't kill him, it's not your fault. Blame the people who killed him."

She hadn't been able to do anything about my back, but I liked her blunt demeanor and her unflinching way of looking at the world. Months later, when my people began to succumb to the illness, he'd approached Kordova again. I knew she might turn me away like Covington had, but she'd always been a doctor first and a demon second. And I was right. Kordova convinced Covington to ally with us, at least for this one fight. It wasn't some utopian united world, but it was something. And as more and more angels became sick, we needed all the help we could get.

A knock interrupted my thoughts. The door opened before I had a chance to answer. Rebekah poked her head in. "Are you decent?"

She wouldn't have cared if I'd said no. Maybe in her mind, it would have been better if I were naked.

Rebekah was…a problem. I hated her for what she'd done to Isaac. Every time I saw her face, I remembered her dangling him hundreds of feet in the air, and then dropping him like an old rag doll.

But when I'd declared my leadership, Rebekah had been one of the first people to pledge her loyalty to me. She'd been one of Gabriel's senior lieutenants for over a century, so she knew where all the bodies were buried—literally and figuratively. She was an important ally to have. I had to look at the greater good. Even if I did dream of wrapping my hands around her throat until the life drained out of her.

And things *were* getting better. I refused to allow part-blooded angels to be treated like pawns anymore. I was working on tracking down the weaker angels—the ones that had been exiled under Gabriel's rule—and bringing them back into the fold. I'd gotten rid of some of my father and Gabriel's more ridiculous rules, like forcing parents to give their children Biblical names in order to give the right "impression" to the humans. The ones who believed in angels probably thought of halos and sparkling wings. As if I'd ever be allowed anywhere near a halo.

The first time I found out that a Throne parent had named their new baby "Brooklyn," I'd almost jumped for joy.

If I had to sacrifice Dale's love and trust to do it…well, nothing in life was free. I'd never deserved her, anyway.

My back ached again.

Rebekah sat down on my pallet, oblivious to my internal dialogue. She angled herself so that the bare light bulb above us shined on her blond hair. I was sure it was intentional. I'd never met anyone more conscious of their looks than Rebekah, which was probably a byproduct of her power. She could shift her appearance to look like anyone or anything she wanted. I wasn't sure I'd ever actually seen her real face. But I was almost certain she didn't look like the Grace Kelly clone she was pretending to be now.

BETH WOODWARD

She tossed her hair over her shoulder self-consciously. "So Amara's whelp has returned."

My response was automatic. "Rebekah, don't say 'whelp.' No one uses that word anymore."

"No one in the human world, you mean." She rolled her eyes.

"Part of our job is to blend in with the human world, to assimilate."

"But maybe it shouldn't be. We are *more* than the humans could ever hope to be. Why should we try to blend—"

"Rebekah..." I'd had this conversation so many times with the older ones—including her.

"Fine." She sounded like a sulky teenager. For someone who disdained everything human the way Rebekah did, she could mimic their expressions perfectly. She took a breath and spoke again. "Some people are concerned about working with the demons," she said.

"'Some people?' Does that include you?"

"Yes." She wasn't trying to hide it. I could appreciate that, at least.

I sat up and faced her. "My job is to protect our people. Our people are dying..."

"We have medics!"

"Medics. Not doctors. None of them are as good as Irene Kordova. None of them even come close." I softened my voice. "Right now, we have a common enemy. That's what we should be focused on. Not our differences."

"Old enmities don't just disappear because they're no longer convenient. And now they want us to work with Amara's daughter..."

"Dale is not Amara."

"She looks like Amara, and she has Amara's abilities. There are also rumors about your relationship with her..."

My back flared again, and I clenched my teeth. "Rebekah, please reassure everybody that I'm doing everything I can to find the cure to this illness and get the Zetas out of our hair. If that means working with the demons, I'll do it, because our people come first. Can you do that?"

"Yes, of course. There is one other matter." Rebekah ran her hand up my thigh. "I wanted to...re-extend my offer. We could be good together."

I stifled a groan. "Rebekah…not again…"

"You may have the power, but I have the respect of our people—something you are still lacking. Many of them are still…upset…about the way you came into power. And I'm a pureblood. I can help you ease your transition."

She stroked me through my jeans. Much to my chagrin, I hardened involuntarily. I moved her hand away. "That's not going to happen."

She hesitated. "I know you're still upset about what happened with the mongrel at the fun park…"

"Don't call him that!" I jumped up, towering over her. "His name was Isaac. And I'm as much of a 'mongrel' as he was."

"No, you're not." She stood, meeting my eyes. I had three inches on her, but she wasn't deterred. "Gabriel was shortsighted. It was never just about blood. It was about *power*. You have it. You've always had it. That's why Gabriel was scared of you. So was Zaphkiel."

It had been years since I'd heard anyone say my father's name, and it still felt like a punch to the gut. Rebekah continued. "Here, Zaphkiel expected this docile, subservient child, one who would be beholden to him. A good foot soldier, he said. And then you came along, with the potential to be stronger than he ever was."

"What's your point?"

"Unlike your father or Gabriel, I know how to share power. You want to make things better for the mongrels? Make alliances with the demons? We can do that, together. And our children…our children could rule the *world*."

She touched my face, but I smacked her hand away. "I'm tired of your games, Rebekah. I don't need that kind of help." I opened the door. "You need to leave."

She strolled to the door, but paused at the entryway. "It's important to understand and acknowledge your weaknesses. You may be strong, but you're still a part-blood. Some of them will never see you as anything but that foot soldier your father expected you to be. But I can help you with that." She left without another word.

I sighed.

Once, when I was young and stupid, I'd taken her up on her offer. It meant nothing. There had never been many women, but none of them meant anything. All that had mattered was avenging my parents and taking over leadership of the Thrones.

Until a blue-eyed woman with curves for days had marched across a warehouse floor and taken my heart with her.

Now I'd lost her. I deserved nothing less. Even worse was the reality that because of me, Dale was going against her instincts, being less than the person I knew she could be.

There was a metal shelving unit in the back of my closet, covered in cleaning supplies and buckets of paint. I inched the unit to the side, careful not to make noise, until I uncovered what I was looking for.

A window.

I opened it and looked outside. Two floors to the ground. Doable. I hoisted myself over the windowsill and jumped.

CHAPTER SIX
Dale

Covington and I walked in silence to a limousine. It wasn't one of those crazy twenty-person stretch limos I used to see on prom night, but something smaller and more understated—well, as small and understated as a limo can be, anyway. As the driver held open the door for me, I finally spoke to Covington. "I need you to get Nik Cohen and Chaz Jimenez and bring them to the safe house, too. I befriended them when I was here last year, so they could be in danger."

"Are you sure that's really necessary?" he asked.

"They know about me, and the Thrones interrogated them last year when I was on the run. If the Thrones can get to them, so can the Zetas."

"Fine. Is there anyone else?" I stiffened at the sharpness of Covington's reply. When he saw my reaction, he softened his voice. "Dale, I'm not a monster. I know you're not here of your own free will, but I don't want any of your friends to get hurt, either. You've met a lot of people over the years. Is there anyone else the Zetas might target to get to you?"

I thought about it. He was right: I had met a lot of people in my ten years on the run. But I'd known very few. I spent that entire decade holding people at arm's length, because I knew I was going to have to leave again sooner or later. My entire life was made up of stories and lies, and it was exhausting. The only time I could be myself was when I was alone.

It probably would have been the same way with Nik and Chaz if it hadn't been for the fact that I'd discovered I was a demon and the Thrones had caught up with me while I was in New York. They'd been inadvertently caught in the crossfire when the Thrones had decided that they might be a viable way to get information about me. The Thrones had questioned them—and, I suspect, tortured them—and when I returned to New York, I had to tell them something. So I told them the truth, the first time in over a decade that I'd given anyone anything real about myself.

As for anyone else. "Maybe if you could have someone keep an eye on Griddles n' Grits, the restaurant where I worked in Kentucky." If I knew anything about the Zetas, they'd already covered up the attack on Tyler and me, and then what happened in the hospital, with some story or another. Rival gangs? Drug wars? People were always ready to believe the simplest explanation, and human-on-human violence was so much easier than "attack by a group of paramilitary, anti-supernatural zealots." If Sally knew some kind of violence had gone down that night, she probably figured I'd disappeared afterward to avoid police scrutiny. If she didn't…well, she probably just figured I disappeared. She was used to that, the hard-luck cases who showed up for a few weeks and then disappeared without a word between one shift and the next. I'd seen it happen four times in just the few months I'd been there. Maybe she worried about them, I don't know, but she didn't go out of her way to do so. She had a business to run, and their disappearances meant she needed to find someone to cover their shifts.

"No one else?" Covington asked.

I shook my head. "No one else."

Covington walked away, leaving me alone with the taciturn limo driver. We went to a brownstone adjacent to Washington Square Park. The driver parked in front of the building, opened my door, handed me a couple of shopping bags with the Macy's logo on them, and told me to go to the fourth floor. Before I even reached the entryway, he'd driven away.

The apartment was generously sized for New York, which basically meant "infinitesimal" for anywhere else: a living space just large enough to fit a love seat and a coffee table, a galley kitchen, and a twisty metal staircase leading up to the two bedrooms. The place had recently been renovated, the smell of paint and wood flooring still lingering. The back wall of the place was exposed brick, adding a little bit of character to the place. Unfortunately, the poster of the New York City skyline and a French movie I'd never heard of were just cliché enough to take it away. I was so focused on the utter triteness of the decor that it took me a while to notice something even weirder: the windows were all covered with blackout shades that had been nailed shut.

A few hours later, the door opened. The same limo driver that had dropped me off led Nik and Chaz inside—blindfolded. I rolled my eyes. "Seriously? Is this *necessary*?"

The driver shrugged. "I don't make the rules." He removed their blindfolds and walked out without another word, shutting the door behind him. I was left with Nik and Chaz staring at me, dumbfounded.

They'd changed in the past year and a half. Nik's hair was chin-length now, and streaked with rainbow colors, and I suspected she was sporting a few new tattoos underneath her winter coat. Chaz looked skinnier than I remembered, and a line indented his forehead that I had never seen before. Nik recovered first. She set her bag down and ran to me, hugging me with enough force to cause me to stumble. "I never thought I'd see you again! What are you doing here? What are *we* doing here?"

"What do you *think* we're doing here?" Chaz didn't bother to hide the bitterness in his voice. "Obviously we've gotten sucked into some demon shit because of Dale. *Again.*"

Chaz dropped his bag on the floor and plopped down on the love seat, his legs dangling over the edge. There was such defeat in his posture, as if life had beaten him down, and he'd ceased to care a long time ago. I looked over at Nik, but she wouldn't meet my eyes. "Guys, I'm sorry. It was just a precaution. There's some stuff going on right now, and I wanted to make sure you were safe."

"The woman who couldn't be bothered to send a text message in the last year and a half wants to make sure we're safe. I'm thrilled." Chaz pulled a throw pillow out from behind his head and covered his eyes with it.

I took a few of those cleaning breaths everyone said were so calming. "I know I should have gotten in touch with you sooner. But a lot of stuff happened last year, and I just…I needed to get my head straight. But I thought about you guys all the time, and when the supernatural stuff started getting hot again, I just wanted to make sure you were protected. That's all."

Chaz uncovered his face. "'Make sure we're protected.' That's why we're prisoners here?"

"You're not prisoners. It's just a safe house. I'm sure you'll be able to go home again in a few weeks."

"We're not prisoners? So what's this?"

Chaz pulled up his pants leg to reveal an electronic ankle bracelet.

"Shit. I had no idea they were going to do that. I'll talk to Covington to see if we can do—"

"Don't bother. It doesn't matter, anyway. If we wanted to leave, you could just mind-control us into staying. Or hell, I don't know, maybe you'd just kill us, too."

I froze, growing cold all over. "What are you talking about?" Because that was the one part of my past I'd never confessed to them.

"Did you think we wouldn't Google your real name and find out about that guy you murdered at your senior prom?"

Tears filled my eyes. "You don't understand. He raped my best friend." And now I remembered the other reason why I never told anyone anything about myself. If Nik and Chaz had any idea, even the slightest inkling, of the other people I'd killed since then, they'd bolt. To hell with the Zetas and the tracking devices on their legs and the might of the supernatural community. They'd think I was the bigger threat to them, and they'd be right.

Chaz's next words confirmed it. "And you played judge, jury, and executioner all by yourself, *because you could.*"

I sniffled and wiped the wetness from my face. "I'm sorry, Chaz. I'm just trying to do the right thing."

"Whatever helps you sleep at night." He picked up his bag and stormed up the metal stairs, slamming the bedroom door behind him.

I sat on the love seat, rubbing my face. Nik sat next to me. "I'm sorry about that. He hasn't been himself in a very long time. Not since he was taken by the Thrones last year."

"Doesn't he know that I'm trying to *prevent* that from happening again?"

"I know. But Chaz…I think he might have post-traumatic stress disorder." She sighed. "When the Thrones took me, they demanded to know where you were and everything I knew about you. I didn't know much of anything, and I told them so. They roughed me up a little, and… things happened…and then they let me go."

My breath caught. "Jesus, Nik. I didn't realize they had hurt you, too."

"It's fine. I get worse from the guys on the subway every day. But Chaz…I think he must have gotten argumentative with them. He's like that, you know, or he used to be. It was…worse for him, I think."

"Fuck." It was all I could say.

"He's stopped doing his art, you know. I haven't seen him touch any of his artwork or supplies since then."

"Nik, you know that I never intended for you guys to get hurt. If I could go back and take this all away for you, I would."

"Not even you have that kind of power, Dale." Nik stood up and went over to the wall, staring that the picture of the city skyline—the one that we couldn't see, because all the windows were blocked off.

"What about you?" I asked her. "Maybe you could help Chaz. You were kidnapped and hurt by the Thrones, too. How are you coping with it?"

She gave me a sad smile. "Who said that I was?"

———◇———

THERE WERE ONLY TWO BEDROOMS in the apartment. Instinctively, I knew Nik and Chaz would be sharing one of them, and I would be by myself.

BETH WOODWARD

As usual. By the time I was able to bring myself to go upstairs, Nik and Chaz had already shut themselves inside the smaller bedroom, speaking in hushed tones. The message couldn't have been clearer if they'd put up a "Do Not Enter" sign. I sighed. At least they'd left me the bigger room.

I went into my room and lay back on my bed. I knew I wouldn't be able to sleep, in spite of the fact that my body wasn't back to 100 percent after my injuries. Instead, I imagined patterns in the popcorn ceiling.

I don't know much time had passed when I heard a knock on the door. Thinking it was Nik or Chaz, I jumped up to open it. Instead, I found Covington standing there. I ushered him inside. "What the hell? Ankle bracelets?"

"Dale, it's just a precaution."

"A precaution. For *whom*?"

"For us." He sat down in the egg-shaped chair by the desk and swiveled it toward me. "They're human, Dale. We're not. Or have you forgotten that we're under attack right now by a group of humans?"

"They're not just 'humans.' They're my friends. And we can't treat them like criminals. They haven't done anything."

"We're protecting the integrity of the safe house. It's blocked from incoming and outgoing electronic transmissions and GPS software, so no one can find you covertly. But if one of them were to walk outside, it wouldn't be any great mystery where we are."

"You don't have an ankle monitor on me."

He eyed me wryly. "Whom would you tell?"

He was right. The Zetas were out to kill me, and the only people in the world who might notice I was gone were either in this apartment or strategizing next to a mural of Ichabod Crane at an abandoned hospital in Tarrytown. And if I hadn't come back, the Zetas would have killed me eventually, and no one would have ever known.

Maybe it would have been better that way.

I sighed. "Covington…I know there are a lot of bad things going on right now, and I'm sorry I can't do more to help."

"Can't or won't?"

EMBRACING THE DEMON   **63**

I sighed. "I *can't*, Covington." Through the wall, I could hear Nik and Chaz. I couldn't hear what they were saying, but I could tell from the tone that Chaz was pissed. Great. One more thing to feel guilty about. "I just can't work with him, not after what he did to my mother. And I don't see how you can."

"John has been a very reasonable leader, from our perspective," Covington said. "He toned down the Thrones' anti-demon rhetoric. He curbed much of the violence against our people. He even proposed monthly meetings between our leaders so we could exchange information pertinent to our people. And this was all before the illness hit. When Dr. Kordova realized how quickly the illness was spreading, our initial fear was that the Thrones had launched a covert attack against us. But soon afterward, John contacted us and told us that his people were getting sick, too."

I sat on the bed. "That's great. I'm glad that he contacted you. But it doesn't change anything."

Covington leaned back into the egg. "Have you ever the term 'fading'?" I shook my head. "Fading is something that happens to the old ones sometimes. After hundreds or thousands of years on this planet they just... give up. First they start to lose touch with reality. They slip in and out of their own minds, forgetting what era they're in. Then slowly, they retreat into their minds more and more often until what's going on inside seems more real to them than what's going on outside. Some of them ultimately commit suicide. But the rest...they just keep fading and fading until one day they're completely catatonic."

"I don't understand," I said.

"Dale...your mother was fading."

I felt like someone had punched me in the chest. I stood up and paced the room, trying in vain to process what Covington was telling me. "That can't be true. I saw her, and she was fine. She wasn't catatonic. Not even close."

"No, she hadn't devolved that much. But she'd been fighting it for a long time. She was...tired."

I was having trouble breathing. "Tired?"

B E T H   W O O D W A R D

"Raoul could see the future. Short-range, but it was long enough. He knew something was going to happen that night. Your mother sent all the household staff away, including me. The only guards there that night were the ones who *wanted* to be there. They knew they would probably die that night. So did she."

Tears ran down my face. "Are you saying that she *wanted* to die? More than she…more than me…" I couldn't finish my sentence. I sat back on the bed before my knees gave out entirely.

Covington reached over and took my hands. "Dale, I spent the last eighty years serving Amara. Ever since she was forced to leave you behind in Pittsburgh, all she wanted to do was be with you, to spend time with you. I think you're the reason she stuck around as long as she did. She was waiting for you."

I didn't bother to stifle my tears now. Covington handed me a handkerchief. "Your John is a legend in our world. The Bloodhound. They say he can find anyone, and he kills without a conscience. He's stronger and faster and better at what he does than any pureblooded angel the Thrones have ever had, yet he was treated like a second-class citizen because he was half human. His ambition to lead the Thrones was never a secret, at least among the demons. But he would never be able to do it without doing something drastic first."

"Something like killing my mother."

"Your mother had been evading the Bloodhound for years. She could have done it again."

"So she *let* John kill her?"

"I don't know. But things are not always as simple as they seem."

I started to cry again, big, ugly, heaving sobs. Covington's handkerchief was useless by then, covered in snot and salt, but there were no tissues in the room so I was stuck. Covington just smiled sadly. "Your mother wanted a better world for you. And now angels and demons are communicating like never before. We're united against a common enemy."

"Fuck that!" I jumped up from the bed. "If she wanted the world to be better for me, she could have *stayed*. Been my fucking mother, for a change." I punched the glass-top desk. It shattered, leaving shards of glass on the floor and my hand shredded. Covington rose, concern on his face. "No. Fuck. Just don't worry about it. It's going to heal in two and a half seconds anyway."

By the time the sentence came out of my mouth, the wounds on my hand were already closing, leaving just the blood behind that was already beginning to feel crusty on my hand. I walked to the other side of the room, enjoying the sound of glass crunching underneath my shoes. It was going to be a bitch to clean up later. But right now…it was destructive. And I wanted to be destructive. "I'm not Amara."

"I know."

"No, I don't think you do. You want me to help 'save my people' or whatever, but I can't. I'm just some high school dropout and runaway who accidentally blacks out and kills people sometimes. I'm not a hero."

"That's not true. Or at least, it doesn't have to be."

"*Amara* was the leader, the strategist, the inspiration. I just look like her. And if she wanted to make the world better for me, she should have stuck around and *made it better*." Anger built up in my chest again, ready to explode again. I wanted to hit something. Maybe the wall. Maybe the stupid egg chair Covington was sitting in. I didn't even know who I was mad at anymore. "None of this excuses what he did. Even if you're right—even if Amara wanted to die—she could have been struck by lightning or hit by a semi or jumped off the Empire State Building. Any of those would have a more than fair chance of killing even a demon, I think. But no. He killed her. She's still dead because of him."

Covington closed his eyes and sighed. "We all have a common goal right now."

"It's not my goal," I said. "All I want is to get the Zetas off my ass. Then I'll go, and I'll be out of your hair."

"All right, Dale." The determination, the resolution, I usually saw in his eyes was gone. Now he was just…resigned. He walked to the door, but before he turned the handle, he looked back at me. "You know, your righteous anger may not be the most important thing in the room."

"Get out." I didn't try to hide the venom in my voice.

Covington left, shutting the door just a little too hard behind him.

I COULDN'T SLEEP. I KEPT thinking about Nik and Chaz, and how they suffered because I'd come into their lives. I thought about what happened at the hospital, the things Irene and Covington had said to me, how they wanted me to help them, to fight with them.

Mostly, I tried not to think about John.

Seeing him had affected me more than I wanted to admit. It was like a drug habit that I had kicked, only to discover I was still addicted when someone dangled another hit in front of me. Not that I'd ever done drugs. Even Tylenol made me loopy, a weird quirk of supernatural physiology. But still, the metaphor was there.

John was my fucking Kryptonite.

It had taken all my strength not to waltz over to him and punch him in the face. I was so *angry* at him for what he'd done to my mother…for what he'd done to *me*. But when I saw him, anger wasn't the first emotion I'd felt; it was relief. For the last year and a half, I'd dreamed of that night at Amara's almost every time I slept. I'd wanted to hurt him. My mind crushed his. But when he'd trip over the edge and fall, I'd grab for his hand. I'd hold him there until he slipped through my fingers and crashed to the bottom.

In real life, I hadn't reached for him. Either way, it ended the same way.

There was a pull-down door embedded into the ceiling, secured with a flimsy-looking padlock. Earlier, Covington had explained that it went up to the roof and advised me not to go up there. "That defeats the purpose of a safe house, don't you think?" he'd said.

The hell with that. I threw on a coat and shoes over my thin pajamas. I dug through the desk until I found what I was looking for: paper clips. I'd learned to pick locks back in high school, from a boyfriend who had little respect for the law and a touch of kleptomania. I wasn't going to be a safe cracker anytime soon, but even I could manage a padlock. If you're trying to keep your stuff safe, the padlock is the security equivalent of "just a suggestion"—and not a very strong one, at that. Seriously, you'd be better off putting a sign that says "steal me" next to your stuff. That way, thieves might assume there's nothing valuable there and leave it alone.

I was out of practice, but it still only took about a minute to pop the lock. I removed it and pulled down the ladder from the ceiling. It creaked loudly, and I cringed, hoping I hadn't woken Nik and Chaz. When they didn't barge in, I brought the ladder the rest of the way down and climbed to the roof.

The roof could have been a New Yorker's wet dream. A few dead plants were pushed along one wall, and several rotting wooden chairs were scattered around. Someone had tried to make this nice, once. But no one had bothered in a long time.

But nothing could beat the view. The safe house faced Washington Square Park, and from where I stood I had a perfect view of the Christmas tree, framed by the Arch. So what if it wasn't Rockefeller Center, and the Arch was a bastardized replica of the *Arc de Triomphe*? New York was magical at Christmastime. I'd only had one Christmas in the city to appreciate it, but that was enough. I hadn't really celebrated Christmas since I was a child—Aunt Barbara never bothered, and I never had reason to once I was on the run—but this city made me want to try. In spite of the time, I could hear car horns echoing below me, reminding me of the other thing I loved about New York City: no matter what day it was, what time it was, it was always so *alive*.

"It's beautiful, isn't it?"

The voice came from behind me. I didn't turn. "How did you know I was here?"

"It's the Thrones' safe house."

Of course it was. "I guess I'll have to tell Covington to relocate us."

"Haven't you heard? We're allies now."

He stepped out of the darkness toward me. Still, I would not look right at him. I was afraid my eyes would betray too much. Or maybe I was more afraid of what his eyes might say. He stepped up next to me at the front of the roof, staring over the waist-high wall into the park below. He lit a cigarette. "I remember when this was a potter's field," he said. "That stupid tree in the corner was never a hanging tree—that's just something they tell the university underclassmen to scare them—but this was a potter's field. So many people died during the yellow fever epidemic, and they just dumped them here."

I stepped away from him, putting some distance between us. "You shouldn't smoke, you know."

"Why? Are you worried about my health, Little Demon? They won't hurt me. They won't hurt you, either."

"No, but they'll hurt the humans who have to breathe your secondhand smoke. Plus, it just smells gross."

John chuckled, but he ground out the cigarette underneath his foot and then took a piece of Wurther's candy out of his pocket, unwrapped it, and put it into his mouth. "You know, it's funny. I started smoking because it helped me blend in with the humans. I started right around the Great War, and it was just the same to me as putting pomade in my hair and wearing those stupid celluloid collars. But then, sometime around the 1980s, people became more concerned about the health effects and they started to quit. So I had to quit, too. They didn't have nicotine patches or gum then, and I don't know how my body would have reacted to them, anyway. So I started sucking on hard candy whenever I wanted to smoke."

I couldn't help myself. "That's why you smell like butterscotch all the time."

He nodded. "Yeah, I guess so. The candy worked pretty well for a long time. But now...now I just can't seem to stop myself."

"The strain of having everything you ever wanted must be terrible."

"You have no idea."

He took out another cigarette, thought better of it, and shoved it back into the pack. I rolled my eyes. "Why, thank you, for doing the absolute *least* you could do and not smoke around me. That totally makes up for all your past transgressions."

"Dale—"

"What do you want, John?"

"You planning on pushing me off the roof again?"

My stomach clenched with guilt. I tried not to let him see my reaction. "I didn't push you; you fell."

He peered over the edge. "A fall from this height might be enough to kill me. Still, it would be messy. The cops would be swarming the house, and people would gather down there for vigils, which would completely negate the point of having a safe house. Of course, maybe you don't intend to push me over. Maybe you're going to take me right here, hand-to-hand. Since I *taught* you hand-to-hand, that might be tricky, although I could be underestimating you. You could have practiced while you were gone. Still, the body would start to decompose after a few days—that much we have in common with humans, I'm afraid—and your roommates would probably complain about the smell. Maybe Covington would help you clear the body, although he'd probably be a little put out since we are, technically, allies now."

I touched his mind. The shield around it was rock solid—and once again completely impenetrable to me. Whatever had allowed me to pierce into it the night he'd killed Amara was gone. *You have to want it more,* Amara had told me, and right now I didn't. John could probably see all this in my expression. He could read me like a book. That had always been my problem. "Why are you here?"

"I want you to help us with tracking down the Zetas and figuring out how to cure this illness. We need you on this raid tomorrow."

"Seriously? Tell Covington he can send all the minions he wants. It's not going to work."

"You think Covington sent me?" He sounded surprised.

I hesitated…and then I stood firm. "It doesn't matter. Either way, it's not gonna happen." I kicked one of the old wooden chairs sitting nearby. It cracked, its leg falling off with a hollow *thunk*, though whether that was because of my mad demon superpowers or the fact that the chair had been sitting out in the elements since before I was born, I don't know. "I didn't come back because I had some big epiphany that I want to be a 'real demon' after all. I came back because the Zetas were trying to kill me, and

BETH WOODWARD

the cops were so far up my ass that they could probably see out of my belly button. Once the danger passes, I'm gone. This world has never done anything good for me, or the people around me. Honestly..." I sat down on the ground, pulling my legs up to my chest. "If I'd known you were here, I never would have come at all. The hell with the police or the Zetas. I would have found another way."

"Fair enough." John picked up one of the other chairs. He pushed down on it, testing its stability, and then sat down facing me. "On the other hand, you're already part of this world whether you want to be or not."

"I wouldn't have even *known* about this world if you hadn't brought me into it!"

"If it hadn't been me, it would have been someone else. Gabriel had been trying to track Amara for centuries. You were a means to an end. Once he found her, he would have killed you. You were a reminder of his failings with Amara—and if there was one thing Gabriel didn't like, it was failure." John's voice remained perfectly calm as continued. "Besides...were you really better off before? Before I met you, you'd been on the run for ten years because of your Rages. You had powers you had no idea what to do with or how to control, and you planned to spend the rest of your life pretending to be someone else."

I leapt up. "Oh, so you did me a fucking *favor*? Oh, well thank you so much for killing my mother to make sure I could reach my full potential."

He stood up. "No, Dale, that's not what I..." He sighed. "For the record, I never meant to hurt you."

"Sure. I was just...in the way." Tears filled my eyes. I turned away from him. "You know, what I don't understand is why you pretended to lo—like me. I would have helped you, if you'd just been a friend. It's not like I have a lot of those, anyway. But you didn't have to fake feeling something for me. You didn't have to pretend you cared."

"I didn't."

The words were so low that I thought I'd imagined them. I looked at John. The cold night wind blew through his hair. He didn't look at me, instead staring out toward the city in front of us. "This isn't about you and

EMBRACING THE DEMON

me. It's about the people who are getting sick, the people who are dying. You can help them. You could be a real asset to this fight."

"They have a weapon that neutralizes my mind control abilities," I told him. "I assume that's why you need me, with all of your 'Dale can do things other people can't' bullshit. But they've already got it figured out."

"Do you think that's all you have to offer?" He looked at me incredulously. "Dale, you're one of the best fighters I've ever seen. I've heard about what happened with the Zetas. You were surrounded, outnumbered, and unarmed, and you still managed to take out several of them. Did you have a Rage?"

I shook my head. "I controlled it."

He grinned at me, the expression so pure and unexpected that I almost smiled back at him. "That's amazing! If you're able to fight like that *and* you can control yourself…hell, Dale, you might be unstoppable."

"They're still not my people," I said.

"Does that matter?" John moved off of the chair and sat on the cement next to me. "Whatever may have happened between us, it doesn't change the fact that I spent ten years following you, learning everything I could about you. I know the things you've never told anyone else. And I know, much as you like to beat yourself up about it, that you're not an indiscriminate killer. I know about the man who was beating his son in Arizona…the Texas Congresswoman running a dog-fighting ring…the man killing strippers in St. Louis…"

"The cops weren't doing anything about it," I muttered.

"No, they weren't. So you got a job in one of the clubs he'd frequented, and you waited for him."

The manager had been reluctant, because I had no experience and because I wasn't the skinny, long-legged type that they usually hired. But he'd also been desperate, because a lot of his strippers had left after the St. Louis Slasher had begun his rampage. So for six weeks I stripped under the name "Layla Devine," and I waited. Then one Thursday night, a man had come into the club, alone. He sat in the back and didn't speak to anyone, which wasn't that unusual, except he gave off an icky vibe that I couldn't ignore. So I paid extra attention to him, making as much eye contact as I could from the stage and offering him a discounted lap dance—which the asshole took me up on, of course. Sure enough, at the end of my shift, he cornered me and covered my face with a washcloth doused in a sweet-smelling chemical—which, if he was following his M.O., was probably chloroform. The next thing I remember, I woke up with blood all over my leotard and the probable St. Louis Slasher had a bedazzled stiletto shoved through his trachea. I learned later that it had gone through his carotid artery, and the blood loss had killed him.

"Those strippers weren't your people, either. Neither was that little boy...or those pit bulls, for that matter. You saved them, anyway. Because that's what you do, Dale. Long before you knew you were a demon or had any special abilities, you were helping people. And now you have the chance to help *millions* of them." He sighed. "Look, after this is all over, you can go back to hating me. God knows, I deserve it. But right now, we have a problem, and you can help. You're not someone who leaves well enough alone. You never have been. It cost you your identity, your freedom, and over a decade of your life, but you are someone who helps. You are someone who *cares*."

I didn't respond. John strolled over to the ledge. "We're leaving tomorrow at ten p.m. on a private flight out of Westchester County Airport. Give them the name 'Virginia Gardner,' and they'll show you to the gate. Dress in black, and wear layers. It's cold in Montana."

He hoisted himself over the ledge and began to climb down.

"Come, or don't come. It's up to you, Dale."

I STILL COULDN'T SLEEP AFTER John left, so I went downstairs to raid the refrigerator. I found Nik sitting on the couch, flipping through the TV menu. "I'm surprised you're awake," I said to her.

"Yeah...I heard a big banging noise, and then I couldn't get back to sleep after that."

EMBRACING THE DEMON

Crap. Guess I hadn't been so stealthy after all. "Yeah, I knocked the chair over on the floor. I can't believe how heavy those damn egg-looking things are."

I opened the refrigerator door. Thankfully, it was fully stocked with fresh food. I ignored the fruits and vegetables and pulled out a Carnegie Deli cheesecake. I grabbed two forks and set everything on the coffee table in front of the love seat. "We're kickin' it *Golden Girls*-style tonight. Dig in."

Nik didn't have to be told twice. She picked up the fork and started working on the cheesecake. "Is there anything you want to talk about?" she asked between bites. "I mean, when Dorothy and Blanche and Rose do this, they're always talking about some crisis that's going on in their lives."

"Or reminiscing about previous shows because the writers were too lazy to write a whole new episode," I said. "No, there's nothing. Other than the fact that people are out to kill me again, I'm great."

We ate in silence for a few minutes, until my stomach started to growl at me. Whether it was the cheesecake or my internal turmoil, I didn't know. I set my fork down. "It's just that…Covington wants me to help with this thing they're doing tomorrow."

"Thing?"

I took another bite of cheesecake, much to my stomach's chagrin. "Yeah, so…supernaturals are getting really sick. They're dying. Covington thinks I can help."

Nik hesitated before responding. "Help? How?"

"They're going on a raid or something. I don't really know."

Nik cleared her throat. "So, uh, what's the problem then?"

I took another bite, chewing slowly before I answered. "They've allied with the Thrones. With John."

"They've *allied*?" Nik leaned back against the love seat, shaking her head. "I didn't see that coming."

"Yeah, me neither." If I ate any more cheesecake I was going to throw up, so I shut the box. They always made binge-eating look so much easier on television. "I can barely stand to say his name. If I have to see him all the time, I'll just…I don't know, maybe I'll beat the shit out of him or start reciting bad poetry."

"Hmm." Nik opened the cheesecake box and took another forkful, chewing slowly and methodically.

"I mean, I want to help. A lot of people are dying, and maybe I *could* make a difference. But I can't work with him, and I can't believe Covington would even ask it of me. Hell, I can't believe Covington would even do it himself, after all those years of serving my mother."

"I think you should go." I stared at her as if she'd grown a second head. "Dale, the first rule of breakups is that you never let the other person know how much they've gotten to you."

I stared at her. "Nik…we didn't 'break up.' *He killed my mother.*"

"I know, but it's the same principle. You would help otherwise, but you're not going to because John will be there. You're giving him too much power in your life. Besides…maybe this could help you get some redemption."

I froze. "What are you talking about?"

"Like for that guy at the prom. Chaz was kind of right about that. It was pretty fucked up what you did."

"Did you not hear the part where he raped my best friend?"

She shrugged. "I mean…it's not really up to us to decide that."

"*Decide?* I saw it! One of his buddies told me that he'd drugged her, and I walked in on him shoving his dick inside her while she was unconscious!" I took a breath, trying to bring my anger back down to a simmer. "You know something? I don't regret killing Brad Kinnard. He was a rich, entitled asshole. Even if Julie had reported him, his WASP-y lawyer would have gotten him off and he would have done it again." It was the first time I'd ever said it, but I meant it. And I didn't regret killing the others, either. Twelve years running away from my mistakes, only to realize maybe they weren't mistakes after all.

Except for Andrew Seymour. Two years ago, I'd woken up to discover I'd decapitated a guy with a kitchen knife, and I still had no idea why. That one still haunted me, still made me wonder who I really was…whether that demon inside would take me over completely.

Nik brought her knees up to her chest. "You're right, Dale. I'm sorry. Of course, he never should have done that to your friend." She hesitated. "I guess it's just easy for me to forget sometimes that you're not really like us."

I shook my head. "I don't know about that. I mean, I thought I was human for twenty-seven years. I only found out about my demon heritage a year and a half ago."

"Yeah, but you've got all these powers. Like, you could pick me up and throw me out the window right now…"

"Well, from an aerodynamic perspective, that might be difficult."

"…Or you could make me feel things I'm not really feeling."

"Whoa! Time out." I formed my hands into a T-shape. "That's not how my power works. Like, at all. I can't read your mind. If you were to think of a number between one and one hundred, I would literally have a one-percent chance of guessing it correctly—because *math*, not mind reading. Also, I can't make you feel anything you don't already feel. I could make you hop on one foot or cluck like a chicken, but if you hate my guts, you're always going to hate my guts. My ability only works on actions, not feelings."

"But are there supernaturals like that? Ones who can change your feelings and emotions?"

"I don't know. Maybe. I've never met one, but that doesn't mean that they don't exist."

Nik wasn't looking at me anymore. Old ghosts were in her eyes.

"Nik…did something happen to you? Back when the Thrones kidnapped you and Chaz?"

She smiled with sad eyes. "Don't worry about it. I'm fine, I promise."

I was about to push her, but then I heard a door open. Chaz stumbled down the steps in a pair of flannel pants and a T-shirt. "You guys had cheesecake down here, and you didn't invite me? Seriously?" He headed for the kitchen and grabbed a fork. He was all bleary-eyed and disheveled, the venom gone from his demeanor. It would have been easy to pretend that the three of us were having a movie night at his apartment, discussing the merits of *Grease 2* or debating whether *Starship Troopers* was actually the best film ever made. But then Chaz turned around and glared at me, and I remembered just how much had changed.

"Don't worry, there's plenty left," I said. "I think I'll just head to bed. I've got a lot to think about."

"So where's this raid going to be?" Nik asked as I started climbing up the stairs.

"Montana, I think."

She nodded. "For the record…I think you should go. If you don't, you're just letting him win."

CHAPTER SEVEN
Dale

I GOT TO THE AIRPORT OVER an hour before the flight, thinking I was going to have to wait in security lines. But when I got to the airport and gave them the "Virginia Gardner" name, they ushered me to a separate part of the airport—no lines, no X-ray machines, no taking my shoes off, nothing. I spotted John first. He was off talking to someone who wore a headset and carried a metal clipboard—the pilot maybe? He saw me and gave me a slight nod, like he never doubted that I would be here today. Asshole.

Irene stood on the other side of the gate, flanked by Mabel and Tina. When I walked over to her, she raised an eyebrow. "So the princess decided to join us after all?"

"I just wanted to say that I'm sorry about your husband. And...I'm here to help with this mission, however I can."

Irene looked at me, and then at Mabel and Tina, a shadow of uncertainty crossing her face. But then she hardened. "Just stay out of my way, princess."

Mabel jumped in. "Irene, maybe you should listen to what she has to say."

"The hell with that! You want to kumbaya with someone who's only here because she feels guilty, that's fine. But your longhaired hippie shit doesn't work for me."

She stormed off. Mabel started to follow her, but Tina grabbed her arm. "Leave her alone." After a second of hesitation, Mabel nodded.

I shifted my bag to my other shoulder. "She seems super nice. Maybe one day we can grab some dinner and see which one of us shivs the other first. But she should be warned, a toothbrush really can be a lethal weapon in the right hands."

Mabel sighed, leaning her tall frame against the window. "She's not usually like this. She's just had a rough road lately."

"I get it, she doesn't like me. She's been playing Mother Teresa, and I was gone. But I'm here now, and I'm helping. I don't know what she wants from me, and to be honest, I'm sick of her sanctimonious bullshit."

Mabel's jaw tightened. "Irene's done a lot of things to help a lot of supernaturals, long before this illness happened."

"So what? I'm just supposed to kowtow to her? I don't think so."

"She helped me!" I froze at the sudden anger in her tone. Mabel closed her eyes and took a breath. "I'm transgender. I wanted sex reassignment surgery, but I didn't think I'd ever be able to have it. I mean, I couldn't exactly go to a human doctor and say, 'By the way, there's a good chance my incision will heal before you're done with the surgery, hope you don't mind.' But about twenty years ago, Tina found Irene and suggested I go see her. The procedures she developed for me were new and unique, and I don't know what I would've done without her. And I'm not the only person she's helped, not by a long shot. Irene's specialized in the care and treatment of supernaturals since before the Civil War."

"So you're saying I should respect her."

"I'm saying you should cut her a little slack. Her husband did just die. I don't know how she's even functional right now. If that had been Tina..." her voice trailed off. Tina put her hand on Mabel's shoulder, as if reassuring her that she was still there.

I took a deep breath. "You're right. I'll try to cut her a little slack."

EMBRACING THE DEMON   79

"That's all I can ask." Mabel smiled. "So, I'm going to get something to drink before the plane takes off. Would you like anything?"

"No, thank you." Mabel turned and walked away, Tina flanking her silently. "Hey Mabel," I called when she was a few feet away. She turned back around and looked at me. "I'm glad that Irene was able to help you."

Mabel smiled at me before she walked away.

A few minutes later, we boarded the plane. It was smaller than the ones I had ridden as a kid, but the seats were more comfortable and spacious. The pilot had spread us into seats throughout the plane—something about correct weight distribution, which made me nervous. But at least I didn't have to sit next to Irene and her accusatory glare—or worse, John and his…Johnness.

A few hours into the flight, Tina made her way to the front of the plane, with John flanking her, arms crossed over his chest. "In forty-five minutes, we'll land in Great Falls, Montana. The Grave is about an hour from there."

"Why's it called the Grave, anyway?" I asked no one in particular.

Tina ignored me. "The facility is underground. There's an elevator from ground level that will take us down into the bowels."

"'The Grave?' 'The bowels?' Will we be visiting the Rectum Sanctorum, too? How about Castle Doomittydeathpants?"

This time, Tina glared at me. "Rebekah," Tina pointed at the blond bitch, who was sitting near the front of the plane, "is going to take the lead for getting us into the Grave. For those of you who don't know, Rebekah has the ability to transform herself to look like anyone."

I perked up. "Wait, seriously? She can make herself look like *anyone*?"

Rebekah stood up, an imperious look on her face. Then, her body shimmered and morphed into a weird, blobby shape. When it stopped, I was staring at an exact replica of myself: same blue eyes, same shoulder-length brown hair, same long-sleeved black Tt-shirt and jeans. "Did you manage to get the birthmark on my ass, too?" I asked her.

I hoped I never stuck my nose that far up in the air. She looked like someone had farted, and it wasn't an attractive look on my face. "I doubt anyone is going to be looking at your ass."

BETH WOODWARD

If I didn't despise the woman so much, I'd be insanely jealous of her mad cool superpower. Wait, who was I kidding? I *was* insanely jealous of her mad cool superpower. I just wanted to throw her out of the plane without a parachute more. But no, I couldn't do that. We were allies now. Greater good and all. Ugh.

Tina, unbeknownst to me, had started speaking again. "…will assume the appearance of one of the Zetas guarding the entrance, and then she'll deactivate the security system and let us in."

"Is that why you need me?" I asked. "To compel the Zeta into telling us how to deactivate the security system?"

"We've had a spy on the inside for about eight months, so we know how to deactivate the system. We'll need you to mind-control the Zetas."

"What, like mind-control one of the Zetas so they'll lead us to the information we need? No problem."

"No, like mind-control *all* of them so we're not found out."

My eyebrows lifted practically to my hairline. John stood up and jumped into the conversation. "All of the Zetas who work in this facility are being biometrically monitored using subdermal implants. Real-time readings of their heart rates, blood pressure, temperature, respiration, and blood oxygen saturation levels are continually sent back to Zeta HQ. It was sold to them as a way of monitoring their health, so that medical personnel could respond immediately if someone had a heart attack or a stroke. But it actually serves as an internal lie detector, alerting the Zetas to any changes in physiology that might indicate someone is betraying the organization."

"This implant, does it manage their Netflix queue, too?" I asked.

Tina spoke up, her voice flat: "These implants have already cost us a life, Dale. That's how they got our mole. We had her on drugs to calm her nervous system. But eventually there was enough discrepancy in her readings to make them suspicious. They executed her last month." She closed her eyes. "I should have known. I should have protected her. *That was my job!*"

Mabel—who had been sitting across the aisle from me—walked to the front of the aisle and took Tina into her arms.

When no one else said anything, John continued. "So the Zetas' main goal is preventing and eliminating insider threats. But the biometric monitoring also works as a backup security system of sorts. If everyone's heart rates and blood pressure spike at the same time, the Zetas are going to know something's wrong and send in reinforcements."

"I can't control their heart rates and blood pressure!"

"No, but you can control what they pay attention to, and keep them doing what they're supposed to be doing."

I considered this. "So essentially, you want me to pull a 'these are not the droids you're looking for' on all of the Zetas."

"Yes." When I stared at him, he grinned at me. "I do occasionally pay attention to the human world, Dale. And I was actually alive when the first *Star Wars* movie came out."

"All right, so how many are we talking about? Five? Ten?"

Tina, who had reverted to her normal stoicism, stood up again, electronic tablet in her hands. "On any given night, there are between a hundred fifty and two hundred people on the overnight shift."

If I lifted my eyebrows any harder, I was going to pull a muscle in my forehead. "Two *hundred*? I've never controlled that many people at once before. I'm not even sure it's possible."

Covington had stayed behind, but he was listening to the whole meeting via speaker phone. "Amara could," he said. "I once saw her stop a riot with thousands of people involved."

Great, Covington, thank you for reminding me how much better off we'd be if my mother were still alive. "I don't know if my powers are as strong as hers. I certainly haven't had as much chance to practice."

"I've seen you control multiple people at once, over a much greater distance than this," John said.

He was referring to the time I'd controlled a group of Zetas who'd attacked us at my Aunt Barbara's house. I'd seized their minds and frozen them in place, giving me and John time to get away. I was able to hold the connection for about a mile or so until it snapped and left me power-drunk.

"First of all, there were only about two *dozen* Zetas there that day—not two *hundred*. Second, I only had to give one command to all of them. Whereas for this, I'm going to have to give multiple commands to multiple people. Think of it like a computer game. If you just wanted the character to walk straight, you could hold down the arrow key indefinitely. But if you wanted him to jump or turn or climb—or do a combination of those things—the sequence of keys you had to push got more involved. Then multiply that by two *hundred*. There are no cheat codes in the *universe* that can help you with that."

Most of the people on the airplane stared at me blankly—except Tina, who nodded. "That makes total sense."

"Thank God someone on this plane was born in the same *century* I was." I held up my hand to high-five her, which she returned awkwardly. "We'll work on that."

John came over and crouched in the aisle beside my seat. "Dale, your powers aren't any weaker than Amara's. That's not how it works."

"How do you know?"

He looked at Irene. She rolled her eyes. Clearly, the appeal of talking to me ranked somewhere between "root canal with no anesthesia" and "watching Adam Sandler movies while having a root canal with no anesthesia."

Irene said, "Supernatural genes are always dominant. So a child with one supernatural and one human parents will inherit all its supernatural parent's abilities. Once you start adding more human DNA into the mix, it becomes more complicated. The supernatural genes will win out, but they're less likely to inherit them in the first place. You could end up with a quarter-blooded child with all of its supernatural grandparent's abilities—or none of them."

"See? I know you can do this."

John reached out to touch my hand, but I pulled it away from him. "Fine. I will do the best I can."

Tina nodded. "Good. According to our intelligence, information pertaining to the illness is most likely on the third, eighth, or tenth level, so that will give us a more concentrated area to focus our search. Unfortunately, the Zetas are pretty old-fashioned, so any pertinent data will likely be on paper. Carrying it out is impractical, obviously, so you'll need to go through and take photographs of anything—anything at *all*—that looks like it might be pertinent.

"We'll all be wearing body cameras, which hopefully will help Dale know when to divert attention away from us. Are there any questions?"

"Yeah," I replied. "Can I still back out?"

<hr>

AN HOUR LATER, WE WERE in our Humvees outside of Great Falls heading toward the Grave, a dozen of us total. I had expected Montana to be mountainous, but it was just the opposite: nothing but flat stretches of land as far as I could see. Granted, I couldn't see *much*. Once we left the Great Falls city limits—though Great Falls was a "city" in the same way a Matchbox car is an "automobile"—the highway was so dark that we wouldn't have been able to see more than a few feet in front of us if we hadn't been using our brights. The whole thing looked like a scene out of a horror movie. I kept waiting for the Humvee to break down on the side of the road so the killer could pick us off one by one.

Unfortunately, it wasn't much better when we got to the Grave. The above-ground part of the facility was nothing more than a rectangular concrete slab, given an eerie glow by the spotlights surrounding the building. Guess I shouldn't have expected more from a facility named after *the place where you put dead bodies.* As we walked toward the building, I heard Mabel say to Tina, "I don't see why you have to go. You can command just as well from the Humvees. We've got the radios and the—"

"Mabel, stop. I'm not made of glass." I could almost hear Tina grinding her teeth.

"I just…I worry about you." Mabel's voice broke.

Tina reached out and touched her arm. "I know. But I spent twenty-one years in the Army. I know what I'm doing. And remember what

Doc Irene always says: just because you're immortal doesn't mean you're unkillable, either."

That was true. I'd seen my mother, the most powerful and influential demon, struck down before I'd been able to save her—by *these very people right here.* I looked at John. He'd traded his suit in for dark jeans and a leather jacket, and he looked more like the John I remembered…which made it that much worse.

I took a breath. I needed to focus. John was just one person, and I had the chance to save the entire supernatural world from extinction.

As Irene had apparently said, immortal didn't mean unkillable.

One of the group, an angel named Mike who wore an afro, peeked into the window. "Two guards at the desk, surrounded by security monitors. Four elevators behind them."

Tina ducked underneath Mike's arms and stood on her tiptoes. "They don't seem to have noticed anything. Leah, Suki, head over to the generator and deactivate the security system."

Two women left, leaving the rest of us to wait. A few minutes later, Tina spoke again. "One of the guards is on the move!"

The door flew open, and a middle-aged guard burst out, cursing to himself. "Damn generator. If they'd just get the parts that we needed…" I was ready to grab his mind, but then I realized I didn't have to. What felt like a heavy blanket had descended upon us, and the air seemed to shiver. Although I could still see everyone, the guard didn't seem to notice anything as he walked right by us. Once he passed, the weight lifted and the shimmering stopped. "Thank you, Naveen," Tina said.

An olive-complected man smiled and nodded. Tina turned to Rebekah. "That's your cue."

Rebekah's body morphed into the shape of the guard who'd just left for the generator. She'd duplicated everything down to the badge the guard used to swipe into the facility. But when Rebekah got to the door and swiped, it didn't work. "Push the intercom. Tell the other guard your badge isn't working."

Rebekah pushed the button, and a tinny voice came out of the speakers. "Yeah?"

"It's me." Rebekah really did sound like the guard had. Whatever my feelings about her personally, her power was pretty cool. "My badge isn't working. Can you let me back in?"

The voice came over the speaker again. "What happened with the security system?"

Rebekah hesitated before responding. "Yeah…looks like maybe it got struck my lightning or something. It's beyond my ability to fix. We'll have to call someone in."

"Got it." There was a buzzing noise, and the lock clicked open. A few minutes later Rebekah poked her head out again, wearing her own face. "Coast is clear."

The rest of us walked inside. The second guard was gone. Rebekah sat down at the desk and morphed again, transforming herself into the missing guard. "Where's the body?" Tina asked.

Rebekah pointed to a door behind her. "Janitorial closet."

"All right, we'll make sure to grab it before we leave. If you need help, hit the emergency signal." She turned to the rest of the group. "Guys, we're heading down. Split up and take floors. Half work your way up, half down. I want to make sure at least two of us run through the third, eighth, and tenth levels. Dale, I want you to head down to the bottom level and remain in the atrium. Make sure you have this on you at all times." She handed me a computer tablet. The display showed a grid-screen view of everyone's body cameras. "I think that'll give you the best macro-level picture of what's going on."

"I'm staying with Dale," John interjected.

"Oh, hell no!" I said at the same time Tina said, "Good idea."

A couple of nervous chuckles went through the group, and I heard Irene muttering something about prissy princesses under her breath. Tina looked me straight in the eye, undeterred by the fact that I had a good four inches and forty (or so) pounds on her. "You're critical to this mission, and you need backup. John trained you. He knows your strengths and weaknesses, and he knows how your power works better than anyone else here."

"Do you know what he did to me?" I asked.

"I don't care. You're part of this now. You do what's best for the mission. You'll need to head down first and grab their minds before we get there. Naveen, go with them, keep them covered."

I sighed, but I didn't argue further. Three of the elevators were labeled "All Floors," and the fourth was labeled "Express to Atrium." I pushed the button for that one and waited, John standing beside me like a sentinel. Naveen stood behind us, tapping his feet nervously. Whether it was because we were taking the express elevator into enemy territory or because of the buttloads of tension between me and John, I wasn't sure.

I'd been expecting some kind of cave or subterranean tunnels. The reality was much more intricate. Each floor was open, with a balcony wrapping all the way around the perimeter in sort of an oblong shape, becoming progressively smaller as they got closer to the top. Each floor was filled with rows upon rows of sliding shelves filled with accordion envelopes. The smell of paper and dust saturated the air, even down in the atrium. Pneumatic tubes ran lengthwise across the balconies, weaving in and out at every floor. There must have been hundreds of them, and every few seconds a cylinder would fly through the tube, traveling to some destination within the compound. Employees skittered around like ants, grabbing cylinders as they came out and loading more into the tube system. But the strangest thing about this place was that it was almost completely silent, save for the *whoosh* of cylinders traveling through the pneumatic tubes. In every office I'd ever been in, you could hear people chatting about their weekends and making lunch plans and saying hello to the coworker who just came back from vacation. Here I heard *nothing*—and given that the Grave was shaped like a glorified megaphone, I should have been hearing a lot more than that. On the fourth level, two people almost bumped into each other at the output of one of the pneumatic tubes. They changed direction and averted eye contact without a word. "Why aren't they talking?" I whispered. "Are they drugged?"

EMBRACING THE DEMON 87

"No," John replied. "They're terrified."

I shivered.

Tina's voice sounded through my earpiece. "Are you ready?"

"Not yet. Give me a minute."

I concentrated, seeking out the minds of everyone in the building. I found John and Naveen first and ignored them, pushing my focus toward the balconies. I decided to start with Zetas I found in the stacks. *Go back to your desks*, I ordered silently. Now, I did hear something: the sound of shoes clicking against the tile floors as dozens of employees returned to their desks. *Stay at your desks. Keep doing your work. Everything is okay.*

I didn't know how effective the last part would be: as I'd told Nik, my power didn't work on emotions. But I figured it couldn't *hurt* anything, so what the hell. "I've got them," I said into the microphone on my collar.

"Good. Heading down now."

Now came the tricky part. As the supernaturals navigated through the labyrinth of floors and shelves and tubes, I had to continue to tell the Zetas to stay at their desks and keep doing their work. Meanwhile, I had to watch the body cam feeds on the tablet to make sure none of the Zetas noticed my teammates.

The elevator doors opened. The supernaturals spread out into the shelves as I watched the feeds. One of my teammates ran into an issue almost immediately when she found herself face-to-face with a Zeta on the fifth floor who had slipped my leash and was headed to the pneumatic tubes. *That's Sally. She's supposed to be here.*

"Hello, Sally," he whispered, barely audible even through the sensitive microphone on our feed. For once, I didn't think my power had caused the glazed look on his face.

Another Zeta intersected the leftmost feed—Irene's body camera. He hadn't seen Irene yet, but he would as soon as he turned around. *Go back to your desk and stay there*, I told him.

He walked away without even turning around.

It kept going like this for several minutes. My head began to pound with the stress of concentration. At one point, Naveen asked, "Is it okay if I drop the cloak around us? It's hard to keep it going this long."

I didn't answer, because I was busy diverting a Zeta that was walking toward Mabel around another corner. I guess he took that as a yes, because a second later the air stopped shimmering as the invisi-bubble around us fell.

"You doing all right?" John asked.

"Huh?" A Zeta turned a corner suddenly and smacked into Tina. Shit. I thought fast. *You just ran into a shelving unit. Your foot hurts. Go back to your desk and rest it for a while.*

"How clumsy of me," the Zeta muttered before he turned around, presumably to go back to his desk.

"Holy shit, it's like that Zeta didn't even see her!" Naveen apparently didn't have a concept of the whole "inside voice" thing.

"He saw her. He just thought she was a shel—" One of the supernaturals wandered too far beyond the stacks and found himself surrounded by the Zetas' desks—all of which were occupied, thanks to my orders. Double shit. *That's just Carl from tech support. Don't worry about it.*

"Carl from tech support? *Is* there a Carl from tech support?" Naveen asked.

I hadn't realized I'd spoken out loud. "It doesn't matter. It—" I stopped speaking again when I saw another Zeta wander into the bottom right-hand frame.

I heard something crinkle next to me, and then John took my hand and put a protein bar in it. "You need to eat," he said.

"I'm fine. It's not like I'm running a marathon or something."

"No, but using your abilities takes energy, too. And your nose is already bleeding."

I couldn't help myself—I reached up and wiped my nose. Sure enough, my hand came back bloody. Grumbling, I shoved John's protein bar into my mouth. I didn't even have time to chew before I had to avert another Zeta collision. But sure enough, it was a little easier this time around and my headache started to dull. After I swallowed the last bite, John handed me a bottle of water. "Don't think this means you're out of the—"

And then we heard the sound of a toilet flushing.

We all swiveled our heads to our right, toward the noise. A door opened, and a man walked out. "What the hell? Who are you?"

I reached for his mind. *It's okay. It's just the cleaning crew.*

His eyes started to glaze over. But there were just too many strings pulling me in too many different directions. I closed my eyes, trying to keep them all within my grasp.

"Dale…" John's voice, filled with concern.

All the strings snapped.

For a second, I froze, my mind free from all the pressure that had been boring into it. But then I realized what had happened. "Oh, shit." I tapped my earpiece. "Abort! We need to get out, now!"

On the tablet screen, I could already see the Zetas, their mind control hazes fading, getting closer and closer to our people. I reached for them with my power again. Even if I could manage to hold them off for a few seconds, it might be enough to get us out of here.

But I couldn't. While I could still feel my ability humming dimly in the background, I didn't have enough mojo left to compel a cat to chase a laser pointer. "I'm tapped out!" I shouted.

"Damn. Plan B, then."

John pulled out the gun that had been holstered on his hip and fired at the Zeta who had just emerged from the bathroom. The Zeta fell. "Serves him right. He definitely didn't wash his hands before he came out of the bathroom," I said.

John ignored me. "Naveen, can you cover us?"

Naveen nodded, but judging by his pale skin and trembling hands, I wasn't so sure. Naveen's invisi-bubble dropped over us again. We ran for the elevator and pushed the button. Thankfully, the elevator was empty when it arrived. We jumped inside and rode back up to the lobby.

…and found ourselves surrounded by dozens of heavily armed Zetas in black BDUs.

Rebekah was still in her disguise as the guard. It hadn't fooled them, apparently, as they had a gun pointed at her head. She looked terrified.

When I stepped out of the elevator, the Zetas began muttering among themselves and checking their watches. One of them stepped forward. Then, he took my chin in his hand, chuckling. "It really is you. We've been looking for you for a long time, girlie."

Another elevators dinged. Irene, Tina, Mabel, and two other members of our team emerged. Mabel saw the Zetas and immediately raised her arms, freezing them in place. "It won't hold for long."

"The rest of the team?" John asked. Tina shook her head. "Then it's time for Plan B."

Tina pulled a grenade off of her belt, pulled the pin, and threw it at the Zetas. "Run!" We didn't hesitate. We ran like hell as the Grave exploded behind us.

The force knocked me off of my feet. "Dale?" John called frantically once the dust cleared. "Dale, are you all right?"

My body chose that moment to lose consciousness.

CHAPTER EIGHT
Dale

WHEN I WOKE UP AGAIN, I was on the airplane, lying flat across a row of seats. An IV line dripped into my hand, the bag hanging from the handle of the overhead compartment. I was still wearing my jeans, but my top had been replaced by a cotton hospital gown.

Irene stood above me, listening to my breathing with a stethoscope. When she saw my eyes open, she nodded. "Good, you're awake. You're going to be fine. You overextended yourself using your powers like that, and then when we were running away you caught some shrapnel in your back. I took a few images with the portable X-ray, and it doesn't look like it hit anything important. I'd like to follow up with a full MRI when we get back, though. Unfortunately, that's not our biggest issue. The Zetas are tracking you."

"I don't understand," I interrupted. "We already knew the Zetas wanted to kill me, which is exactly what they did. What makes you think they're tracking me?"

"How else do you think they found us, princess? There are no other Zeta compounds nearby. The nearest is Billings, and that's over two hundred miles away."

Shit. I took a deep breath. "Right. Okay. So first things first. If they were tracking me on their watches, it must be some kind of GPS chip or something. So do you think maybe it's in my clothes—"

"I think it's in *you*."

Before I could ask Irene what she meant, she pulled a device out of her bag that looked like a combination of the handheld bar code scanners they use at the grocery store and an old Gameboy. She pushed a button and began to move it over my body. When she reached my right thigh, it began to beep. "Found it," she said. "I'm going to need you to take your pants off. Try not to pull out the IV catheter when you do, because I'll just have to put it back again." I hesitated.

"What's wrong?" Irene asked.

"I just…I don't like getting undressed in front of strangers."

"Dale, I'm a doctor. Anything you've got I've seen hundreds of times before, and given all my supernatural patients, I've seen a lot of configurations *no one's* ever seen. You're fine."

"It's not that." I shrugged. "What if something happens? It's inconvenient to have to run for your life while naked—not to mention cold."

She sat down in the row across from mine. "I know you and I didn't get off on the best terms, but…regardless of what I think of you, I'm a doctor first. I won't do anything to hurt you."

I nodded and pushed myself up. My legs felt weaker than I expected, and I had to use the seat back for balance. My body had been taking a lot of damage lately and, supernatural healing or not, I was not invincible. My shoes were already off—someone must have removed them when they brought me on the plane—so I pulled my pants off and draped them over the back of my seat.

Irene took out a scalpel from her bag and a syringe filled with a clear liquid. "This is a local anesthetic, calibrated specifically for supernatural physiology. You'll feel a slight pinch when it's going in."

Something stirred in the back of my mind, a memory that was not quite there. "Is it a big needle?" I asked, although I wasn't even sure where the question had come from.

She pulled the protective cap off, revealing a thin needle about an inch long. "Just normal-sized. It won't hurt too much, don't worry." I must have stared too long, because Irene said, "I need you to lie down again."

The leather was warmer than I expected, probably from my own body heat. I felt a slight burn as Irene stuck me with the syringe, and I closed my eyes. I felt the pressure of the syringe, but the area was numb so it didn't hurt. About ten minutes later, she said, "Okay, you can open them up again. I got it out." She held up the offending object for me: a black cylinder about the size of a grain of rice.

I sat up. The incision in my leg had already healed, and the only evidence of it was the bloody gauze next to me and the slight pink discoloration of my skin. I stood up and put my pants on again.

Once I was dressed, Irene peered through the privacy curtain. "Rosa, can you come in here please?" A dark-haired woman peeked behind the privacy curtain. "I need you to take this somewhere. I don't care where, but it's got to be remote, and far away from any supernatural activity. Then take the long way back to throw them off the scent."

"No problem." Then she disappeared.

I gaped at the spot where Rosa had been standing less than a second earlier. Irene chuckled. "Teleporter. She comes in useful for these kinds of ops. Also, if you're ever looking for a cheap vacation, she'll take you anywhere in the world for a hundred-fifty dollars and a six-pack of beer. One time Rosa took me and Greg…" her voice trailed off, "…but that was a long time ago."

"I know I said it before, but I really am sorry about your husband. And I'm sorry about compromising the location of the hospital."

She shook her head. "It isn't your fault. Any of it. I should have thought to scan you back when we were in Kentucky. I knew the Zetas were after you, but I didn't think…I've just been so distracted lately."

"Don't beat yourself up too much. You've been busy trying to save two races of people. It takes a lot out of you."

"Well, technically—"

Suddenly, John burst through the privacy curtain, with Tina close on his heels. "I tried to stop him," Tina said. "Can I shoot him now?"

John spoke at the same time. "I'm sorry. I just had to make sure Dale was all right." He looked at me, an emotion I couldn't identify in his eyes. "You are, aren't you?"

"Yeah, I'm fine. I just overexerted myself."

"Good." Then he leaned in and kissed me.

I was so stunned at first I didn't think to push him away…and then I didn't *want* to push him away. The kiss resonated through my body from my lips to my toes, the zing between us—a side effect of John's power—dancing over my skin. He pulled back, just a little, and I almost whimpered at the loss. But he did not disappoint. He kissed his way up my neck, stroking my cheek with one hand, the other wandering up the back of my shirt. "Just go with it," he whispered. "Please."

Someone cleared their throat.

Irene and Tina still stood behind us. Irene looked bewildered. Tina just looked bored. "Usually people go into the bathroom to join the mile-high club," she said.

I flushed. John turned to them and offered a charming smile. "I'm sorry. I'm just so relieved that she's all right." He stroked my cheek tenderly. The effect was devastating. Tears started to fill my eyes, and I buried my head into John's chest to hide them from Irene and Tina. John wrapped his arms around me in a bear hug. "Oh, sweetheart. I was so worried about you."

I pulled my face away from his chest and took a breath. "Me, too." I wasn't sure if that was the answer he wanted, but it seemed like the thing a girl would say to her…boyfriend?

"Dale…I thought he killed your mother," Irene said. Oh, good, I wasn't the only one confused here.

"It's…it's complicated?" I replied. That much was true, at least.

"Apparently so, princess," Irene said. Great, I was back to princess again. Just when I thought I was getting somewhere with her. "All right, well, we'll leave you guys to your…business. The plane should be landing in about an hour."

Irene and Tina both retreated through the privacy curtain. I heard Tina muttering, "That was just gross. Can I *please* shoot him now?"

I turned back to John, who sat down in the seat Irene had just vacated. "What the fuck was that?"

"I needed a plausible reason to get you alone."

"And *that* was the best you could come up with?"

He shrugged, a mischievous smirk on his face. "I figured if they thought we were about to have hot, wild sex on the leather seats, they'd leave. I was right."

"Ew. Now I'm going to think about all the other people who might have had hot, wild sex in these seats. You do clean this plane after every flight, right?"

"Dale, we have a problem."

"I know, the Zetas are tracking me, and the location of the hospital has been compromised. I'm sorry about that. I had no idea. But Irene got the tracker out, and Covington is working on moving the sick patients into a new location. I'm sure between the two of you—"

"No." John stood up and peeked outside the curtain. Then he turned back to me. "We have a traitor."

———————◇———————

I FROZE. "WHAT DO YOU mean, a traitor? Irene just pulled a tracker out of me. That's how they found us."

"This airplane has been hardened against interference from any outside electromagnetic sources. So have our vehicles. I've tested them myself. Whatever device they had implanted in you, their monitors wouldn't have registered it from the outside."

"So? Maybe they locked on to me once we were in."

He shook his head. "As Dr. Kordova said, the nearest Zeta site is in Billings, and our intelligence indicates it's a small satellite facility. Only about fifteen people work there. There were at least ten times that many Zetas in the lobby. To bring in that many Zetas—and *martial* Zetas, at that—they would have had to bring people in from Idaho and North Dakota. There's no way they would have had time to arrange that, even if they picked you up as soon as we arrived in Great Falls. Someone leaked our plans to them. And the only people who knew about our plans are Covington…and the people on this plane."

I shook my head. "Maybe your intelligence is wrong? Maybe the Great Falls location has more people than you think."

"Maybe, but it doesn't fit with their M.O. Their sites are mainly located in populated areas—cities and larger towns—to fit with their recruitment goals. That area outside of Great Falls is mostly farmland."

I sighed. "Why are you telling me this?

"Because you're the only person here that I trust."

I scoffed. "Half of the people on this plane are your own people!"

"I know."

His voice was so bleak that it almost broke my heart. I fought it. Of course I felt sympathy for him. I'd loved him, once. But he'd still murdered my mother.

Still…John and I seemed to be on the same side in this, and a lot of people would die if we didn't help them. I thought about Irene's husband, about the sadness that filled her eyes whenever she talked about him. "So what do we do?"

He ran his fingers through his hair. "I wish I knew."

The intercom dinged, and the pilot announced we would be landing in a few minutes. John folded up the map and put it back in his pocket, just as Mabel came through the privacy curtain with her hand covering her eyes. "Are you decent? We have to go back to our seats, but no one else was willing to come back here to check."

I laughed, but it sounded fake. "Yeah, we're good. Tell everyone they can come back."

Fifteen minutes later, we were disembarking the plane. John had gotten off the plane in front of me, since his seat was in front of mine. I jogged to catch up to him. He strode hurriedly, his arms crossed, his lips pursed together in a thin line. I grabbed his arm and turned him toward me. "Baby, weren't you going to say goodbye before I have to go back home?"

Some of our fellow passengers chuckled as they passed by us without a second thought. After John's spectacle earlier, I must have looked like every stereotype of a clingy, insecure girlfriend ever.

Humiliating though it was, it wasn't actually a bad cover. I wasn't sure whether anyone understood my sudden transformation, but they weren't willing to ask me as long as I had my tongue stuck down John's throat. I pulled John into a corner, which was the closest we could get to privacy in the middle of an airport. "I want everything you have on the Zetas, including whatever we managed to gather in this raid. If you want my help with this, no more secrets. You need another set of eyes on this thing." I could tell he was hesitating, and it pissed me off. "You told me about this because you don't trust anyone else, and I don't know if that's frightening or just sad. But you don't know what to do next. People are dying, and you need help to fix this. And I'm the only one who can help you."

He sighed, but then he nodded. "You're right. I'll give you everything. No more secrets."

CHAPTER NINE
Dale

COVINGTON MET ME OUTSIDE THE airport and took me to a new safe house, this one located in Jersey City. It was a one-level apartment, sleek, modern, and minimalistic, like I'd died and ended up in an IKEA catalogue. It probably would have been more impressive if the windows hadn't all, once again, been covered with blackout shades nailed into the walls.

I found my bedroom and crashed immediately, not waking until the next morning. When I awoke, several boxes filled with documents were waiting for me in front of my bed. I wasn't sure how John had gotten in without me noticing, but it didn't bode well. Normally I was a light sleeper, but my poor body had been through so much lately. Even supernatural healing has its limits.

I was still reviewing the documentation when John knocked on the door that evening. Nik answered the door, wearing an oversized tank top and shorts, her short hair pulled away from her face with a bandanna. When she saw John in his leather jacket and khakis, she plastered on her most charming smile. "Well, hello there. Are you here to…install some pipes, perhaps? I have some plumbing that's in dire need of examination."

I rolled my eyes and pushed myself between Nik and John before she could further steer the conversation down Porno Lane. "Actually, he's here to see me. We're going to go up to my bedroom and…talk." Just in case my innuendo-laced words weren't enough, I stroked my palm down his chest, stopping just short of his belt buckle. I felt him stiffen. Happy trail, indeed.

She huffed. "Well, fine. Be like that. But I'm just so *bored*. All I did was try to step out the door to talk to the security detail yesterday, and my ankle monitor starts going off like I'd tried to murder someone. And now they moved us to a new place because of it?"

John frowned. "Why were you trying to leave?"

"I wasn't trying to *leave*. Like I said, I just wanted to chat with the security detail. Chaz has been such a sad sack lately, and the woman they sent up to check on us yesterday morning when I screamed because I saw a spider in the shower? Un-be-lievably hot."

I groaned. "Nik, can you please try to keep your libido in check for just a little while longer? I know it sucks, but we're really trying to keep you and Chaz safe. And trying to leave the residence so you can get laid is a whole new level of stupid."

She laughed, but there was an odd note of sadness in it. "Dale, you would be amazed at the level of stupid I can come up with."

Before I could press her on what she meant, Nik retreated into her and Chaz's room and shut the door. I led John toward my bedroom.

John sat down on the bed, looking uncomfortable. "Why did you do that?"

"It's our cover, right? I mean, if anyone finds out that you've been coming here, we want them to think that we've been hooking up." And if a surge of possessiveness had surged through me when I saw Nik flirting with him, well…there was really no need to analyze that too much, right?

"And Chaz?"

I glanced toward the wall between my room and the room Nik and Chaz shared. "I haven't seen him since I got back. Nik must be funneling him food, but I'm really beginning to worry that he's got bottles of pee stashed away in there like he's Howard Hughes or something."

John studied me. "You know, you don't have to stay here with them if things are…tense. We can relocate you."

I rubbed my temples. I felt a headache coming on. Between the stress and the abuse of my power, I'd probably be the first half-blooded demon ever to give myself a stroke. "No, that's not necessary. They're my friends, and I can understand why they're frustrated and upset. I need to try to make things right with them."

"They were only part of your life for a few months, and Chaz especially seems to have written off your friendship entirely. You don't owe them anything."

"I know, but…maybe it's different when you don't have anyone else."

John opened his mouth like he was about to say something, but he closed it again. "Have you figured out anything about the Zetas?" he asked.

"Well…I have some thoughts." I flipped open the binder. "It says that the Zeta Coalition originated after World War II, when human politicians first learned about the supernatural population."

He cringed. "Some stupid kid started showing off his powers to his human friends. That was during all that McCarthy Era/Red Scare bullshit, and everyone was paranoid about everything. The human's parents called the feds, and the kid got taken in. No one ever saw him again. But not long after that, we started getting wind of this government organization to combat 'the supernatural menace,' as if we're something out of an old sci-fi movie. But as far as we know, the Zeta Coalition hasn't been associated with the government since the early 1990s."

"Yes, but they still operate like a government entity." I turned to another page. "It's hierarchical, with a rigid organizational structure. If we take out the senior leadership, the rest will just fall apart."

"Problem is, we don't know where that senior leadership is located. We've had undercover operatives embedded with the Zetas for years now, and we've tripled that number since the illness emerged. These people are notoriously tight-lipped with information."

EMBRACING THE DEMON

"Exactly. Which is why we have to get them to bring us to the information." I went over to one of the other boxes—the one filled with the bits and pieces of information we'd managed to retrieve during the Montana raid. "The Zetas have a pastor named Selwyn Schilling in their organization, based out of Lincoln, Nebraska. He's become increasingly popular in the Lincoln area over the past few years, and they're opening up a new church there. First services are next Sunday."

"So?"

"The church is a front for Zeta recruitment. So we should go in there and just…let ourselves be recruited."

He gave an exasperated sigh. "Dale, we can't just go up to them and say, 'Hey, we hate supernaturals, and we're interested in joining. Now give us all your secrets.'"

"No, we can't. So we have to give them something they really want. Something they can't resist."

"And what exactly would that be?"

I gave him my best smile. "Me."

———————◇———————

My plan was simple: John would pose as human who had discovered an evil demon bitch (i.e. me), and somehow managed to imprison me. Of course, John the Human would have no idea that the demon bitch who had mindfucked his brain during sex—again, my idea, preying upon all those testosterone-laden assholes' worst fears about women. No, that would just be a happy coincidence. The process of leading the Zetas to me would help John get into their good graces and worm his way into their inner circle. Basically, I was the bait. It was brilliant.

"That is the stupidest idea I've ever heard," John said.

He correctly pointed out that the Zetas were not just trying to imprison me, but to kill me, so once he turned me over I was pretty much dead. He also pointed out that, even if the plan did work, it would likely take several meetings over the course of weeks or months to get into the Zetas'

BETH WOODWARD

good graces. There was also the slight problem that the Zetas still had that potion to strip me of my powers, which would eliminate my main offensive capability.

I sat down on the floor with my knees against my chest. "All right, fine. Possibly this plan was a little more risk-intensive than I thought. Back to the drawing board."

"Not entirely." John sat down across from me. "We can't risk turning you over to the Zetas. But that doesn't mean we can't use you as bait—or at least, the idea of you. We pose as a married couple, go to the church services, and approach Reverend Sel. We use the same story: that I was coerced into sex by a demon with mind-control powers. Without the tracker you're completely off the grid, so the Zetas are probably desperate for any sort of information that would lead back to you, and who knows more about you than you do? We can give them just enough to entice, but not enough to compromise you."

"There's one problem with that. The Zetas have been chasing me for God knows how long. What if they recognize me—or both of us?"

He grinned. "But Dale...that's your area of expertise."

Two days later, John and I got on the private airplane again and flew to Lincoln, Nebraska.

There was a vehicle waiting for us in the airport parking garage, a black Toyota Tacoma with the keys in the ignition. How and why no one had messed with it in the airport garage, I don't know, but John climbed in and started the engine as if it were the most natural thing in the world. I got into the passenger's side, and we headed to our temporary home. "Did you get the identifications?" I asked. John motioned to the glove compartment, where I found two Missouri driver's licenses with our pictures on them under the names of Aaron and Laura Hill.

"Perfect! Here's our story. You are thirty-three, and I'm thirty. We've been married for three years. You're a long-distance truck driver, and I'm an eighth grade social studies teacher. We want to have children—"

"Does it matter if we want children?" John asked.

"Yes, that will literally be the first thing that people ask." I'd seen it happen to newly and not-so-newly married women I'd met in my travels too many times to count. "It's a thing: single women get asked when they're going to get married, and married women get asked when they're going to have a baby, and women with a baby get asked when they're going to have their second. It's a never-ending cycle of people butting into your shit."

"If you say so," John replied, making it very clear that he'd both not spent enough time in the human world, and never had a uterus.

I continued. "We met through an online dating website—"

"I've heard things about those 'online dating websites.' Don't people consider them a little risqué?"

"Only if you're geriatric." Of course, John technically made geriatrics look like young whippersnappers, but this was not the time to get into a discussion about supernatural biology.

John pulled into the driveway and put the car into park. Then he turned to me. "I shouldn't question you. I know you know what you're doing. I'll go with whatever you come up with. This is why I need you here." And then he smiled at me, like he had all the confidence in the world that I could pull off a covert espionage operation.

And maybe he was right. In a way, this was what I'd been practicing for my entire adult life.

Our house was a newish suburban split-level with three bedrooms, walking distance from Capitol Lake Beach. I wasn't sure that it would count as a "beach" anywhere but the Midwest, but hey, it had water and boats and sand, and you'd take what you could get when you were thousands of miles from an ocean.

All the houses around us were so clean and new, with basketball hoops and cars parked neatly in the driveways. The neighborhood was all decorated for Christmas, with lights and reindeer and those blow-up Santas in the yard. The sky was blue with puffy clouds, and a light dusting of snow covered the grass. Everything was flat, no hills to be found, giving it the surreal quality of a movie backlot. I half expected a slasher movie villain to jump out of the bushes and start attacking us with a chainsaw.

It was a Thursday afternoon when we arrived. Since this was a supernatural-sponsored mission, I had a bigger budget for our disguises than I usually did—and you really can do *anything* with the right amount of money. I spent most of the day Friday at the local mall, getting my hair done, buying clothes and makeup, and choosing a wardrobe for John. By the time I returned to the house I had soft layers and chunky highlights—a style that probably would have looked dated in New York, but seemed to fit the aesthetic of the other women I'd seen while wandering through the stores. Laura wore a lot of earth tones, I decided, and applied her makeup with a heavier hand than my own. I also purchased brown contact lenses to hide my blue eyes, as well as some makeup putty and spirit gum, which allowed me to change the profile of my nose and chin.

John's disguise was simpler. For Sunday services, he would wear a pair of dark jeans and a blue button-down shirt, one of the heavier ones that you don't have to iron. I'd made him dye his hair dark brown and comb it down neatly, parting it on the left side. I'd have to watch that; his normal spikiness had more to do with his tendency to run his fingers through his hair than excessive use of hair product, and I wanted to make sure that Aaron Hill did not retain any of John's mannerisms. Overall, it was a look that said, "Ugh, my wife forced me to dress decently for church."

It was perfect.

He shifted his weight between his feet. "All right, for the finishing touches." He reached into his pocket, pulled out a ring box, and set it on the kitchen counter. I gasped. I couldn't help myself. John may have betrayed and nearly broken me...but my traitorous heart didn't seem to care.

I opened the box. Inside was a platinum engagement band with a square-cut diamond in the center, large enough to be conspicuous but not gaudy, and a matching wedding band with more diamonds embedded in the metal. They were beautiful...and not even remotely my style. But they were perfect for Laura Hill, with her chunky hair and her too-perfect makeup. And if anything could bring me back to reality, it was that: fake rings for a fake marriage to a man I had loved once upon a time. "I didn't think about getting rings."

"Yeah, I figured that when I didn't see any with the clothes you bought yesterday. I ran out to the store and got them last night. Got one for myself too."

Sure enough, there was a plain platinum band on his left hand, thicker and more masculine than mine. "They're perfect," I said as I slipped the rings onto my finger. "I'm glad you thought of it. Someone definitely would have noticed if we weren't wearing wedding bands." I couldn't believe I had missed such a big detail. But none of my previous identities had been married—and I wouldn't have been able to afford rings like this even if they had been.

"One last thing." John put two auto-injectors on the counter between us; I only knew what they were because a friend of mine in middle school had a severe peanut allergy, and I'd watched her mom inject her when she'd accidentally eaten some peanut butter cookies while we were at the mall. When Angie started wheezing, her mother had whipped the EpiPen out of her purse and jammed it into her thigh. I'd never seen anyone move so fast.

"I didn't think supernaturals suffered food allergies," I said.

"What? Oh…no, these aren't EpiPens. It's called the Changeling Serum. Irene formulated it. Remember the supernatural detectors that Isaac had in his tunnels?" I nodded. "There's a good chance the Zetas have access to the same technology. The Changeling Serum will block your—well, your *demonness*, for lack of a better word—for six hours. If you hit one of those supernatural detectors, for all intents and purposes you'll *be* human. Downside is, your powers will be blocked during that time, too. It's similar to the serum the Zetas dosed you with when you were attacked."

"That's a big downside."

"Unfortunately, it's not the only one." He picked up the injector, pulled the cap off, and plunged it through his jeans without so much as a twitch. "The serum is emotion-sensitive. Something about the chemicals that flood your system when you feel strong emotions, particularly anger or fear. The serum reacts to the chemicals, and the effects are negated."

"Negated?"

"Your powers come back, but every supernatural detector in the place will be going off like fireworks on the Fourth of July."

Just what I needed. I'd be powerless and terrified of being killed by the Zetas...but also completely unable to feel that terror, lest I negate my serum and reveal myself. "Just don't ask me not to think about elephants," I muttered.

We planned to attend the Sunday morning service at ten. But that morning around four, I heard a noise. I went downstairs and found John sitting on the couch, staring into nothingness. There was a paperback book on his lap, but he appeared to have forgotten about it. "That book's not going to read itself, you know."

He looked up at me. "Sorry, I didn't mean to wake you. I'm just having trouble sleeping."

"That pretty much seems to be the story of my life lately." I walked into the kitchen—which was connected to the living room in that open floor plan style everyone seems to rave about on the real estate shows—poured some milk into a mug, and popped it into the microwave. When it was finished, I pulled it out, and then I hesitated. I could have stayed in the kitchen. Maybe I *should* have stayed in the kitchen. But we were both nervous about the same thing, and it seemed silly to leave him alone. Whatever had happened between us in the past, we were partners now. We both needed to be in top form if we were going to survive tomorrow.

Besides...I was lonely. And maybe he seemed a little bit lonely, too.

I sat down on the couch next to him. "Are you nervous?" I asked. "I thought this kind of thing would be old hat to you."

"I'm an assassin, Dale, not a spy. Most of the time, I just kill people."

I wasn't sure what to say to that, so I didn't say anything. I sipped on my warm milk as John opened his book and stared at the same page for a long time. Finally, he gave up the pretense of reading and turned to me. "I don't think you should come tomorrow," he said.

I put my mug down. "Wait...are you serious?"

"I think I'll focus better without you to worry about."

I stood up and shook my head. "Great. That's just fucking great. I guess I'll just head off to the kitchen where I belong then. Would you like me to make you a sandwich while I'm there?"

"It's not like that."

"Oh really? Then what's it like?"

He tapped his foot against the floor, a staccato beat on the hardwood. "I've always worked alone," he said. "I'm not used to…worrying about anyone else."

"How inconvenient for you."

I started back toward the kitchen, but John grabbed my arm and spun me back toward him. "The Zetas are trying to kill you!"

"I *know*! I was there, all three times." I yanked my arm away. "You lost the right to worry when you betrayed me."

I went to the kitchen and began digging through the pantry. I didn't know what I was looking for. Maybe something sweet? Hell, arsenic was looking good at that point. I heard footsteps, until John's shadow loomed over me. I sighed. "I've said what I need to say."

"I haven't."

I didn't turn around right away. I wouldn't give him the satisfaction. But I couldn't just stare into the pantry forever. I grabbed a package of Oreos and sat down at the breakfast nook. "All right. So talk."

"Did I ever tell you how my parents died?"

This was not the direction I expected him to take the conversation in. "Amara killed them, and you wanted revenge. I get it."

"No, you don't." He sat down across from me. "My mother's name was Mercy Goodwin. She was born in the Massachusetts Bay Colony, probably around 1660. She was the third of nine children, seven of whom survived past infancy, and their resources were always scarce. The Goodwins struggled to make sure all their children were fed. But Mercy had something the others didn't: she was beautiful. Striking. And as she grew into a young woman, that caught the attention of the local elites."

I didn't think I would like where this story was going. I took a cookie out of the package and bit into it, needing *something* to do other than stare at him.

John continued. "After the War of Purity, angels kept most of their activity underground for a long time. Officially, they didn't mate with humans. Unofficially…well, once you let a cat like that out of the bag, you can't exactly put it back in. Angels may not have believed humans to be their equals, but many had no problem rutting with or even raping them. Sometimes a child would result. Those early children were either abandoned to their human parents…or killed. But after some years had passed, my father—"

"Zaphkiel, right?" A while after shit had gone down and I'd left New York, I'd put together a sort of flowchart/family tree so I could try to wrap my head around who's who in the supernatural world. Not that I ever intended to come back.

"Yes, that's right. Zaphkiel realized that if he were to mount a war against the demons, he was going to need a bigger army. Demons had continued to procreate with humans, and their numbers dwarfed ours. Gabriel proposed a solution: start a breeding program with a select number of humans that would be under Thrones' control. They used whatever means necessary to convince the human families to give up their kin—money, blackmail, but especially religious propaganda. I believe that's how we became so linked with human religions. They'd try to get humans who were between the ages of ten and twelve—young enough to be malleable, but old enough to be of breeding age fairly quickly. They jokingly referred to the humans' living quarters as 'the stables.'"

A picture started forming in my head. "Your mom got taken to the stables, didn't she?"

He nodded, his lips pressed into a tight line. "Zaphkiel told my grandparents that he needed Mercy to help him do God's work. And when that wasn't enough, the money he offered did the trick."

He took a shaky breath. He was building up to something, but I still wasn't sure what. "So did you grow up in the stables?" I asked.

"It was all I knew when I was a kid." The look on my face must have been pretty horrified, because he chuckled. "It wasn't as bad as it sounds. It's not like I slept with the horses or anything. It was…crowded. There were dozens of us on the compound, men, women, and children. Often at night, groups of angels would come by. All the adults would have to stand outside in a line, and the angels would pick which ones they wanted. There were no walls in our quarters, so I could see the outlines of them fucking in the darkness. Sometimes you'd hear the women cry. Sometimes the men, too. Especially the new ones. On the nights when I couldn't sleep because of all the sobbing and noise, Mother would hold me tight and sing to me until I drifted off."

"I think you would have been better off with the horses," I said.

He shook his head. "It wasn't as bad for me as it was for a lot of the others. My mother belonged to Zaphkiel, so none of the other angels would touch her. Some of the women would be pregnant one right after another after another. Many of them would die. For the men…physically, it wasn't as difficult for them. But mentally…so many of them based their whole identities on being providers and protectors. Without that, they had nothing.

"But I was just a boy. I didn't know any better. I also belonged to Zaphkiel, his only child. He always made it clear that I wouldn't lead because of my human blood, that I was merely going to be a foot soldier. But I think…he was proud of me in his way, of how strong and capable I already was. And my mother got to spend her time caring for me, since she wasn't pregnant all the time. I had love, which was more than the other children got."

He stood up and walked across the kitchen. He got a glass out of one of the cabinets and filled it with water from the sink. He stood there longer than he needed to, letting the water overflow and drip down his hand. When he finally turned the faucet off, he had to empty some of the water into the sink so he could come back to the table without spilling. When he sat down again, he didn't touch the water. "One night, when I was about seven or eight, Zaphkiel came to the stables to see my mother. My mother told me to go outside to play, but it was cold and I didn't want to go out by

BETH WOODWARD

myself, so I hid in the pantry. There was a little knothole in the door, so I could see them from my hiding spot."

He sighed. He wouldn't meet my eyes. "I don't know how long I was there before they came in—Amara and her people. My father was...busy with my mother, and Amara caught him unawares. She slit his throat. My mother screamed, and she tried to run, but..." he swallowed, "...the weight of my father's body pinned her there. Amara slit her throat, too."

My eyes filled with tears. "John, I'm so—"

His voice was shaky. "Amara and her people killed everyone that night, all the children I'd grown up with, all the people I loved. And I watched. I covered my mouth with my hands so I wouldn't scream, and I just... watched. I was too terrified to do anything else. Even after it was over, I wouldn't come out for hours. By the time I did, my mother was already c-cold."

"John, you were just a child. If you had come out, they would have killed you, too."

"I know. And yet a part of me still thinks that I should have done something. That I should have tried."

He didn't say anything else. I stood up and walked across the kitchen, needing to put some distance between him and me. The tears that had been threatening started to drip down my face. "I get it," I said. "You watched Amara murder your parents. And you wanted to avenge them. I get it."

"No, you don't get it!" He whirled me around to face him. I hadn't even heard him get up. "I've lost *everyone* that I've loved. Everyone. I don't want to lose you, too."

I pulled out of his grip. "You lost me, too. The night you killed my mom."

I headed to my bedroom without looking at him again. I think if I had seen his eyes, I would have lost it. "I'll be ready to go at nine-fifteen tomorrow," I said.

CHAPTER TEN
Dale

THE FEW TIMES AUNT BARBARA had taken me to church, they were very old-fashioned and rigid, all stained-glass windows and organs echoing through the pews. This church was...something else.

The church building was new, the smell of paint and new carpet still fresh in the air. Between the recessed lighting and the shiny white walls, the room was so bright I felt like putting on my sunglasses. Instead of pews, this church had separate, theater-style seats, arranged stadium-style so you could always get the best view. There was a band playing in the front, complete with electric guitars, a longhaired bass player, and colored spotlights shining on them. The whole place was just so...not churchy. I felt like I had accidentally walked into a concert at the local community college, except for the cross on the front of the lectern and the fact that the band was singing about God's love instead of orgasms and heroin.

Then, the lights dimmed, and a booming voice echoed through the room. "Ladies and gentlemen, please welcome the Reverend Selwyn Schilling."

Elvis's entrance theme blasted through the room, and everyone jumped out of their seats. A spotlight zeroed in on a man in his mid-forties racing up the center aisle, high-fiving everyone he encountered along the way. The crowd screamed and cheered, reaching across other people for the merest chance that they might be able to touch him or brush his clothing—or hell, just touch someone who had touched him. The whole spectacle was so ridiculous that I had to stop myself from laughing and breaking character. Instead, I whispered to John, "His name is fake."

"What makes you so sure?" he asked.

"Come on! *Selwyn Schilling?* With a name like that, he should be busking in Diagon Alley during the Quidditch World Cup." When John stared at me blankly, I raised my eyebrows. "*Harry Potter.* Seriously, you've never heard of *Harry Potter*?"

"Was that a sequel to *Star Wars?*"

I sighed and turned back to the spectacle.

By this time, Reverend Sel had finished his sprints up and down the aisle, and he stood in the front of the room, not the least bit sweaty or out of breath. He reminded me of the host of one of those old game shows, all blinding white smile and Ken doll hair. As the applause and the screaming died down, Reverend Sel smiled and waved again, and the crowd exploded again.

If I'd rolled my eyes any harder, they would have gotten stuck.

And then he began to speak. "Welcome, my friends! I'm so glad you could all join me in our gorgeous new church. Many thanks to our generous donors who made the construction of this new building possible. God is great!"

More applause and cheering. My ears were starting to ring.

"Since I see so many new faces in the crowd today—welcome, to all of you—I'd like to present to you one of my favorite sermons. It may be the most important sermon we give here in the Church of the Holy Light. Today, I'd like to talk to you about sparrows."

"Sparrows?" I muttered under my breath. Apparently, I wasn't the only one confused; some people around me were frowning and whispering, too. Others, however, sat with their hands folded in their laps and smug smiles on their faces, like the people who had read the *Game of Thrones* books on the day the Red Wedding episode aired. Guess we knew who had seen Reverend Sel's sermons before.

EMBRACING THE DEMON

"Sparrows are great little birds, and they've always led great little lives. They're hearty, they sing beautiful songs in the morning, and they can nest just about anywhere. Sparrows have lived happily among us for a very long time...until cuckoos began laying eggs in their nests."

"Wait, are you sure we're not attending a conservation lecture?" I whispered. John shushed me.

"Cuckoos, for those of you who don't know, are a very different kind of bird. They're parasites. They lay their eggs in the nests of other birds. Oftentimes, the cuckoos will push the sparrow's eggs out of its nest to lay its own, and then the sparrow will be fooled into taking care of the cuckoo chicks instead. Then after the eggs hatch, the cuckoo chicks will steal the food and the resources from the baby sparrows, so they'll grow strong while the baby sparrows become weak and frail. Sometimes, the cuckoo chicks themselves will even push more of the baby sparrows out of the nest. The babies that have grown up as their brothers and sisters...and the cuckoo chicks will just push them out of the nest."

Reverend Sel paused dramatically. "My friends...we have cuckoos among us."

I shivered, my fight-or-flight response kicking in. John grabbed my hand, willing me to stay put.

"These are people who walk among us every day, but they are not like us. They don't believe in the same things we do, they don't hold the same values that we do. They are not children of God—though they may pretend to be. But the reality is, *they do not belong here.*"

I tightened my grasp on John's hand. He whispered into my ear, "Stay calm. Everything's fine. This is what we came for."

John's words, and the pressure of his hand on mine, reassured me. I didn't want to think too much about what *that* meant at the moment. I took several slow breaths and tried to focus on Reverend Sel's voice. "Now, just so we're clear, I'm not talking about people who don't look like you do or don't live in the same kinds of neighborhoods or who maybe don't even believe in the same God. No matter what, we have to remember we're all part of the same race: the *human* race. No matter if we're black

BETH WOODWARD

or white or green or purple, we're all the same on the inside, where it counts. But these cuckoos…they *aren't* like us. And as long as they remain in our neighborhoods and our schools and our workplaces, they will take from good people like you and me. They take the jobs that are rightfully ours. They take the education opportunities that rightfully belong to our children. And pretty soon, they'll push all the rest of us sparrows out of the nest completely."

There were mutters throughout the audience. That didn't surprise me. What surprised me is how many of them seemed to *agree* with this crap. I thought of my own life—living on the fringes of society, taking whatever shit job would pay me under the table—and I wondered what they really thought I was taking from them.

"So you probably want to ask, 'Why Reverend Sel, just how do I spot these cuckoos, anyway?' Now, that's the tricky part—and I warn you, my friends—this might be the part that's the most difficult for you to understand right now. The tricky thing about cuckoos is that they look exactly like us. Your nextdoor neighbor might be a cuckoo. Your child's teacher. A waitress at your local diner. But there are things you should watch for. For example, have you ever met someone and then run into them again years later—ten, twenty, maybe even thirty years—and realized they looked just the same? 'Just great genes,' you think. 'Maybe they've had some work done.' Maybe. But maybe not."

Based on the reaction of the crowd, anyone who had been hitting the Oil of Olay too hard was suspect. Shit. John took my hand again, willing me to relax.

"But there are other things to watch for, too. Have you ever seen something that you just weren't able to explain? Like maybe something on a table moved by itself. Maybe someone was standing in a crowd one minute, but disappeared the next. Maybe you've even had thoughts that didn't belong to you, or did things that you never wanted to do. And you rationalized it. You thought it was your imagination or your mind playing tricks on you. And we all do it. It's human nature. But I'm here to tell you that it's not your imagination, and it's not a trick. I've seen these cuckoos, these not-human creatures, with my own two eyes. They are powerful, they are strong, and they are *among us.*"

Reverend Sel lowered his voice, his stance relaxing. "But there is hope, and I'm looking at it right now. You, me, all of us…*we* are the hope. Genesis chapter one, verse twenty-seven, tells us that God created mankind in His image. We belong here on Earth, because God willed it so. But these creatures, no matter what they look like, no matter what they call themselves, are abominations. But there are more of us than there are of them…and we have the will of God on our side. Thank you very much."

The room burst into applause. I followed suit, because I knew it's what Laura Hill would do, but I felt cold on the inside. I met John's eyes, but between his dyed hair and his wash-and-wear button-down, he felt like an alien to me. Or maybe I was the alien, in a room full of people who wanted nothing more than to dissect me. John gave me a tight smile. "I think it's time we spoke to Reverend Sel."

AFTER THE SERVICE ENDED, JOHN and I walked up the aisle, joining the line of parishioners waiting to greet Reverend Sel. It was crowded, and it took a long time to get to him because we wanted to wait until the other parishioners cleared out. When it was finally our turn, John stepped forward and held out his hand. "I'm Aaron Hill, and this is my wife, Laura," he said with the broad mid-Southern accent he'd adopted for this persona. "We just moved to Lincoln from St. Louis, and we heard so many great things about you. And this new church of yours looks great!"

Reverend Sel shook both of our hands. I made sure to keep my face nice and scowly, which seemed to take him aback. He hesitated slightly after he withdrew his hand. "Well, I'm so glad you two could make it. I hope you will attend the service again next week."

"Actually," John said, "we wanted to speak to you. You see…" He lowered his voice. "I think I've been targeted by one of those cuckoos you talked about."

BETH WOODWARD

I folded my arms and sighed heavily. I may have tossed an eye roll in there for good effect. Reverend Sel looked intrigued. Not salivating yet, but it was a good sign. "Is that so?"

"Yes." He ran his hand through his hair—a gesture that belonged to John, not Aaron Hill, but it worked here. "She, uh...she seduced me. I didn't want to. I love my wife. But it's like she..." he lowered his voice, "she took over my mind."

I rolled my eyes. "This is ridiculous."

"Baby, I know you don't believe me, but it's true."

"You dragged me hundreds of miles away from my home and family, moved me out to this hellhole, and *then* I find out that you've been fucking some *whore* on the side!" Everyone around me gasped. "Oh, I'm sorry, can you not say 'fuck' in church? What about 'whore'? Mary Magadalene was a whore, did you fuck *her* too?"

Reverend Sel held his hands up in a conciliatory gesture. "Mrs. Hill—"

John spoke up, "I told you it wasn't like that. I didn't want to! I just...I couldn't stop it. I couldn't control my body, I couldn't control *anything*."

"That's convenient. 'Baby, I just couldn't help myself, her pussy hypnotized me!' I didn't know she had a hypnopussy!"

Reverend Sel interjected again. "Mrs. Hill—"

"Oh right, can't say that one either! How about vagina? I didn't know she had a hypnovagina!"

"Mrs. Hill!"

I stopped. Everyone in the church was staring at us now, not bothering to hide it. I scrubbed my face with my hands, tears welling up in my eyes. (Crying on cue had been a very helpful skill on more than one occasion.) "I'm sorry. It's just...Aaron is the love of my life. I never thought he'd do something like this to me."

I sat down in a seat in the first row, shaking and sniffling. Reverend Sel, however, was much more focused on John. "What did this woman look like?"

John hesitated, like he was thinking about it. "Maybe about five foot four. Black hair, but I think it was dyed, curvy, but not real big, fair skin... really striking blue eyes."

EMBRACING THE DEMON   117

I rolled my eyes, praying that the damn contact lenses wouldn't pop out and reveal the real color underneath. "'Striking.' Of course they were."

Reverend Sel rubbed his chin. "Mr. Hill, I do think you had an encounter with one of those 'cuckoos' that I spoke about. And I know exactly how you're feeling, because…something very similar happened to me. Several years ago, when I was still an associate pastor in another congregation, a woman approached me after one of the services; I think it was the same woman you met. She flirted with me aggressively. I told her I was married, but she didn't care. Before I knew it, she had taken me back to her place and was…having her way with me. I had to do everything she said. I knew what I was doing was wrong, but I couldn't stop it." He sighed heavily. "Afterward, I felt horrible, and I told my wife everything." Reverend Sel turned to me, tears in his eyes. "She didn't believe me, either. We divorced two years ago. I pray that you two won't suffer the same fate."

This guy was lying hard enough to set off every polygraph in the state. I'd never met Reverend Sel before, I'd certainly hadn't gone to *church* anytime in my adult life, and I would never use my powers to rape someone. The thought horrified me, and I hoped John didn't think I was capable of it. I wanted to look over at him, to try and read his thoughts, but I knew I'd break character if I did. So I settled for staring at Reverend Sel, skepticism in my gaze. "Look, I don't know what kind of 'bros before hoes' thing you're going for here, but don't bother. Aaron and I are going to have to figure this out for ourselves, one way or another. C'mon, Aaron, let's go."

I grabbed John's arm and led him toward the door. This was all part of the plan. We couldn't appear too anxious, otherwise Reverend Sel might get suspicious. It was like going into a car dealership and walking away when the sales person didn't meet your price. Even if it took weeks, eventually Reverend Sel wouldn't let us get out that door.

"Would you be willing to let me take you somewhere?" Reverend Sel called after us.

Bingo.

CHAPTER ELEVEN
Dale

WE ACCOMPANIED REVEREND SEL TO his silver Chevy Suburban. John held the front door of the car open for me. I ignored it and climbed into the back seat. John shut the door and came around to sit in the back with me. I scooted away from him and moved as close to the door as I could possibly get without physically throwing myself out of the car.

Reverend Sel glanced back at us from the driver's seat as he pulled out of the church parking lot. "You two doing all right back there?"

"Yes, sir, we're just fine," John said. I rolled my eyes.

"It's going to be about an hour to get to where we need to go. But if you need to stop to use the restroom or anything, just let me know."

We sat in silence until Reverend Sel pulled onto the highway. Then he spoke again, apparently uncomfortable with the silence. "So, uh, I'm so glad that you two could join me today. I'm so excited to introduce you to the members of my group. We're not the only ones who have been affected by the supernatural menace, and I think you'll find that everything makes a lot more sense once you've seen what they have to say."

I made a disdainful noise. "Aaron, don't you hear how ridiculous this sounds? They're probably some kind of cult or something. Next he'll be telling us we have to drink poisoned Kool-Aid so the aliens will take us into their spaceships."

John rubbed his temples. "I really wish you would just trust me."

"How can I possibly trust you? You made me think you loved me, and then betrayed me in the worst possible way!"

Whoops. Too much truth there.

"I understand. But I'm so sorry. I will be sorry until the day that I die."

There was a charged silence between us for a minute, a moment that belonged to Dale and John, not to Laura and Aaron. I shot John a look, trying to get him back on track. When he didn't say anything, I took the reins. "If you were really sorry, you never would have slept with that... that *whore!*"

Reverend Sel cleared his throat from the front seat. "You know, the church does offer marriage counseling on Tuesdays and Saturdays. Whatever else is going on here, I think you two would really benefit."

Reverend Sel's voice seemed to push John back into character. "Thank you, Reverend. We'll keep that in mind."

"I know this sounds strange, but I promise it's real. Mr. Hill, you've experienced something that no human should ever have to experience. Here, you'll be among people just like yourself who know that those beings *don't belong here*. And Mrs. Hill, I can understand why you're skeptical. I was, too, before I saw the truth with my very own eyes. Just try to keep an open mind, all right?"

Neither John nor I responded. After a few minutes, Reverend Sel gave up and turned the radio on to a nineties alt-rock station. We spent the rest of the ride listening to Green Day and Oasis.

Traffic was good, and we made it to our destination in less than an hour: a gold-covered skyscraper in the middle of downtown Omaha. Even the windows had a reflective gold surface, which shone brightly in the early afternoon sun. The building was wider at the base, but narrowed to a point at the top.

BETH WOODWARD

Of course the Zetas' HQ would be a giant gold penis.

"Welcome to the Obelisk," Reverend Sel said.

We parked in the garage and got into an elevator covered from floor to ceiling with gold-hued mirrors. Reverend Sel hit the button for the top floor. Muzak played over the speakers, a slow-tempo, mellow song with a repetitive melody. Since we were on, apparently, the world's slowest elevator, the song ended before we got to the top…and then immediately started again. I thought it was a glitch, until it happened again. "It's the same song over and over," I said. "I don't recognize it."

John listened. "It's 'The Girl from Ipanema.'"

"What's it about?" I wasn't sure whether it was a question Laura Hill would ask, but I felt like it was too important not to.

"It's just about a pretty girl who walks down to the ocean."

Reverend Sel had an intense look of concentration on his face. "I never noticed before. How about that!"

The elevator door opened into an office suite. Unlike the garish gold of the exterior and the elevator, the offices were very…beige. Just beige. There were people working at desks and answering phones and typing on their computers, all very office-like things. But I didn't see any personalization anywhere—no pictures, no candy dishes, no cutesy stuffed animals, not even a funny mug declaring the drinker's incurable coffee addiction. Every single person in the office was dressed in a black suit—all genders, young and old. It didn't look like a uniform, because there were subtle differences from person to person: one person might have a button-down blouse and a pencil skirt, while another might have a turtleneck and slacks. It was as if they had all, coincidentally, woken up and decided to wear almost exactly the same thing.

And then when the song ended, they all paused. When it started up again seconds later, they resumed their work as if nothing had happened.

Four men dressed in the Zetas' BDUs met us and patted us down for weapons. After they found nothing, Reverend Sel led us into a conference room with a rectangular table in the middle, where about a dozen people sat, all wearing identical stern expressions—and shockingly enough, black suits. Reverend Sel gestured for John and me to sit down at two empty seats at the head of the table. Once we were seated, an older man with thick white hair, very silver fox-looking, leaned forward. "I understand you had an experience, Mr. Hill."

So much for pleasantries. John took a breath. "Yeah, that's right. A few weeks ago I was on my route—I'm a truck driver, you see. I was at a rest stop outside of Peoria to get some food, and this woman sat down next to me. She was pretty, I'm not gonna lie, and we got to talking. After we were finished eating, she said that she found me attractive and she'd like to go back to my truck and fu—pardon me, I mean, have intercourse. I told her no, that I was happily married, and she got real quiet for a few seconds. Then she said, 'You will take me back to your truck and have sex with me.' And then I was taking her back to my truck." He covered his face. "I didn't know why I was doing it. I didn't want to. But it was like…I had no control over it."

"That's what they call 'thinking with your dick,'" I muttered.

John wheeled around toward me. "Jesus, Laura, how many times to I have to tell you it wasn't like that!" He ran his hands through his hair. It was a very John gesture, but it worked well for the emotionality of this moment. "It was like my body and my brain weren't my own anymore. I still have nightmares where I see her face above me, and I tell my body to move or push her away, and I just—can't."

"What did the woman look like?"

He gave them the same description he'd given Reverend Sel. I held my breath, hoping that they wouldn't notice any resemblance between John's description of the mysterious demon and me. A couple of them were staring at me pretty hard, and it made me nervous. How long did I have before my shot wore off? John had been right about the Zetas having supernatural alarms; one of them was mounted on the wall by the door, its blinking green lights mocking me.

The Zetas around the table started bombarding John with questions. What was the exact date of your encounter? What was your exact route? What's the name of your company? What were you delivering? What was the name of the truck stop? We had prepared for this, and John answered the questions with just the right amount of *how the hell am I supposed to remember that* hesitation. One of the women at the table left the room during the questioning—to confirm the details of John's story, I suspected. John had assured me that our identities were airtight, and that if they did enough digging, they would be able to verify that Aaron Hill was a long-distance truck driver with Fernando Corp who would have been passing through Peoria on the night in question. Our Social Security Numbers were real. Our driver's licenses would pass even the most thorough law enforcement check. I wished I'd had half of these resources available when I was on the run.

A man to our right—who had not asked any questions before—spoke up. "What did it feel like?"

John hesitated. "It was like…imagine if your brain was made out of silly putty, and then it got sliced through with a machete."

Reverend Sel—who hadn't spoken the whole time we were there—suddenly burst into the conversation. "You see? It was her. It had to be her. I was there that day in Pittsburgh. I remember how it was."

Ah. So that was how Reverend Sel fit into all this. "That day in Pittsburgh" was the day the Zetas swarmed my aunt's house to capture and/or kill me. Aunt Barbara had been foolish enough to run out into the horde of large men with guns—not so much trying to protect me as narc me out to them—and she'd gotten a hole in her head for her trouble. So much for doing her civic duty. The only way for John and me to escape had been for me to grab the minds of all the Zetas and keep them frozen in place until we were a good distance away. I didn't regret it one iota.

Was that why the Zetas were trying to kill me?

Reverend Sel continued, oblivious to my musings. "The machete through clay—that's *exactly* what it feels like. Only someone who'd actually experienced it would know that."

Guilt stabbed through my chest. The story about the truck stop might have been an invention, but I *had* forced my way into John's mind once. John had spent centuries building shields to keep people like me out, and

I'd been so hurt and angry that night that I'd bulldozed right through it. And apparently, it felt like I sliced his brain up with a machete.

I stood up and walked over to the window. I needed to do something, needed to get away from John's overwhelming presence. The view of Omaha was distorted just a little through the thick glass. It was probably bulletproof or something. Or maybe demon-proof. I wondered how it would hold up to Irene's telekinesis.

I felt everyone's eyes on me, and I remembered that I was still supposed to be Laura Hill. I looked at John. "You know this is bullshit, right? You screwed up, and now you're trying to justify it with some crazy story about mind control. And now this crazy cult is using you, probably so you'll give them money—which they're obviously not lacking, because it's easy to prey upon scared, desperate people."

The missing woman returned to the room and whispered in the Silver Fox's ear before returning to her seat. After she finished, Silver Fox stood up. "You have doubts, Mrs. Hill. That's understandable. All we've offered you are stories without evidence. I'd like to show you both something. Follow me."

Silver Fox walked out the door toward the elevator. John, Reverend Sel, and I followed. When we got in, Silver Fox pushed a button labeled "BZ," and the elevator descended so rapidly that my ears popped. We exited into a wide hallway with white cinder block walls. I shivered. "You must save a bundle on heating costs down here."

"We don't worry too much about heating down here." There was a hint of amusement to his tone.

We went through a set of double doors. The first thing I noticed was toilets lining the walls on both sides, each one spaced about eight feet from the last. To the right of the toilets were anemic-looking cots, each one covered with a thin blanket that wouldn't have done jack shit to keep out the chill in the room.

Then I saw the people.

There were men and women, some barely out of adolescence, all dressed in white jumpsuits. Some sat on the beds or the floor. Others paced the

BETH WOODWARD

space between the toilets and the beds, which was probably only about four feet or so. One man sat on the toilet, pants down, clearly taking a dump, staring at us defiantly as we passed. There were more than a dozen of them in there. Not a single wall or privacy screen separated any of them. "What is this?" John asked.

"This is a...research laboratory of sorts," Silver Fox said. "These are our specimens."

I shivered again, this time not because of the cold. "Reverend Sel told us that they were predators. Dangerous. So why aren't they attacking us?"

"Because they can't." Silver Fox looked at the man who had just gotten up from the toilet. "Number 42806, please approach the barrier."

The defiant glare vanished from the man's face, replaced with anxiety. But he did not move. Silver Fox spoke again, his calm tone never wavering. "Number 42806, approach the barrier. You know what the consequences are for noncompliance."

This time, 42806 approached us reluctantly, getting closer until he was about a foot away from Silver Fox, where he stopped abruptly. Silver Fox didn't seem to mind the invasion of his space. "Now penetrate the barrier."

All the blood leached from 42806's face. "But sir—"

"I will not ask again."

Then 42806 reached forward, his hand shaking. His whole body started to convulse violently, and the acrid smell of urine filled the air. Then he collapsed on the floor. I stared at the still-twitching body. "Is he dead?"

"Unconscious. The barrier often causes them to lose control of their bodily functions. Thankfully he emptied his bowels before our little demonstration."

"It works on the same principle as an electric fence for your dog, but with stronger currents," Reverend Sel said. "The trick is, we have to implant the 'collar' subdermally, somewhere they can't find it. I caught one of them once scraping her own skin off with a jagged piece of metal she had hidden from us somehow. She was bleeding like a stuck pig, but she was still scraping away looking for the damn thing."

"I would never use an electric fence on my dog," I muttered before I could stop myself.

Silver Fox smiled. "Neither would I." He took out a small bottle of hand sanitizer from his pocket and coated his hands liberally, adding alcohol to the pungent mix of smells. "I have something else to show you. Follow me."

Silver Fox started walking again, leaving 42806 in a heap on the ground, still soaked in his own urine. We followed because, well, what the fuck else could we do? I was beginning to think this mission had been a very bad idea.

John laced his fingers with mine. I wasn't sure if the gesture was appropriate for Aaron and Laura Hill—or hell, for the two us—but at this point, I was desperate for any comfort I could get. It was strange to feel his touch without the familiar zinging between us, just his skin on my skin. It felt foreign somehow. Even so, I squeezed his hand so hard that I dug my nails into his skin. He said nothing, just squeezed me back with equal fervor.

Silver Fox led us to what looked like a classroom, complete with child-sized desks and a chalkboard in the front of the room. Unlike other classrooms I'd seen, the walls were bare, devoid of the finger paintings and "What I did on my summer vacation" essays you saw in every other classroom. Silver Fox signaled Reverend Sel. "Bring 71206 in here," he said.

Reverend Sel returned a few minutes later, holding the hand of a young girl. She was maybe about seven or eight years old, with black hair and piercing dark eyes, and she was entirely too thin. She wore the same style of white jumpsuit. Silver Fox turned one of the desks around so it was facing us, and he gestured for the girl to sit down. She did, and then looked up at him without a word. "Fatima, I would like you to show these people your powers," he said.

Fatima cupped her hands. A sphere of white light formed in her palms, growing until it was about the size of a baseball. She looked over at Silver Fox, who nodded at her. Then, she threw the ball against the wall. It hit with a loud *crack,* sending a plume of smoke and dust into the room. John and I covered our mouths, but neither Reverend Sel nor Silver Fox moved.

BETH WOODWARD

When the dust cleared, a large, black crater remained in the wall, still smoking. Silver Fox gave the girl a tight-lipped smile. "Thank you, Fatima. You will get a treat after dinner tonight. Reverend Sel, please take her back to the nursery."

Reverend Sel led her out of the room. Silver Fox took out his hand sanitizer again. "We find it helps with the little ones if they view us as their allies rather than their captors. A substitute family, so to speak." He squirted his hands and rubbed them together. "The advantage of taking them young is that they're easier to mold. Once you establish a system based on reward and punishment, they *want* to cooperate with you. Some of my predecessors were, I think, too liberal about leaving the young ones with their guardians, particularly when their guardians were human. You can't control all the variables that way. Fortunately, we've learned from our mistakes." He looked directly at me.

What the hell? Did he know who I was? Was Silver Fox on to us? I studied him, trying to catch any hint that his remark had been intended for me, but he had moved on without missing a beat. "Come along. I have more to show you."

He took us back to the elevator, where Reverend Sel was already waiting. As we rode to the top floor, Silver Fox spoke again. "The girl you saw down there is not unique. Many of the creatures we've captured have otherworldly powers, everything from telekinesis to psychic ability. Aaron, we believe that the woman who victimized you was one of these creatures, a woman who has the ability to control minds. We're very interested in any additional information you can provide us. We've been searching for her for quite some time, you see."

The elevator doors opened, and we headed back into the conference room. But outside the door, something caught my eye.

There was a large memorial spanning the width of the wall perpendicular to the conference room. I had been so focused on not getting killed before that I had failed to notice it. But now something caught my eye. Across the top were the words, "Wall of the Fallen." Underneath were several rows of black-and-white photographs, about thirty in all, the type of head-and-shoulders shot you saw in yearbook photos—and mugshots. Next to each photo was a name, the dates of birth and death, and a brief description.

I got closer.

One of the photographs on the lower right-hand side of the memorial drew me in. It was of a man in a conservative suit with dark hair and olive skin. He wasn't smiling in the photo, but I knew if he did, one of his canines would be a little bit crooked. I couldn't see the color of his eyes, but I knew they were a brown so dark that the pupils were nearly hidden in their depths. I knew he smelled like Acqua Di Gio and that he used cherry ChapStick and that he had calluses on his palm. I also knew that I'd left him with his head no longer attached to his neck.

Andrew Phillip Seymour, his plaque said. *Killed in the line of duty while working undercover on Operation Cuckoo in Raleigh, North Carolina.*

My hands shook.

It had been a good date. He'd taken me back to his condo, and we were making out in his kitchen. His hands wandered to the zipper of my dress, a silent question, and I whispered the answer into his mouth: yes. He unzipped me, and the dress fell to the floor. We both laughed as we made our way across the room...

"Laura?" John's voice came from somewhere in the distance.

We were naked, kissing on his leather couch, his hard length rubbing against me. He stroked my clit with the heel of his hand. Fuuuccck. It had been way, way too long. "Let me make you feel good," he said. He knew just how to touch me, how to apply exactly the right pressure to unglue me. I came apart in his arms, moaning and gasping. I felt a prick on my leg.

"Laura, are you all right?" John voice again.

I pulled away from him and felt around the couch. A syringe was tucked between the couch cushions, a large hypodermic needle protruding from it. "I don't know how that got there," he said. There was still a drop of blood on my right thigh.

I remembered what happened to Julie during the senior prom. My best friend had been drugged and raped, and I couldn't stop it. I could only

avenge her. And now this bastard was trying to do the same thing to me.
"You drugged me."

"One of my friends is diabetic. He must have left it here."
There were still droplets of liquid in the vial. "You drugged me!"
"It isn't like that!"

I never gave him a chance to explain. I grabbed the santoku knife from the block in his kitchen...

John touched my shoulder. "Hey, are you all right?" But I still couldn't speak.

Andrew Seymour had been a Zeta operative.

He'd been working undercover on something called "Operation Cuckoo" when I killed him.

The Zeta operative that we'd captured kept talking about cuckoos.

Supernaturals were getting sick, and Andrew Seymour had injected me with something.

And now the Zetas were trying to kill me.

It was all connected. It had to be. My skin started to buzz where John was touching me. "Dale," he whispered softly enough that only I could hear. The warning in his voice was still clear.

An alarm blasted through the room. "Intruder alert! Unauthorized non-human. thirty-third floor." Red lights flashed. Shit. The serum suppressing my demon side had worn off.

But at least I wasn't helpless anymore.

I whirled around, and found Silver Fox looking at me. "I thought it might be you. We heard you were coming last week, but we had to be sure, you understand. Can't go slaughtering innocent humans."

The stairwell doors opened. Dozens of men in the Zetas' black uniform poured out. The elevator doors opened, releasing another group of men. Silver Fox smirked as the men charged toward John and me.

I thought about Andrew Seymour, about all the time I'd spent worrying that I was crazy, that I'd killed him for no reason.

I thought about all the sick angels and demons at the hospital, how they would die without a cure.

EMBRACING THE DEMON   **129**

I thought about whatever the fuck was in that syringe, how it was still probably swimming through my body.

When the red haze bled over my vision, I didn't fight it. I took a deep breath and let the Rage take over.

CHAPTER TWELVE
John

I KNEW I'D LOST HER WHEN her eyes glazed over and became something unrecognizable to me. I'd seen the tail end of it once before, the day that Isaac had been killed at Funland Park. But that was nothing.

The Rage had taken over. *This* was Dale unleashed.

She went after the old man first, pulling a chunky gold necklace over her head and wrapping it around his throat, an impromptu garrote. The more the man struggled, the tighter the garrote became. He collapsed, strangled by the force of his own body weight.

The old man's death spurred the rest of the Zetas into action.

I hadn't talked to Dale much about weapons when we were training together; she'd gotten one look at a handgun and nearly passed out. But maybe I hadn't needed to. Dale *was* a weapon, kicking and slashing and punching without hesitation. The Dale I'd trained had been so afraid of hurting someone that she'd always held back. She was afraid of her power, afraid of what she might do with it. Rage-Dale feared nothing, went straight for the kill, used anything she could get her hands on as a weapon. A Zeta jumped up on her back, trying to use his body weight to bring her down.

She slammed him against the wall, grabbed a pair of scissors off of the nearest desk, and stabbed him through the throat with them.

The Zetas had only given me a cursory pat-down when I came into the building. Big mistake: I always had concealed weaponry on me. I grabbed the hair combs out of my pockets and triggered the hidden springs, causing sharp blades to pop out. I gutted the first of my attackers, slicing his throat open before the man even had a chance to strike.

Another Zeta put a blade to my neck; I disarmed him easily enough with a miniature nightstick.

But there were only two of us, and dozens of Zetas—and I suspected they'd be coming at us from different floors in a moment. But our numbers gave us one small advantage: guns were risky to use in close quarters like these, even under the best of circumstances. With so many Zetas flooding the area, they would be more likely to hit one of their own.

I didn't have the same concern. I pulled out the tiny gun I had concealed in my shoe and fired.

I hit three Zetas with my first three shots. My fourth shot missed, but my fifth caught another in the arm.

Something lodged into my arm—a dart of some kind with a needle attached to the end. The buzzing awareness I usually felt around other supernaturals disappeared, along with my awareness of Dale's presence. It felt like a limb had been cut off. They must have used the same potion on me that they had used on Dale—and in fact, when I looked over at her, I saw that she had a matching dart still stuck in the meat of her thigh through her slacks. It didn't matter. It wouldn't stop either of us from fighting. I dropped my first gun to the ground and removed a second from my other shoe. "We need to get out of here!" I shouted.

I didn't know whether Dale would understand me while she was like this, or whether she'd trust me if she did. I'd given her plenty of reasons not to. But she nodded once, just a quick cut of her head. When I pulled my shirt collar over my mouth and nose, she did the same.

BETH WOODWARD

I twisted the top of my signet ring and released a fine mist into the air. The Zetas began to cough and wheeze until collapsing on the ground into unconsciousness. I ran toward the building stairs, trusting Dale to follow.

After we'd run down a few flights, I heard people running up the steps toward us. I was prepared to grab Dale's hand and pull her into a hiding spot, but she had already reacted. She opened the door to a utility closet on the landing of the stairwell and ducked inside. I followed. Seconds later, we heard the thundering footsteps of the Zetas running by. "We need to go," I whispered once they passed. "They'll figure out what we've done pretty fast, and then they'll find us."

Dale didn't reply. She still had that cold, detached look in her eyes. She opened the closet door and strolled out, seemingly unconcerned. She walked out of the stairwell and right onto the twenty-eighth floor. "Dale, what the hell are you doing? Are you crazy?" Dale ignored me and kept walking through the offices, leaving me with no choice but to follow.

Most of the employees had evacuated when the alarms went off, leaving just the martial forces behind. She palmed a letter opener lying on one of the desks so quickly that I wondered if she was even aware of it. But when a remaining Zeta, dressed in khakis and a button-down, charged at us, she slit his throat without a second's hesitation and kept walking, leaving his body behind. It felt wrong to me. My Dale would have agonized over the carnage. Maybe she would have made a sarcastic remark to cover up her angst, something like, "Guess he didn't get the memo that it was time to go."

But this Dale remained silent. She strolled past the dead body to the elevator bank and pushed the down button, leaving a bloody fingerprint behind. "Dale, what happened to trigger this?" I asked. She didn't answer. "I thought you were learning to control your Rages."

The elevator dinged. Dale stepped inside and pushed the button for the lobby. Once again, I followed.

As plans went, it was risky but not terrible. The Zetas were still busy trying to chase us through the stairwell. Maybe this way, we'd manage to escape unnoticed.

The elevator doors opened into the lobby...which was filled with hundreds of Zetas in black uniforms.

Shit.

But Dale was already fighting, her hair swirling around her face, her body covered in blood. And she was beautiful.

I stepped into the fray, a blade in one hand, a gun in the other, prepared to fight until the end.

But there were just too many of them. As soon as I could take one down, four more would appear. Dale fought beside me, a whirl of contained anger and terrifying efficiency. But she was tiring, and some of the blood covering her clothing was her own.

We would fight to the end. But we didn't have much longer. "Dale, I love you," I shouted.

I'm not sure whether she heard me, but she never stopped her whirl of kicks and punches and slices.

Then a Zeta grabbed her from behind and cut her throat.

I roared, grabbing Dale's limp form before she could fall to the ground. Then I pushed my way toward the front door, cutting down as many as I could who stood in my way.

We weren't going to make it.

Then the plateglass windows on the front of the building exploded. Rebekah and a team of Thrones burst into the building...and oh, thank God, they'd had the good sense to bring Irene Kordova with them. I used the opportunity to run out through the shattered windows, carrying Dale with me, straight to where Dr. Kordova was standing. "She needs help."

Dr. Kordova's eyes widened upon seeing Dale's condition, and we loaded her into the back of an ambulance they'd brought with them. (Probably at Kordova's insistence.) Kordova pressed gauze pads to Dale's throat to stop the bleeding. But even with Dale's supernatural healing, blood soaked through quickly and Kordova had to keep swapping out the pads.

But then Dale opened her eyes. "John," she whispered.

I squeezed her hand. It didn't matter that she would remember that she hated me in a minute; I just needed to touch her. "Don't try to talk. Your throat got cut. But you're going to be okay."

"No, no, I have to. I can't wait." She sat up, ignoring the trail of blood still running down her front. "It's me," she said, tears in her eyes. "I'm the reason everyone's been getting sick. I'm your Patient Zero." Then she passed out.

———◇———

"Hell." Kordova held more gauze against Dale's throat, quelling the flow from the wound Dale had torn open. "What happened?"

"We were fighting. One of the Zetas cut her throat." I didn't say anything about Dale's Rage. Dale tried so hard to keep her Rages hidden from the world, and I doubted that Dale trusted Kordova enough to share that piece of information. I wouldn't do that to Dale. I'd broken her trust enough.

"What did she mean, she's Patient Zero?"

"I don't know." But I had my suspicions. Dale had been mesmerized by the Zetas' Wall of Death before she fell into the Rage. She had seen something. I think you need to run some tests on her. But keep it quiet."

"These are all your people," she said.

"I know." And that made it that much worse.

I hopped out of the ambulance and found Rebekah. She stood outside the building, directing the other Thrones and relishing her role as general—maybe a bit too much. "Where the hell are the demons?" I demanded.

She looked at me, her green eyes filled with false innocence. "You're in charge, John. I didn't think it would be appropriate to speak to them without your permission."

Bullshit. But Rebekah's timing was fortuitous, so I couldn't exactly argue. We had bigger things to be concerned about. "There are supernaturals imprisoned on basement level BZ. They've got them restrained with some kind of electrical device that's been implanted into their skin. You'll need to deactivate it before you can get them out. I think the Zetas have brainwashed some of them, particularly the younger ones. They may see you as the enemy, so be careful. I've got to help Dr. Kordova evacuate Dale, so you'll have to meet me later."

Rebekah nodded. "Where will you be?"

I searched my memory. "Is the Plainsview Park Mall complex still operational?"

"Yes. They just upgraded—"

"Good. We'll head there."

"You're taking her *there*?" Rebekah didn't bother to hide the contempt in her voice. "That's a Thrones holding."

"And as you said, I'm in charge of the Thrones."

I got into the ambulance and gave directions to the driver. Then I climbed into the back with Dr. Kordova. Kordova had taken precautions, covering herself with a mask and a double layer of latex gloves tucked into her shirtsleeves. I didn't even bother; whatever Dale had, I'd already been exposed to.

Dale was still unconscious, though she had stopped bleeding. "Idiots," Dr. Kordova muttered. "They want so badly to kill supernaturals, so you think they'd know to cut off the entire head."

"I'm glad they didn't think of it." Dale looked so fragile, her skin pale, her normally animated body motionless. I wanted nothing more than to take her away from this, away from the world of angels and demons forever—just like she wanted.

But I couldn't. *Patient Zero*, Dale had said. My stomach churned when I thought of the implications of that. Kordova needed to find out what it meant for Dale…and for all of us.

Was Dale a spy? Had she been a Zeta plant all along? Or had the Zetas turned her during her eighteen months away? She certainly had enough reason to hate us all.

We arrived at the Plainsview Park Mall complex a few minutes later. The driver parked in front of the old Sears, but not before he hit a large pothole that no one had bothered to fix.

We'd bought the building about ten years before, when the mall had finally shut down after years of declining sales and increased vandalism. We had many similar complexes throughout the world; one of our specialties was taking spaces that human society had abandoned or forgotten and converting them for their use. The appropriation strategy had been Isaac's idea many years ago, back when he was still an active member of the Thrones. *We have to hide them from humans,* he'd said, *but they'll never notice us if we use the places they don't want anymore.* It had worked extremely well for us, and Gabriel had been pleased. Of course, none of that had mattered when Isaac got sick and Gabriel had exiled him.

A wave of grief struck me. Isaac had been one of the few people I had considered a friend—maybe because Isaac had been too quietly stubborn to let me keep him at arm's length the way I did everyone else.

Isaac would know what to do right now.

Isaac, who remained thoughtful and steady even under the worst of circumstances. Isaac, who could read anyone like a book and intuitively understood what made them tick.

And Isaac had trusted Dale.

That fact nagged me. Even when Dale was at her most stubborn, her most petulant, Isaac had trusted her. Hell, he had even *liked* her, their simple and strange friendship something John had been unable to understand. But he couldn't deny their affection for one another.

But that was before. Before Isaac died. Before I betrayed her. Before Dale vanished for over a year.

And now I could only go by my own instincts, the instincts of an assassin. Spending nearly three hundred years as a trained killer didn't give me much insight into the psyche, human or otherwise.

Dale had every reason to hate me. I'd lied to her. I'd killed her mother. That would have been bad enough, but Dale believed my feelings for her had been a lie, that the times I'd touched her and kissed her and made love to her had all been a ruse.

The irony was that my feelings for Dale were the only part that *hadn't* been a lie. Damned inconvenient, but not a lie.

Kordova, the ambulance driver, and I entered through the old food court, Kordova and I pushing Dale's stretcher. A group of teenagers sat at the beat-up tables that had been left behind when the humans abandoned the mall. Now that the Changeling Serum had worn off, I immediately recognized them as angels.

Whoever had placed them at the door understood that aggressive-looking teenagers would scare most people away. Unfortunately, whoever had placed them there was a few decades out of touch with human culture, so they were dressed as hoodlums straight out of a James Dean movie: rolled-up shirtsleeves, ducktail haircuts, and cigarettes tucked behind their ears. If Dale were awake, she'd probably make a *West Side Story* joke.

They glared at us. "This is private property," one of them said, as two others stood up and approached in the most menacing way they could muster.

"Who's in charge here?" I asked.

The oldest teen sneered at me. "As far as you're concerned, *we're* in charge here." The teen stopped in front of John, angling into his personal space. "I hope you wrote your will, old man."

The side effect of a job like theirs was that it gave these kids a hell of a superiority complex. I strolled up to him. To his credit, he didn't back down, just spit at me with all the contempt he could muster. I wiped the spit away and picked up the teenager by the neck. "I really don't have time for this today." I tossed him into one of the empty tables, which broke when he hit it.

The remained teens jumped out of their chairs and scattered. "Who are you?" one of them asked.

"I'm the Prime, and if you don't recognize me on sight then they really haven't been doing a good job. Now I'll ask again: *Who's in charge here?*"

——————◇——————

THE PERSON IN CHARGE TURNED out to be a short-haired woman with a military bearing named Eleleth. She was a pureblood—although not a particularly strong one, but she seemed to make up for it in the dominance of her personality. She shook my hand firmly and looked me in the eyes. "I

BETH WOODWARD

apologize for the inconvenience. Our door guards can get a little too into their roles at times."

"I can handle a few children. What I don't understand is why they didn't recognize me immediately. All our children should be taught to recognize Thrones' leadership, especially the ones that will be guarding the doors. You never know when we'll need to use any of these facilities as a refuge. So why can't your kids recognize their Prime?"

"Frankly, the transition of power was very recent—"

"The transition of power was a year and a half ago."

Eleleth exhaled. "Yes. But you're a mongrel. We never expected you'd stay in charge."

I fought the urge to run my fingers through my hair. Now that Eleleth had gotten Dale and Kordova settled in a pod—converted offices that were used as both hospital rooms and prison cells, depending on the circumstances—I felt anxious. I wanted to check on her to see if she was okay. But there were other things I had to do first, protocols that had to be understood. I couldn't afford to give away my unease. "Things are different now."

She studied him. "You don't look much like your father."

"No." My power, my strength, and my longevity had all come from Zaphkiel. But my blond hair and brown eyes had belonged solely to Mercy Goodwin. It had made things difficult for me when I was younger, and I always wondered if I would have gotten further ahead if I'd looked more like my father. But I'd proven myself on my own terms.

Dale, on the other hand, looked almost like a clone of Amara. Genetics were an odd thing.

Eleleth faced me, her posture rigid. "I cannot fathom why Zaphkiel would have procreated with a *human*. He might as well mate with a cockroach or a mosquito."

"I've yet to meet a cockroach or a mosquito who could paint the Sistine Chapel or build the pyramids."

"Oh, no doubt, humans have made a great impact on the world. What choice do they have? Otherwise they'd be forgotten the moment they die."

EMBRACING THE DEMON

139

I gritted my teeth. "I am not Zaphkiel, and I did not make his decisions. But I'm here now, and I am the Prime by right of blood." The blood I'd inherited, and the blood I'd spilled.

"I fought on the side of the angels in the War of Purity to prevent abominations like you from existing. We may have lost, but we were never defeated. When Zaphkiel and Gabriel came up with a plan many years later to augment our forces by purposefully breeding mongrel children, I voiced my objections. They ignored me. I remember Zaphkiel said, 'What better soldiers can you find than ones who will always know their place, ones who will always remember their inferiority?'"

"I've always believed that people should be given a chance to prove their own worth."

Eleleth folded her arms across her chest. "Then maybe you should go do that. Among the humans, you'd be a god. But here, you were always meant to be a pawn."

Hell. How many children had this woman beaten down with her cruel words? How many fragile minds had she damaged before they'd even had a chance to form? I stepped toward her, taking advantage of the fact that I towered over her by more than a foot. "I can sense you," I said. "Pureblooded or not, you're not as strong as I am. I know it. More importantly, *you* know it. My reputation has preceded me for years. I'm the Bloodhound. I don't just find people; I assassinate them. And no one has ever found a body of mine yet."

Eleleth took a step back, her eyes widening almost imperceptibly at the implied threat. But I saw it. "Go tell your people that there's been a change of command," I told her.

Supernaturals are long-lived. The biggest difference between us and humans is the length of time we've been around. Being an assassin meant that I had to blend in with the human world on a regular basis. I had to imitate their clothing, their speech, and their culture so that I wouldn't

BETH WOODWARD

give myself away as something "other." But most supernaturals don't have as much day-to-day contact with the human world—and if they're not around humans at all, they don't bother to try. The Plainsview Park Mall complex exemplified that. A woman wearing a long dress with a bustle walked next to a man with spiked hair and safety pins through his nose. A woman in a button-up cardigan and a poodle skirt spoke animatedly to another woman wearing a belted chiton. Many of them wore clothing combinations that had no regard for style or historical accuracy, like the dark-haired woman who wore a corset with a miniskirt or the man with the Afro who wore knee-length breeches and a leather bomber jacket. I saw one man walking around who wore a multicolored raincoat and galoshes over a toga, although I wasn't sure why because we were indoors and it wasn't even raining.

The mall itself still looked very much like it probably had when it closed down, with its gray tiled floors and neon storefronts. The stores, however, were a different story. As Eleleth and I walked to the apartment where I would be staying, we passed a milliner, a five-and-dime, a malt shop, an apothecary, a bookshop, and a haberdashery. A horse-drawn popcorn wagon—minus the horses—stood in the middle of the walkway, and a line of people waited to buy bags from a man in a red-striped suit jacket. On the other end of the mall, inside the area where the anchor store used to be, there were market stalls selling meat and produce. I bet they loved it here, in this little oasis where they didn't have to hide, a place that only changed at the rate they wanted it to. I had to give Eleleth credit: she'd created a haven for the Thrones here.

But signs of modernity had crept in despite them. Each of the stores was protected by a retinal scanner that controlled the security gates. Wheeled automatons—wait, no, they were called *robots*—whizzed by, taking deliveries to the shops, cleaning the floors, taking out garbage, and basically doing the things that none of the angels here could be bothered with. These robots—black, cylindrical, and roughly the size of a kitchen trash can—had been one of Isaac's last inventions, before he'd gotten sick and his parents had kicked him out of AziziCorp—the technology company that was a front so they could do research and development for the Thrones. Gabriel—and Isaac's family, for that matter—were idiots. Why had they let a talent like Isaac's get away? Small drones flew through the air—with video cameras attached to them, I suspected, another Isaac trick. The whole thing was topped off by the large fountain in the center of the mall, which had been retrofitted with lights to turn the water different colors. It might have just been decorative, but I suspected it was used as a signal to warn the residents of possible danger.

Right now, the water was red.

At some point along the way, someone must have realized that cars coming into and out of the "abandoned" Plainview Park Mall all the time would pique some interest, so they converted the stores on the second floor into apartments, adding front doors and covering the large windows with retractable blinds. Problem solved: the Thrones stayed on site, and the local humans had no idea they were even there.

Eleleth took me to one of these apartments on the second floor and handed me a six-digit code. (Since it was temporary lodging, it had a numeric keypad on the door in lieu of a retinal scanner, she told me.) The apartment was clean and furnished, but tiny, consisting of little more than a phone booth-sized bathroom, a kitchenette without an oven or stove, and a Murphy bed that had been tucked into the wall to give the apartment the illusion of space—not that it worked. I pulled the Murphy bed down from the wall and fell asleep over the covers.

I woke up when I heard banging on the door. A quick glance at the digital clock next to the bed told me I'd been out for nearly twelve hours. Kordova's voice came from the other side of the door. "I need to see you, *now*."

I sat up, trying to wipe the sleep-fog out of my head. "Is it about Dale?"

She hesitated. "It's about everything."

Kordova had claimed what had once been the mall's security office, and somehow, in the hours that I'd been unconscious, had managed to turn it into a scientific haven. It didn't surprise me too much, despite Eleleth's hostile attitude. Kordova might have been a part-blood, and a demon, but her reputation preceded her. She'd been treating the supernatural community for a century and a half, and she didn't discriminate based on whether you were an angel or demon, part-blood or pure.

On one side of the makeshift lab was a long table with a centrifuge, a microscope, and other scientific equipment that John could not identify. On the other were video feed monitors. Each monitor showed different parts of the mall, from the neglected parking lot to the central fountain. Several of the feeds were shaky and moving, which told me I'd been right about the drones. But I only paid attention to one feed: the one into Dale's room.

The room contained only a hospital bed, a nightstand, and a desk. I wasn't even sure why there was a desk there, since they hadn't left her anything to read or write with. There was a door to a bathroom opposite the bed, although the inside was, at least, not viewable on camera. Dale lay on the bed, wearing nothing but a hospital gown. She had her legs curled up against her chest in a fetal position. Most people would have thought she was sleeping. Most people would have been wrong. Her face was puffy and red, and there were traces of tears on her cheeks. "Why are you holding her in there like that? Because of the illness? We could at least make her more comfortable. Get her some books or—"

"John." Kordova whirled around and face me. "Has it occurred to you that Dale is probably our leak?"

My blood grew cold. "That's not possible. The Zetas are trying to kill her."

"She *says* the Zetas are trying to kill her. But do we really know that? She shows up a year and a half ago—coincidentally, in the city where the illness originated. She had no connection with the supernatural world at all, but suddenly she's involved with the most important angels and demons in the world?"

"She was involved with them because I brought her—"

"And then she disappeared. But a few weeks ago, just as we're starting to close in on the Zetas, she shows up again out of nowhere saying that the Zetas are trying to kill her. And of course you and Covington go into rescuer mode. But both of our missions since she came back have backfired. Oh and, coincidentally, she happens to be the source of the illness."

"That wasn't Dale's—" But then I remembered something the old Zeta at the Obelisk had said. *We heard you were coming last week.* I hadn't had a chance to think about it at the time, but now… "How did Rebekah find out where we were?"

"When you and Dale hadn't been in contact for a few days, she ran a search of all your known aliases. You pinged in Lincoln."

"When was this?"

"She started looking yesterday morning." She glanced at the clock. "Saturday morning, that is. We flew into Lincoln Saturday night."

Which didn't jive with the old Zeta's timeline. I rubbed the bridge of my nose. "So Dale is the source of the illness, then?"

"Yes." Kordova hit a button, and a picture came up on a projection screen—something that looked strangely like hairy caterpillars swimming in the ocean. "It's a virus. Specifically, I believe it's an engineered virus infused with self-replicating nanotechnology. It's pretty amazing, actually. This technology isn't even supposed to exist yet, but the Zetas have—"

"Focus, Kordova. What's going on with Dale?"

"Right. She's basically our Typhoid Mary, totally asymptomatic herself but spreading the virus to others. Her viral load is ten times what we've seen in normal patients. But that's not the only thing. The virus has already—"

The door burst open before Kordova could finish her thought. Rebekah stood there, out of breath, her hair mussed—which told me, more than anything else, that it was serious. "Something's happening in the old movie theater."

I dashed to the monitors and flipped some switches on the security panel, trying to bring up the feed for the theater. There was no audio, but the image couldn't be more clear. Eleleth stood in front, her face contorted in anger, while the people in the seats raised their fists to cheer her on. "They found out that Amara's daughter is here," Rebekah said before I could ask the obvious question.

"What? How?"

Rebekah gave me a dubious look. "Amara hasn't kept a low profile through the years, and the chit could be her twin."

Something about Rebekah's answer struck me as off—too quick, too confident. But I didn't have time to contemplate that now. I hadn't had a chance to replenish my hidden cache of weapons after the Obelisk battle. I had managed to find a 9mm that someone had left in the ambulance, and I tucked it into the holster concealed on my hip, and I still had about half a dozen knives on me. It would have to do. I turned to Kordova. "I want you to come with us. I'll need someone to explain why Dale needs to be here, why this is so important." *And they don't trust me.*

Kordova nodded. I thought she was hesitant, but no…she was staring at a spot on my arm, a spot I usually kept covered with my sleeves. Shit. I pulled my sleeves down, and the three of us rushed to the theater.

The theater was still painted in the teal-and-purple color scheme that had been so popular back in the 1980s, and I caught a hint of stale popcorn in the air. I barged into Theater 1, Rebekah and Kordova behind me.

The seats were nearly full, and everyone turned around when they saw me. Everyone except Eleleth, who was still stomping on her soapbox in the front. She sneered at me. "Look who it is. Our esteemed leader."

I marched up the aisle. "What the hell do you think you're doing?"

"What am I doing? You've some nerve, asking that. I'm not the one who brought an enemy into our domain."

A chorus of agreement went through the theater. I glared at them until they fell back into silence. Then I turned back to Eleleth. "What are you trying to accomplish?"

"I want her out," Eleleth said.

"No." I turned to the audience. "Dr. Kordova here has managed to isolate the illness that has taken so many in our community already. Amara's daughter is integral to that work." John gestured toward Kordova, who nodded in agreement.

"Integral?" Eleleth spat the word. "You mean she's sick. You brought the sickness to our doorsteps."

"No," I said firmly.

"But she is infected," Kordova said.

I shot her a look. *Now* she chimes in? But Kordova folded her arms, holding firm.

"We haven't had anyone get sick here in *months*, but you brought the infection back to our door?" There was a surprising hint of vulnerability in Eleleth's voice.

"That's why she's been in isolation—to protect all of you." It was a good line. But I hadn't been thinking much about the residents of Plainview Park Mall when I brought Dale here. All I'd been thinking was that it was close and convenient, and I needed to get Dale somewhere that Kordova could examine her. If a few of the Thrones at the Plainview Park Mall had to die in the process—hell, if *I* had to die in the process—then that was the price of keeping my people safe. It was the price of keeping *her* safe.

"We had five people die here within two months when the epidemic started, and three more since then. But there's been no one since June! No one! There are *reasons* we want to stay isolated here. But of course you wouldn't think about that. All you wanted was to protect your demon whore!"

Eleleth lunged at me, trying to wrap her small hands around my throat. She had fury on her side, but I had training and experience. I grabbed her arms and twisted, throwing her to the ground with little effort.

Eleleth jumped up and came for me again, producing a gun from the side pocket of her cargo pants. I'd bet money that gun had fractal bullets in it.

I jumped up on the back of the theater seats and ran across the row, ignoring the people whose heads I narrowly missed—and whose heads I didn't. Rule number one of shooting was that moving targets were much harder to hit than still ones. Not *impossible*, but harder—and I didn't think Eleleth was a good enough shooter to do it with any accuracy. If she had that kind of potential, Gabriel would have stationed her at one of our bigger sites: New York, Tokyo, Paris, maybe Los Angeles or Chicago if she were intent on staying in the United States. The fact that she was in a old shopping mall in Nebraska spoke volumes. I also didn't think she would shoot at me when she would risk hitting one of her own people.

BETH WOODWARD

Caring was a weakness. I knew that quite well.

Eleleth lowered the gun, and I used the opportunity to jump off the seats and knock her off her feet, causing the gun to fall from her hand. She reached for it, but I was faster. Distantly, I heard Kordova shouting at us, but I was too caught up in the fight to care. I pinned Eleleth to the ground and pointed the gun at her head. "Who the hell do you think you are?" I asked. "You said you were loyal to my father. Do you know what Zaphkiel did to traitors?"

"At least I'll know I died trying to protect my people from the illness you brought to us."

"But that's what I've been trying to tell you!" Kordova shouted, no small amount of frustration in her voice. "We're all infected already."

I froze. "What do you mean? All of us here in the mall?"

"No. All of us here *on Earth*. That's why I had so much trouble isolating the virus. I couldn't compare it to uninfected samples because there *were* no uninfected samples. We're not all sick…but that nanovirus lurks inside all of us."

———◇———

THERE WAS A LOT OF arguing and a lot of shouting. I could handle that. But it was the crying that got to me, the muffled sobs of people who suddenly realized *they* might be in danger, too. *You were always in danger*, I wanted to tell them. I hadn't needed Dale's confession or Kordova's blood analysis to know the truth. Every last one of them was a target for this virus. It was just a matter of spinning the roulette wheel and seeing where it landed.

I muttered something about needing to use the bathroom and excused himself, returning to the shoebox Eleleth and her Thrones called an apartment. I closed the automatic blinds. I had just taken off my shoes when there was a knock on the door. I found Kordova standing in front of the entryway, a stern expression on her face. "Take off your shirt."

I grinned at her. "Why, Dr. Kordova, I'm flattered."

Not so much as a twitch. "Now."

"But I'm afraid I just don't feel the same way about you. I hope we can still be friends, though."

She pushed into the apartment and slammed the door behind her. "Take off. Your damn. Shirt," she said through gritted teeth.

I lowered his eyes before I pulled the navy Henley over my head. There, on my left arm, was what Kordova had been looking for: an inflamed, star-shaped rash. "How long?" she asked.

"It first appeared two days ago."

She pressed a finger to the site. It turned white with the pressure, then quickly darkened back to red when she released her hand. "Two days ago? Hell, John. Were you too busy playing footsie with your girlfriend to bother quarantining yourself?"

The last of my control snapped. "We've been studying this thing for *months*. Even before this discovery with Dale, you knew there was no evidence that exposure makes us more or less likely to develop symptoms. Gregory got it, but you didn't, even though you've been exposed to sick patients nonstop for the past year. Dale's walking around with a viral load that should down an elephant, and she's fine. You dress up like you're walking into a nuclear containment zone because it makes *you* feel better— like a child with a stuffed bear."

She folded her arms across her chest, a sheen forming over her eyes. My words had hit their target. Good. "We need to get you back to the hospital," she said.

"No."

She was all business now. "John, the only way we can make sure you don't hurt yourself once the hallucinations start is to keep you in secure containment."

"That isn't necessary. The rash only presented two days ago. I have a few weeks before other symptoms appear."

"You're being irresponsible. Do you know how many people you could hurt if you go active? Do you know how many people count on you?" She paused. "It doesn't look like your leadership over the Thrones is exactly… stable."

"It's fine." The rash on my arm started to itch again. "Everything's fine."

"Sure."

"Immortals don't adjust to change well. Gabriel had been in charge for over three hundred years. He was my father's second-in-command. It's going to take some time."

"Time that you won't have if hallucinations cause you to kill yourself or someone else."

"Time that I won't have if I'm strapped to a bed and the virus kills me, anyway." Kordova shook her head. "I'll be careful. I'll bring restraints with me wherever I go. I'll take whatever medication cocktail you can come up with. I'll—"

But my speech was interrupted by another knock on the door. I opened it and saw the James Dean punk I'd thrown into a table earlier. I'd gotten the chance to talk to him briefly after our confrontation in the food court. His name was Simon, and he seemed to have a good head on his shoulders when he wasn't following foolish orders from his superiors. I was thinking of offering him a job working for me when he came of age, because he deserved better than Nebraska.

"I'm sorry to bother you, sir, but I can't find Eleleth," he said. "I think—I think she's gone after your demon."

CHAPTER THIRTEEN
Dale

I *FUCKING HATE HOSPITALS.*

That was my first thought after waking up, because even though everything else was fuzzy, it was very clear that I was in a hospital of some kind. From the IV dripping into my hand (again) to the white-on-white decor to the antiseptic-and-tongue-depressor smell of the room, everything screamed hospital. How many times had I woken up in a hospital bed recently? I was starting to lose track.

My second thought was, *Why the hell am I in a hospital?* I searched my foggy brain.

Foggy. I'd had a Rage. Shit.

Bits and pieces came back to me.

We'd been at the Zetas' building in Omaha.

I saw the memorial plaque for Andrew Seymour, saw that he'd been working undercover on something called Operation Cuckoo, and it had all clicked. *That* was why the Zetas were after me, not because of my mother and not because of our confrontation at Aunt Barbara's.

Operation Cuckoo.

For two years, I'd been punishing myself for killing Andrew Seymour, wondering whether I'd just snapped and murdered an innocent person for no reason. Now I knew. Two years ago, I'd thought he was trying to drug and rape me. But now that I knew he was connected to the Zetas, I knew it had to be something much more sinister than that.

But how the hell did I get into a hospital? Was I in enemy hands? If so, why hadn't they killed me yet?

I yanked the IV out of my hand, thinking about how Irene would bitch me out if she saw me, and I inspected myself. Physically, I seemed all right. Still a little woozy from the Rage, but that was normal for me. The skin around my neck was pink and tender, like it had just healed, but I couldn't for the life of me remember how or when I'd been injured. I was cold, but that probably had more to do with the fact that I was wearing nothing but a hospital gown with no underwear or socks.

I tried the door. Locked. I put all my strength behind it, but to no avail. Whoever was holding me had demon-proofed the door. There were no windows, no mirrors, nothing I could use to get myself out.

In the corner of the room was a small white device with a flashing red light. It could have been a motion detector or even a fire alarm, but I very much suspected it was a security camera. I looked up at it. "Okay guys, whoever you are. I'm awake. Come and get me."

No one answered. So I waited.

I kept drifting in and out of consciousness on the hospital bed because there wasn't much else for me to do. There was a bathroom, so I was able to shower, washing my body and hair with a bar of yellow soap.

At one point, someone slipped a tray of food in through a slot in the door. I was more interested in the slot than the food. Unfortunately, there was a solid six inches of door between me and the outside, leaving me unable to even slip a finger through—let alone use it to jimmy the door open. Whoever had imprisoned me in here had thought of everything.

At one point, I looked up at the flashing red light and said, "You know, if you're just going to leave me in here, you could at least bring me a TV or something."

No one answered. Of course. It left me more convinced that I had fallen into the hands of the enemy somehow.

And so my boredom continued.

I was asleep on the bed some time—maybe hours, maybe days—later when the door finally opened. A short-haired woman wearing a tank top and cargo pants. Her eyebrows were furrowed together, her fists were clenched, and she looked like she was ready to tear me limb from limb. "Are you from AAA? If so, you really need to rethink the Five Diamond Award you gave to this hotel. I mean, the concierge couldn't get my Broadway tickets, these linens are definitely not thousand-thread count, and the amuse-bouche was merely satisfactory."

And then she jumped me.

People *really* needed to rethink the whole "let's try to take Dale in hand-to-hand combat" thing. Aside from it being annoying, did they not realize I'd trained with John—who thought that grabbing me in the dark and throwing his full body weight on me was not only good instructional technique, but also a lot of fun. And as much as I was ashamed to admit it, it had been. This was less fun, since this woman was way more serious about killing me than John was. But she was emotional, and she was sloppy.

When she grabbed me around the back, I slammed her into the wall and then shoved my body weight forward, throwing her over my head and onto the floor. She caught my leg from the floor, kicking out my knee and causing me to fall onto my back. She climbed over me, pinning me to the ground with her body. So I head-butted her, hard. While she was distracted, I rolled us over so that I was on top, and then I slammed her head into the floor. "Stay down!" I ordered, pushing all of my power behind it. Whatever my injuries had been, my powers were intact. This was a good thing.

And then John and Irene burst in, accompanied by a a kid who looked like he'd dressed as Fonzie for Halloween and forgotten to take off his costume. I rolled my eyes and stumbled into the bathroom. "Thanks for the rescue, guys. Don't know how I would have done it without you." My face was smeared with blood. I wet a threadbare washcloth and wiped myself clean.

BETH WOODWARD

John took his 9mm out of its holster and shot the woman between the eyes without saying a word.

I stared at the body for a minute before I could manage to say anything. "She wasn't going anywhere, you know. There is a such thing as 'due process.' I know that's a foreign concept in your world, but—"

"Sit down, Dale," John said.

I sat on the edge of the bed, facing John and Irene, and trying really hard not to stare at the dead body. "So what's going on?" I asked. "Was I captured? Is that why I have these luxurious accommodations?"

Irene gritted her teeth, but John showed no reaction. "What do you remember about the fight at the Obelisk?"

I scrubbed my face with my hands. "Not much. I had a Rage. It's all fuzzy after that."

Irene broke in. "What's a—"

"Later," John said firmly. "Dale, do you remember what triggered the Rage?"

I clenched my fists. "I saw a picture on their Wall of the Fallen. It was Andrew Seymour. I, uh…" I looked at Irene, not exactly sure how much I wanted to reveal. "I killed him in Raleigh two years ago, but I could never remember what happened, what triggered the violence. But I saw the picture, and then I remembered." I took a deep breath before I continued. "Andrew and I had gone on a date, and afterward we came back to his condo. While we were messing around, he injected me with something. I felt the pinch, and he tried to deny it, but I found the syringe. I thought he was planning on raping me. But on the memorial wall, there was a description next to Andrew's picture that said he was working undercover on something called 'Operation Cuckoo' when he died."

"Reverend Sel kept talking about cuckoos," John said.

I just nodded.

Irene stood up. Apparently she found it easier to get into professor mode that way. "Once I knew where to look—or rather, *who* to look at—it was shockingly easy to find. The Zetas infected you with a self-replicating nanovirus. But the way the virus is built…if they'd released it into the air or contaminated the water supply, it wouldn't have done anything. They needed a host for the virus to start spreading: you. And you have been the perfect host. Your viral load is more than a hundred times what we've detected in any other patient, but you remain symptom-free. They specifically calibrated this virus to your DNA so that you would be their optimum Typhoid Mary. This wasn't an overnight operation, not by any stretch. Science has come a long way with nanotechnology, but anything even *close* to what the Zetas did is decades down the road. They must have been working on this for *years*."

"The Zetas have been on to you for a very long time," John said.

"But how is that even possible? How would they have been able to calibrate—" I stopped mid-sentence when the answer hit me. "Aunt Barbara."

The last time I'd seen Aunt Barbara—a year and a half earlier, when John and I were trying to track down my mother—she'd mentioned that she'd once talked to "scholars" who knew about the existence of angels and demons. Minutes later, the Zetas swarmed the house, notified by the supernatural detection alarm Aunt Barbara had installed in her entryway. "When I was a kid, she used to take me to 'doctor's appointments' every few months, even though I never got sick. They'd take my blood and my urine and scrape cell samples from the inside of my cheeks. I was too young at the time to realize there was anything strange about it."

Irene nodded. "They must have gotten your DNA when you were a child and then developed the virus specifically to be compatible with your system. It's possible that Andrew Seymour injected you with that tracker the night he infected you, but my guess is that they had it on you much longer than that."

I shook my head, unable to process the enormity of all this. "So if I'm their Typhoid Mary, why are they trying to kill me?"

Irene gave a one-shouldered shrug. "You've done your job now—extremely well, as a matter of fact. The infection has spread. They don't need you anymore, but your DNA could help reverse-engineer the virus."

I froze suddenly as something dawned on me. When I had walked through the hospital ward in New York, all the caretakers had been dressed like they were walking through a nuclear fallout zone. Now, John and Irene were sitting in my room, in their street clothes, calmly telling me that I carried the viral load of an elephant, and the door was open. I jumped off the bed and backed away from them, covering my nose and mouth with my hand. "You can't be in here," I said.

"Why not?" Irene asked. She was the doctor. Why the hell wasn't she getting it?

"No, I'm sick. I could infect you!"

John and Irene glanced at each other, unspoken words passing between them. Irene spoke before John could. "Don't worry, that ship has *long* sailed." She stood up, slipping back into doctor mode. "After we figured out that you were the source of the illness, I went back and retested all my samples—including the ones that were gathered before you came back to New York. They were all infected, every last one of them. These were people who never had any direct contact with you, and they were gathered not just nationwide, but *world*wide."

"How is that even possible?" I asked.

"The virus did exactly what viruses are supposed to do. We estimate that most people infected about ten others, and as the original source, you're even more contagious than others. There's a good chance you single-handedly infected most of the Northeast. It explains why New York was the epicenter of the initial outbreaks. And then, people did as people do—they traveled, they moved—and the virus spread. I suppose it's possible that we could find someone in Siberia or Timbuktu or somewhere who isn't infected, but I'm not optimistic." She removed the clip that held her hair in place, and her curls spilled out in a random poof around her face. It was the first time I'd seen her look so disheveled. "I know it was a coincidence that you came to New York right after you were infected, but the Zetas couldn't have planned it any better if they tried. The virus is present inside all of us, regardless of whether we're showing any symptoms or not."

"Fantastic." I sat back on the bed and rested my head against the back, which was elevated into a sitting position.

"The good news is, I have your samples now, so even if the Zetas do manage to kill you, I can still work on curing the virus."

I quirked my eyebrow. "Not much for tact, are you?"

"'Tact' is just 'lying nicely.' But the other piece of good news is that only a small percentage of the infected seem to be showing symptoms—I'd estimate about five percent."

That made me sit up. "That doesn't make sense. The Zetas spend years developing this virus, only to release something that only affects five percent of the supernatural population? Why would they do that?"

She shrugged. "Could be they made a mistake, released it prematurely or overestimated the impact. Or…it could be that the symptoms we're seeing so far aren't the intended effect."

I glanced over at John. He stood by the doorway like a statue, a scowl on his face, his arms folded across his chest. No help there. "What do you mean?" I asked Irene.

"Different bodies can react differently to the same contagion. You've probably seen it in the human world. The same infection that gives one person the sniffles can land the next one in the hospital. A lot depends on their overall health, but also on their genetic structure. Some people have mutations that make them uniquely vulnerable to certain illnesses. Within the supernatural world, we don't have as much expertise since many of us don't get sick, but it stands to reason that the same thing would be true."

"I still don't understand." But I was afraid that I did…and it really wasn't a good picture.

"Those five percent might just be having an extreme reaction to the contagion. That might not be the intended effect of the nanovirus."

"So what's the intended effect?"

Irene sighed. "Hell if I know."

I rolled my head back against the mattress. "So what do we do?"

"Right now, we go back to New York. I need to get back to my patients, and you can go back to the safe house and…I don't know, knit? Macramé?"

"So that's it? We just go home?"

She shrugged. "What else do you want? The Obelisk is locked down tight, if they're still using it at all, and our people are already going through all stuff we managed to grab during the raid, and we have no idea whether any of it will be useful. There's not a damn thing we can do here that we can't do in New York."

"Why do you even care?" John asked.

"It just doesn't feel right, is all. It feels like we should be doing something more."

"That ship has definitely sailed, Dale."

There was a harsh undercurrent to his tone that I didn't understand, and I tried to remember if something had happened that could have angered him. Had I said something or done something while I was in the Rage? Is that why he'd left me alone down here for so long? "What crawled up your butt and died?"

John met Irene's eyes. "I'd like some time alone with Dale, if you don't mind."

"Sure." Irene left, shutting the door behind her.

John took out a small remote from the pocket of his jeans and aimed it at the camera in the corner. The flashing red light clicked off.

He remained silent for a long time, pacing back and forth in the room, ignoring the dead woman's body as if it wasn't even there. He still had Aaron Hill's dark hair, but he was running his fingers through it haphazardly the way I'd seen him so many times before. "Why did you do it, Dale?"

"Do what?"

He continued as if he hadn't even heard me speak. "I get it. Our world holds nothing for you, means nothing to you—you've made that very clear. But I never thought you could be so hateful."

Hateful? "What are you implying, John?"

"All those innocent people. They had lives and families, and now they're dead because of you."

I froze, my body growing cold. "It wasn't my fault. I didn't know I was infected. I had no idea I was spreading the nanovirus."

"Not the nanovirus. The *leak*. What happened? Did they get to you back when you were a teenager? Was the whole Andrew Seymour thing just a ruse? Or maybe you cut a deal with them so that they wouldn't try to kill you."

I gaped at him. "I have no idea what you're talking about."

"We didn't have leaks before you came back. And now you're here, and all of a sudden we're a Goddamn sieve!"

"It's a coincidence."

"Pretty convenient coincidence, don't you think? They must have known if you pulled out your damsel-in-distress doe eyes that Covington would help you, and that if he didn't, *I* would. We were so naive. But you are a better liar than anyone else I've ever met."

"Why are you saying this? I thought you said you trusted me." Tears filled my eyes. "Why the fuck would I leak information to people who are trying to kill me?"

"They found us in Montana. The tracker explained how they zeroed in on you so quickly, but not how they managed to mobilize so many troops to the middle of nowhere so quickly. They couldn't have tracked you through the airplane. I double- and triple-checked those safety features myself. And that old Zeta said he had *heard* we were coming. Dale, there were only two people who knew we were coming to Nebraska: you and me." He exhaled heavily, the weight of the world on his chest. "What am I supposed to think?"

"I don't know. But I'm not the leak."

He sat down in the chair Irene had vacated, a defeated look on his face. "Shit."

Shit was right. The Zetas at the Obelisk had known we were coming somehow. If John and I were the only ones who had any clue we'd be in Nebraska, *how had they known*? We'd been so careful. We'd only talked about our plans at the safe house.

The safe house. Where the one person who had despised me since I got back to New York currently resided. How could I have been so stupid?

John must have seen it as soon as I hit upon the answer. "What is it?" he asked.

"Chaz."

CHAPTER FOURTEEN
Dale

JOHN AND I FLEW BACK to New York on a private airplane. We didn't say much. I kept thinking about the things Nik had told me, about her worry that Chaz had developed post-traumatic stress after he'd been kidnapped by the Thrones. "I think you should let me talk to him first."

John didn't say anything for a minute. "I'm not sure that's a good idea," he finally said.

"Chaz has been through a lot in the last year and a half, and most of it is because of me. If I hadn't brought him into my fucked-up life, he never would have been kidnapped by the Thrones. And if he hadn't been kidnapped, he wouldn't have any reason to work with the Zetas."

"Chaz has made choices. He has to face the consequences of them just like everyone else."

"But he wouldn't have even known those choices *existed* if it hadn't been for me!" I hesitated. "I'm not saying that he shouldn't face the consequences of his actions. I'm just saying…maybe a friendly face will make it a little easier for him to talk, and maybe a little bit of understanding will help him understand that we're people, just like him."

"I doubt it."

I sighed and rested my head against the window, listening to the humming of the plane's engine. I was so tired. All I wanted to do was sleep, but when I closed my eyes, thoughts whirled in my head about Chaz, and about what John would do to him if he turned out to be our leak. Whatever relationship John and I once had, he was still an assassin. He'd been willing to kill the man who'd raised him—not to mention the mother of the woman he'd been sleeping with. What was one human comic book artist who was obsessed with old movies and knew how to rock a Ziggy Stardust look?

I already knew the answer: nothing. But Chaz wasn't nothing to me.

A few minutes later, John spoke up. "You can play good cop, if you want. But I'll be right there with you, and I *will* play bad cop if I have to. You'll also need to be armed."

"I don't know if—"

"And be prepared to use your powers if you have to."

———————◇———————

It had only been a week since I'd left New York. It felt like much longer. Not much had changed in the safe house since I'd left. It was messier, clothing and art supplies scattered all over the living area. Someone had put up a Christmas tree on the coffee table, an artificial one that made Charlie Brown's tree look like it belonged at Rockefeller Center. One of those electric scent diffusers had been plugged in behind it, probably in a smell like "Winter Green"—let's just ignore the fact that "green" is not a smell.

As John and I walked in, Chaz stumbled downstairs, dressed in nothing but a T-shirt and pajama pants, his hair sticking up in all different directions, still rubbing sleep out of his eyes. When he spotted us, he groaned. "Jesus. I haven't even had my fucking coffee yet."

"Where's Nik?" I asked.

He shrugged. "Work, probably. I'm not her keeper."

"Jesus Christ, Chaz, you were supposed to *stay* here!"

He dropped a pod into the slot and pushed a button to start the single-cup coffee maker. "We have *lives,* you know. We can't just stay here waiting until you decide to grace us with your presence."

"I'm trying to look out for your safety! If the Zetas realize we're friends, they could try to kill you, too."

Chaz looked suddenly awake. "Oh, *now* you're concerned about our safety. Where the hell were you for the last eighteen months?"

John cleared his throat and gave me a look. I ignored him. Instead, I sat down at the table. "You're right. I'm sorry. I'm a shitty friend. I dropped this massive bomb on you, and then I disappeared. Then I came back into your life, announced that you were in danger again, dragged you away from your home at Christmastime, and disappeared again. I suck."

Chaz sat down at the table with his coffee. "Yes, you do."

"But I don't deserve what you've been doing." I couldn't bring myself to say it, couldn't bring myself to accuse Chaz of betraying us all, of being an accessory to all those deaths...of being an accessory to *my* near-death.

Chaz turned away from me, staring at the wall. "No, I guess you don't."

It wasn't an admission, but it was close. I glanced at John. He came to the table and sat down silently.

Chaz was shaking, his hands barely able to hold up his coffee cup. I took it from him and set it on the table. Tears started to run down his face. "What happens when we get too old for you?" he asked.

I looked over at John, who shrugged. "Chaz, you do realize that I fudged my age when I was here before? I'm actually like, eight months older than you."

"That's not what I'm talking about!" Chaz slammed his hand against the table, hard enough to knock his coffee cup off, the brown liquid splashing onto the hardwood floor. No one moved. "You're never going to age. You're never going to die. One day I'm going to be at an old folks' home, pissing into a diaper, and you're going to be exactly the same as you are now."

I stared at the remnants of Chaz's coffee seeping into the cracks of the floor. "I haven't really thought about it," I whispered. I'd been more concerned with surviving the here and now.

"And to top that all off, you have *superpowers*. If Buffy the Vampire Slayer and Charles Xavier had a baby, *it would be you*."

I didn't know what to say, so I remained silent, waiting for Chaz to continue.

"Imagine spending your whole life thinking that you were special somehow, believing that some how, in some way, you could be something great and unique in the universe. But then you find out that you're not… and the person who is sleeps on a dirty futon in your best friend's apartment and wears a pair of jeans with a hole in the crotch for three weeks because she can't afford a new pair."

My eyes stung, but I would not cry—not here, not now, not in front of him. "Is that why you started working with the Zetas? Because some white trashy bitch from Pittsburgh got superpowers and you didn't?"

"What's a Zeta?"

His puzzled frown and the crease between his eyes seemed to be genuine. I was about to answer him when John jumped in. "This is ridiculous! Someone has been selling us out to an organization dedicated to exterminating supernaturals. Hundreds of people are dead already—and they're trying to kill Dale in particular. I have no problem breaking every bone in your body; it'll make Dale upset, but she's got bigger reasons to be angry with me. But if you tell us what you know, I promise you'll be treated fairly."

Chaz looked back and forth between John and me. "You think I sold you out?" Anger and offense bled through his voice. But then he started to laugh, a brittle, broken sound. "Of course you think I did it. I probably would too. I've been a complete asshole. I know that. But I've spent over a year in therapy dealing with my inadequacy issues, and just when I thought I had them under control, you show up again."

"That's not enough of a reason to sell me out!"

"Goddammit, I *didn't*!"

His voice broke on the last word. I turned to John. "I think he's telling the truth."

"It's not enough. Use your powers on him."

EMBRACING THE DEMON   **163**

"Don't you think—"

"We know the leak is coming from here somehow. Chaz is still the most likely suspect. If he's telling the truth, he has nothing to be afraid of."

Tears slid down Chaz's cheeks as I reached for his mind. It was as I expected: completely unblocked and oh-so-vulnerable to me. "I'm so—"

I froze when I felt the butt of a gun pressing against my head. "I don't think so, demon bitch."

Nik.

———— ◇ ————

THE GUNBARREL WAS A COLD kiss on my scalp. "Nik, we were just trying to talk to him."

"Talk, my ass. It looked like you were about to mind-rape him."

A chill ran through me. "It's not like—"

She pressed the gun into my head harder. "Like hell it isn't. You violate people, make them into your puppets. Well, I'm sick of it. I'm not going to be anyone's fucking puppet."

"Nik, we're just trying to find out what Chaz knows about the Zeta Coalition. That's it. I'm not trying to turn anyone into a puppet, and a lot of lives are at stake here."

She started to laugh, a strange, maniacal sound I had never heard from her before. "You still don't get it. Chaz isn't your leak. *I* am."

You could have heard a pin drop in that room. John rose from his seat, giving Nik a menacing glare. "Let her go."

Nik's voice had a mocking edge to it. "No, I don't think I will. And if you try anything, her brain stem will be splattered all over the wall. I don't think even a demon could recover from that."

We were at a stalemate. John's face remained impassive, but I could see the wheels turning behind his eyes. Chaz, on the other hand, was anything but stoic. "Nik, what the fuck are you doing? Dale's our friend."

"She's not like us, Chaz! When the chips are down, who do you think she's gonna choose? Us or them? She was ready to rip your secrets right out of your head."

"But they said people are dying," Chaz said.

"Not people. Monsters. They're not from this world, and they don't belong here. We're nothing but cockroaches to them. All the Zetas are trying to do is take back what rightfully belongs to us—to *humans*."

While Nik and Chaz were talking, I reached toward her with my mind, and found...nothing. It was as if she wasn't even in the room. I thought Nik must have shot me up with the serum that inhibited my mind-control abilities without my realizing it. But when I reached for John and Chaz's minds, they were exactly as I expected them to be: John's impenetrable fortress, Chaz's all-too-vulnerable expanse. If I hadn't felt Nik and her gun behind me, I would have thought there were only three of us in the room.

John caught my eye. I shook my head almost imperceptibly—as much as I dared with the gun still on me. But Nik still noticed. She pistol-whipped me on the side of the head, so hard that I could hear a ringing in my ear. "Don't try to talk to him. There's only one person in this room you should be thinking about: me."

"Nik, you have to know that I'd be a far greater prize to the Zetas." John inched toward her. When Nik cocked the gun, he froze. "Dale's only been in our world a short while. She believed she was human until last year. But I'm the leader of the Thrones. I know all their secrets. You want intelligence? I can give that to you. But only if you let Dale go."

Nik hesitated—just long enough. I grabbed the knife hidden in my belt buckle—the one John had forced me to carry—reached behind me, and stabbed her in the stomach.

CHAPTER FIFTEEN
Dale

THE ENTRANCE TO THE SUPERNATURALS' new hospital was located on the west side of Manhattan, concealed as a television repair shop across the street from the Javits Center. When you went inside, you would descend a set of stone stairs into an underground tunnel built from brick and cinder block. Round lights lined the ceiling, casting a greenish tint on everything.

Beds lined the sides of the tunnel, jutting out into the tunnel horizontally, leaving us only about two feet of space to walk through. Every single one had a patient in it, secured to the beds by their wrists and ankles. Another sick supernatural getting ready to die from the Zetas' virus. Some cried, some screamed, some were completely silent. All were obviously in pain. One had dug her nails into her palms so hard that the skin of her hands was shredded. Another had nearly bitten through his own lips. The smell of blood and urine filled the air, and I struggled not to throw up.

Many of their loved ones sat next to them, looks of desperation in their eyes. There was nothing they could do to ease their pain. But at least now that we knew we were all carriers of the Zetas virus and thus could develop the disease at any time, the sick weren't being denied human contact in the days and hours before their deaths.

After I stabbed Nik, John handcuffed her. Then he called Irene while I worked on crudely bandaging her wound with the gauze and medical tape I found in our first aid kit. Irene arrived about twenty minutes later and promptly shoved me out of the way. We couldn't take Nik to a human hospital, because we couldn't risk that she'd start blabbing about angels and demons and get herself committed—or worse, run away and hook back up with the Zetas again. But without treatment, Nik would likely die. The wound wasn't deep, but it needed stitches, and Irene wanted to treat her with antibiotics to prevent infection. Unlike the rest of us, Nik was only human. And I don't know how I would have lived with myself if I had killed her.

So we took Nik to our hospital. Chaz, who insisted on coming with us, sat in the back of the van with her. How the people at the Javits Center failed to notice a heavily sedated, handcuffed woman being carried into a television repair shop, I'll never know, but a lot of strange things happen in New York City. When we got inside, Mabel found us. Without a word, she and Irene immediately rushed Nik off to a side chamber, slamming the door behind them. Tina, who had been our driver, sighed. "Guess I should get you away from the grossness."

Tina led us to an alcove off of the main tunnel, far enough away from the sick patients that their screams were at least muted. There were chairs lining the walls, the pea-soup green ones that looked like they came out of a 1970s classroom. John, Tina, and I sat down. Chaz leaned against the wall, gazing back toward the sick bay. "What is this place?" I asked.

"The old cow tunnels," John replied. "This is the Meatpacking District. People used to complain about the cows blocking up traffic in the street. It smelled, too, like shit and piss and death. So the city built these cow tunnels so that factory workers could walk the cows across Twelfth Avenue without blocking traffic. Didn't help the smell, though."

Tina shuddered. "Yet another reason why I'm a vegetarian."

"When was this?" I asked.

John shrugged. "Around 1870, I think. They weren't used very long. Once refrigerated train cars came into common use, they became obsolete. Everyone pretty much forgot about them, and a lot of historians think they're just an urban legend. The Thrones renovated them back in the eighties; the city was building the Javits Center at the time, so no one noticed the extra supplies heading underground to reinforce the old brickwork and wire them for electricity."

"No one would even think about it, because they didn't know this place existed," I said.

John gave me a conspiratorial grin. "Exactly."

Chaz pushed himself off the wall. "Would you stop talking about the fucking cows?" He turned toward us. His face was flushed. "My best friend has a *stab wound*, and she's being worked on by a doctor who has every reason to hate her."

I rose. "Chaz, I'm sorry. I didn't want to stab her. I just…I didn't know what else to do."

"I don't know that there was anything else you could have done. She had a gun pointed at your head. But that doesn't change the fact that she's on an operating table right now that's probably contaminated with fossilized manure."

I fought the urge to laugh, knowing how badly Chaz was hurting, but "fossilized manure" was almost too much to resist. Tina, however, had no such reservations, and a loud snort escaped her. Chaz glared at her, and she shrugged. "Poop makes me laugh."

Chaz sighed and re-focused his attention on me. "You're going to kill her, aren't you?"

I looked at John. He hadn't moved from his ugly schoolroom chair. "I don't see any other options," he said. "I have an angel employed with the Thrones who can erase memories, but that's only short term. Two, three days at most. Her relationship with the Zetas has been going on much longer than that."

Tears ran down his cheeks. He didn't even try to wipe them away. "Whatever she's done, she's still my best friend. Hell, she's my *family*, way more than a lot of the people I'm blood-related to. And she was *your* friend, too, Dale."

"She tried to kill me tonight."

"She never pulled that trigger. She could have, but she didn't. The Zetas have been trying to kill you for months. But she didn't pull the trigger." Chaz grabbed my shoulders. "Please. I don't know if she's scared, or she just got involved in something she didn't understand, but you know who she really is deep down."

I took a step away from him. "I thought I did…but now I don't know. I never thought she'd do something like this. But it's not up to me whether they execute her."

"You're the one who said your mom was some big, important demon. They'll listen to you!"

I couldn't look at him. "It's not my decision."

Chaz stormed away without another word. I started to follow him, but John's voice stopped me. "Let him go. There's no way out of here except back through the TV shop, and my people there will stop him if he tries to leave without us." John's voice softened. "Give him some time."

"But maybe he has a point. Maybe we should just—"

Irene and Mabel came out at just that moment, interrupting my statement. They both looked tired, although it had only been a couple of hours since we'd brought Nik in. Mabel stretched across the chairs and rested her head in Tina's lap. Irene remained standing. "Is she all right?" I asked.

"She's *alive*," Irene replied. "The stab wound nicked the small intestine, so infection is a major concern. I've started her on antibiotics, but…I just don't work on human patients very often. I don't know how her system will respond."

"We just need to keep her alive long enough to question her," John said. My jaw dropped. John saw the horror on my face but he shook his head. "What do you think will be easier for Chaz: if she dies of a stab wound, or if she dies because we execute her?"

EMBRACING THE DEMON   169

"*Regardless*, I'm going to do my job," Irene said through gritted teeth. "I may not work on human patients often, but I'm certainly not going to allow one to die just because it's more convenient for you."

They stared each other down, and I felt like I was in the middle of a Mexican standoff. I broke the tension with another question. "So why wasn't I able to use my powers on her back at the safe house?"

"It appears that the serum the Zetas created works both ways. If a supernatural is injected, it blocks their powers. If a human is injected, it blocks *them* from *others'* powers. The good news is, humans apparently metabolize it much faster than supernaturals do. The effects only last about ten minutes or so."

Great. Fantastic. That only left one question. Luckily John asked it, because I wouldn't have had the stomach to:

"When can we interrogate her?"

<hr />

Nik woke up about two hours later. "I'm going with you," Chaz announced when Irene came back to give us the news.

"I don't think that's a good idea," I told him. "This is going to be difficult. It'll be emotional, and possibly..." I glanced at John, "...messy. I'm not sure I want you to see that."

"But it's not about you!" Chaz stood up, meeting my eyes unflinchingly. "Everyone in that room is going to be against her. I don't know why she did the things she did, but I know that she's my family. She needs an ally...an advocate."

"Sounds like she needs a lawyer." Tina leaned against the back of her chair, her head resting against the wall, the rebel kid in class who really didn't give a damn—if that kid carried more weapons than a military unit and could shoot fleas off of dogs, that is.

"Well, you're not going to give her a lawyer, are you?" Chaz turned back to me. "And I'm not naive enough to think that you won't be using your... abilities...when you question her."

Nik's words from earlier echoed through me. She'd called my powers "mind rape." I shivered. "Yeah, okay, you can come."

Nik's "room" wasn't so much a room as it was a hole in the wall with a door. It was about five feet wide by seven feet long, and my guess is it was once used as a storage closet. Exposed pipes lined the ceiling, and the only light came from a bare light bulb dangling down. Nik's small, metal-framed bed looked like something that came straight out of the Cold War. There was an IV in her right arm and a blood pressure cuff on her left. Wires protruded from her chest, leading to an intimidating-looking machine that was silently monitoring her heart rate in the background.

Nik herself was paler than I'd ever seen her, and her skin had taken on a yellowish tinge. Sweat coated her body, even though it was chilly in the tunnels, and her dark brown hair looked greasy and limp. Worst of all, she was cuffed to the bed, manacles attached to both her hands and feet. When Nik saw me enter, she didn't even bother to move—not that she could have moved much, anyway. She just looked up at me and said, "Come to finish the job?"

Tears filled my eyes, but I held them back. "We just need to ask you some questions."

"You mean you need to force me to tell you everything I know."

I heard some commotion behind me, and then Chaz's voice. "Let me in. That's why I'm here, asshole." Chaz pushed past John's muscular frame into the room and sat down on the bed next to Nik. He picked up her hand, already covered in bruises beneath where the IV was taped down, and squeezed it in his. "They just want to save their people, Nik. That's all. I know you didn't mean for anyone to die."

Nik took a shaky breath—the first hint of genuine emotion I'd seen from her since she'd revealed herself. "No. I didn't want anyone to get hurt."

"I know, sweetie. It's going to be okay."

Chaz turned to me and nodded. I reached out for Nik's mind. It was all too easy to find now, and completely unshielded. *Oh, Nik. Why the hell didn't they teach you how to protect yourself?* "You will answer my questions, and you'll answer them fully and truthfully."

EMBRACING THE DEMON   171

"Fully and truthfully." There was no fight within her, just a look of resignation on her face. I hated seeing it there.

But it was what it was. "Okay, let's begin."

The questioning took hours. As I grew tired, Mabel brought in a chair for me and shoved it in front of the bed so I wouldn't have to stand anymore. At various points, one of the others—or more than one of the others—would push their way into the room, cramming themselves in wherever they could find a space, to add to what I'd said or ask a question of their own. Then I'd have to redirect it, because I'd only told Nik to answer *me*. I'd been working with my ability long enough to know its limitations. I could direct someone to do what I wanted them to do, but only *exactly* as I directed them. It was like when I was a kid, and my aunt would tell me to pick up everything off of my bedroom floor or I wouldn't be able to watch TV. I'd pick everything up—and then purposely leave it all on the bed or covering the dressers because I knew it would piss her off. Technically, I'd followed her instructions. I'd just ignored her intent. As defiant as Nik was being, she would exploit every loophole she could if I let her.

We learned that Nik had been working with the Zetas since shortly after I left New York last year. She'd gone to a New Age store in Tribeca. When she mentioned angels and demons, the clerk had directed her to a meeting—which turned out to be a front for Zeta recruitment. When they realized that Nik had been my roommate, and that she knew what I was, she climbed the ranks of their organization pretty quickly.

The Zetas' primary headquarters was outside of Washington, DC. Although the satellite offices had some autonomy, their leadership was centralized within their headquarters. The head of the Zetas was its director, a man named Dalton Black, and beneath him were six associate directors—five men and one woman. (The Zetas, Nik informed us with more than a hint of bitterness in her voice, were a very testosterone-heavy organization.) Take them out, and you'd dissolve the entire leadership structure of the organization.

But, even with the leadership destroyed, the satellite offices would continue to try to operate independently. "We know what we're doing is right," Nik said. "Angels and demons don't belong in this world, and as long as anyone with any amount of power is left, we'll continue to fight."

Damn. Well, that wasn't the answer we were hoping for.

It was late into the night and I was battling a headache when John finally said, "I think that's everything we need. Unless anyone else has any questions, I think we can go."

John, Irene, Mabel, and Tina shuffled out of the room. Chaz remained, holding Nik's hand firmly. I stayed, too, in spite of the fact that I felt like someone was taking a hammer to my temples. "Why did you do it?"

Nik closed her eyes. "Chaz was in bad shape after you left. He wouldn't eat, barely slept, and he kept having nightmares."

"Seriously, Nik?" Chaz muttered.

She ignored him. "He must have gone to half a dozen therapists in those first few months. He went on anti-anxiety meds. He took up yoga and meditation. But nothing seemed to help. When I found out there was a group of humans who knew about angels and demons, who had dealt with them before, I thought, 'Maybe they'll understand what Chaz is going through.' After I realized it wasn't some sort of group therapy session, I decided to keep Chaz away from them."

Chaz gritted his teeth. "I wasn't the only one in bad shape, Nik." Nik pursed her lips. "C'mon. Tell them about the nights you couldn't sleep at all, or that when you did you'd wake up calling her name. Tell them how you kept trying to find—"

"Don't." Nik's voice was full of daggers, and Chaz wisely shut up.

I studied her. The gregariousness and the charisma I thought I knew were completely gone, replaced by something far more brittle and hollow. "What happened to you, Nik?"

I didn't put the force of my power behind it. But maybe Nik was just too far broken to notice. Her eyes welled with tears. "They didn't hurt me physically, the way they did Chaz. I wish they had. There was a woman. God, she was beautiful. She made me...she made me..." Nik swallowed hard, "...she made me *feel* things. Whenever she was there, it was like she was the sun and the moon and the stars. I would have done anything for her. I came into that room certain I would never say anything about you, Dale. And then I told them everything I knew, because I *wanted* to. Because I would do anything to make her happy, to make her love me the way I love her. And then they let me go…and I haven't seen her since." Tears were rolling down her face now. Chaz grabbed some tissues and tried to wipe them off, but she turned away from him.

"I'm sorry that happened to you," I said. "It makes sense, that you would be kidnapped and develop feelings for the one person who seemed to care for you. Have you…I mean…would you consider going to a therapist? I'm sure we could find someone who knows about supe—"

"I didn't have Stockholm Syndrome, you idiot!" she snapped. "Don't you get it? She *made* me feel those things. It was her power. She could make you feel *anything*. She could have asked me to burn down the world, and I would have done it. Gladly. *That's* why I started working with the Zetas. Because no one should have that much power over anyone."

I looked over at John. His posture was rigid, his arms folded across his chest. "Do you know any angels with this power?" Because if Nik was right, this woman was incredibly dangerous…but could also be an incredibly powerful ally.

But John shook his head. "I don't know of anyone with that power."

I turned back to Nik. "I'm so sorry any of this happened to you. I didn't mean…I never wanted…You and Chaz were my friends."

"Friends?" She lunged toward me, only to be yanked back by the cuffs on her wrists. "*Friends* don't leave town when you need them the most! *Friends* don't drop big fucking bombs into your life and then vanish from the face of the planet. *Friends* don't have to drag you to a fucking safe house because just being associated with them might make you a target!" She rolled her head back against the pillow and sighed. "I know this isn't a big deal to you. I know you have all the time in the world—literally. But these are our *lives*. And for almost two years, neither one of us has been able to live them, because of you."

I couldn't speak. I felt like someone had punched me in the chest, like I couldn't take a full breath, and the headache had intensified to the point

BETH WOODWARD

where I was about ready to rip off my own skull just to let some of the pressure out.

I got up and left the room, using the walls to support myself as I stumbled. I opened random doors until I found a bathroom, and then I barely made it to the toilet before I vomited.

I heard a voice from the still-open door. "You're sick." John. Of course, it had to be John.

"No shit, Sherlock." I flushed the toilet and pushed myself up.

"And you're bleeding."

I swiped my hand across my face. Sure enough, it came back bloody. I hobbled to the sink and splashed my face with cold water, washing away the remnants of blood and puke. Then I pulled several paper towels out of the dispenser just in case it started to bleed again.

"You should have told me you weren't feeling well."

"It's fine. I've just never held it that long before. Maybe it's like a muscle, and you just have to work it before it gets strong. I just need to do some brain push-ups or something."

His lips turned up at the corners and he shook his head. "C'mon. I'll take you home."

"But Chaz—"

"He wants to stay here with Nik. Dr. Kordova said she'd keep an eye on him."

I had no other reason to object, except that I really wasn't feeling up to dealing with John at the moment. On the other hand, taking a bus or a taxi back to the safe house sounded like the most miserable thing in the world at the moment.

When we left the television repair shop, there was already a town car waiting for us, complete with a driver wearing a dark suit and a cap. I stretched out across the back seat, resting my head in John's lap, not caring that I still hated him and that he'd hurt me so much. In that moment he was warm and comfortable, the electric zing of his skin against mine feeling more like a massage than a lightning bolt. The contrast against the cool leather was nice, and I fell asleep before we even pulled back onto the street.

When John woke me up, it took me a second to realize that we were not at the safe house. Instead, we had pulled up in front of a fancy-looking high-rise. "Where are we?" My voice was still raspy from sleep.

"My apartment building."

I jerked away from him. "What the hell?"

"Dale, the safe house has been compromised. Covington or I can set you up in a new place later today, but it's three a.m. and there's not a damn thing we can do right now."

Part of me wanted to fight him, but he was right and I was too drained—physically and emotionally—to bother. John greeted the doorman and the concierge as we walked into the elevator (already there, like it had been waiting for us) and we took it up to the top floor.

John's apartment looked like what you would dream a New York City apartment would be after you'd watched a few episodes of *Sex and the City* but before you started paying attention to pesky things like "cost of living" and "being able to pay your bills and still eat." It was large, and airy, and had floor-to-ceiling windows overlooking the Empire State Building, now dark for the night.

But for all that it had, the apartment was missing something. It was as if someone had opened up a Crate and Barrel catalog, selected a random page, and said, "There, make this apartment look like that": all clean lines and modern aesthetic and no personality. There were no pictures, no cheap knickknacks from various vacations—hell, even the stainless steel trash can in the kitchen was empty. Everything about it screamed out, "this is just a place to sleep," and it made me surprisingly sad. John had gotten everything he wanted. Amara was dead, he'd avenged his parents, and he'd finally succeeded his father as the head of the Thrones. But in spite of all that, he still lived in an apartment with not so much as a refrigerator magnet to show he actually existed.

John emerged from the hallway, carrying a set of towels, oblivious to my musings. "C'mon, I'll show you to your room."

The bedroom was just as gorgeous, and just as austere, as the rest of the apartment. A queen-sized bed dominated the space, covered with a fluffy white duvet. But what really got me was the fact that the bed was covered with women's clothing, neatly folded and stacked. I picked up a pair of jeans. It was my size. "I had someone run over to the safe house to pick up your clothes earlier tonight," John explained. "She said you didn't have much."

I fought the urge to roll my eyes. "Yeah, well…when you're running for your life, you tend to pack light."

"So I asked her to go out and get a few more things for you, things that were a little more your style than all those Laura Hill clothes you wore in Nebraska."

I was about to snap at him that he didn't know what my style was…but the truth was, the stuff on the bed was exactly the kind of stuff I would have picked out on my own. Jeans. T-shirts. Fleece hoodies. Warm sweaters. I spent so much of my life wearing clothes as disguises that, when left to my own devices, I tended to choose comfort over appearance. John, maybe mistaking my silence for annoyance, shrugged. "At least they're not covered in blood, like all the clothes you had to wear while we were on the run last year."

"Give me time." I picked up the bath towel John had brought for me. "I'd like to take a shower, if that's all right."

"Of course." He opened a door and flipped on the light. "This room has a private bathroom, so you can take as much time as you need. There should be a toothbrush and some toothpaste in the top drawer. Oh, also…" he opened the medicine cabinet and handed me a small glass bottle. "It's eucalyptus oil. Human painkillers don't work with our physiology, so we've had to find alternative methods through the years. Rub some on your temples while you're in the shower. It should help with your headache."

I thanked him and retreated into the bathroom. Twenty minutes later, I was clean and no longer had vomit breath, and my headache had subsided to a dull ache. I got dressed in a pair of flannel pajamas, with a long bathrobe over the top. But the icing on the cake was the slippers, which were extremely warm and felt like they'd been lined with clouds. I vowed to find out what brand they were and buy at least ten pairs.

But when I returned to the bedroom and climbed into the bed, I found that I couldn't sleep in spite of my exhaustion. I went into the living room and sat on the couch, staring out the window at the New York skyline. I don't know how much time had passed when John came out and found me there. "Can't sleep?" he asked. I shook my head. "It's been a stressful day. I think I have some chamomile tea in the pantry somewhere."

John headed toward the kitchen, but before he could get there, I spoke. "Is it me?"

He turned around, his eyebrows knitted. "What are you talking about?"

"My mom left me—twice. Aunt Barbara hated me. And *you*..." I swallowed the tears that were creeping into my voice. I would *not* cry in front of him. "Well, we both know what happened there."

"Dale..."

"Nik's right—I did leave her and Chaz when they needed me the most. I did the same thing to Julie back in the day."

"You tried to help her."

I chuckled bitterly. "Some help! I murdered her prom date and didn't stick around for questions. The police were probably up her ass for months. Like she really needed that, after what happened." I shook my head. "After all these years, I'm still not sorry for what I did to Brad Kinnard. I know I should be. I know I'm supposed to be. But I'm not. I still think the fucker deserved what he got. But if I'd stuck around, if I'd faced the music for my crime, maybe I could have spared Julie...something."

John sat down on the couch, his body angled toward mine. "You did the best you could."

"Did I? Because maybe my best isn't good enough, when I was making the same damn mistakes ten years later. Shit gets too hot, and I run away—and this time, I didn't even have a Rage to blame for it."

"So don't run again." I looked up and met John's golden brown eyes, which seemed to be staring straight into the shriveled husk I called a soul. "The next time things get hot, don't run. Deal with the fallout."

"You think it's that simple?"

"It's that simple…and that complicated. But you're not alone anymore. You have people who will help you. Covington, Dr. Kordova, Mabel and Tina…me."

The room suddenly felt hot. I went to the kitchen and poured myself a glass of water, keeping my eyes averted from John's as I sat at the table—which was basically as far from John as I could get without bolting from the room—and drank it. John didn't move from the couch, but I could still *feel* him there, could still smell the scent of warm butterscotch that was so distinctly *John*. It pervaded his whole apartment, and I wondered if it was just the candy he ate or if he'd actually gone out and bought those sugar-scented plug-in things from Bath & Body Works or something. I wouldn't put it past him.

When I finished my water, I poured a second glass, not because I was thirsty so much as I needed something to do with my hands. John ran his fingers through his hair. He seemed anxious, not an emotion I was used to seeing on him. "It wasn't you," he said finally.

"What wasn't me?"

It took him a long time to respond. "After Amara killed my parents, I could only think about one thing: getting revenge for their deaths. As the years passed, that evolved into a goal of taking over the Thrones. I knew I could be a better leader than Gabriel…better than my father, even. And I knew I could make the Thrones into what it always should have been: protection and aid for *all* angels, not just purebloods. People like Isaac never should have been tossed out in the street, and people like me never should have been used as pawns in the stupid war that angels and demons have been waging on each other for millennia. And for what? You won. Clearly procreation with humans is a thing, or we wouldn't be here."

"I guess Amara liked to hold a grudge."

"Yeah, exactly. If she didn't, my parents—my *mother*—wouldn't have been murdered right in front of me. And if Gabriel wasn't led around by his dick, Amara would have been dead centuries ago for that transgression."

I felt like I'd been slapped. I looked out the window and stared at the still-dark Empire State Building.

John sighed. "I'm mucking this up."

"No, it's fine. I mean, well...it's not *fine*, exactly, but, you know...truce or whatever."

"No!"

John slammed his hand against the couch. The wooden frame cracked loudly and the couch collapsed to the floor. My words came out in a rush. "Jesus, John! You know it's like four o'clock in the morning. Your neighbors are probably calling nine-one-one right now." John ignored the damage and crossed the room to me. He looked almost feral, with his hair in disarray and a resolute expression on his face. "Seriously, John, you really should call the concierge and let them know that no one's being tortured up here. I mean, just as a courtesy."

"Dale, shut up."

I shut up.

John took a deep breath. "For over three hundred years, everything I did—all my training, all the jobs I took, everyone I interacted with—led to the same goal: killing Amara. And I never hesitated, not once, until a summer night in Brooklyn when a redheaded girl smiled at me while 'The Safety Dance' played in the background."

"But you went through with it anyway."

"Maybe I made a mistake." I finally looked at him. He was as pained as I'd ever seen him, his eyes filled with an emotion I could not identify. "In three hundred years, I never imagined I could lo—care for anyone the way I cared about you. I didn't think I was capable of it. I went through with my plan because I wanted to help part-bloods like Isaac—and yes, because I wanted to avenge my parents. But then you were gone, and I realized... maybe the cost was too high."

I studied him. His hair was disheveled, there were dark circles underneath his eyes, and I saw something in his features that I'd never seen before: remorse. I thought back to our time together searching for Amara. Even then, he'd seem conflicted. If I'd been paying a little bit more attention, I would have realized—*should* have realized—that there was more going on with him than he let on. But maybe I hadn't wanted to see. Tears filled my eyes. "You hurt me so much."

"I know. I'm sorry."

"You were the only person who ever knew everything about me, all the people I've hurt, all the terrible things I've done…and then you turn out to be nothing like I thought you were."

He reached out, slowly, cautiously, and ran his fingers through my hair. Part of me wanted to push him away. But it just felt so good that I couldn't bring myself to do it. "For whatever it's worth," John said, "I'm here. And I'll be here as long as you want me to be."

I closed my eyes and rested my head against the couch, remembering the time we'd spent together the previous year. It had been tainted by the angry haze of Amara's murder. But sometimes, when I was alone and everything was quiet, I couldn't help but remember all the rest of it: jumping onto moving subway trains and car chases through New York City to escape the Thrones. Training together at Funland after the park had closed.

Frantic, desperate, *incredible* sex in the backseat of a stolen car after watching my aunt get gunned down right in front of us.

In a strange way, they had been the best weeks of my life.

I opened my eyes. John's gaze met mine, his hand still resting against my hair—an almost nonexistent touch, like he feared I'd push it away at any moment. A month earlier I would have. Hell, six hours earlier I would have.

I kissed him instead.

He was gentle, almost hesitant, and he tasted like warm sugar. Tears filled my eyes, because I'd missed him so much. For a brief moment in time, he'd been my best friend, and I wanted desperately to sink into him. To forget. But I couldn't.

I pulled away.

I didn't say anything for a long time; I wouldn't have been able to form words if I'd wanted to. "I shouldn't have done that."

"Dale…"

EMBRACING THE DEMON 181

"Just chalk it up to temporary insanity, all right? I just…wanted to feel less alone for a minute."

I got up and started to walk away. I'd made it all the way to the door when I heard his voice. "You're not alone," he said.

I froze. "What?"

He met my eyes with his golden brown ones. "I'm so sorry I hurt you, Dale. In all my years, I've never regretted anything more. I know you'll never forgive me, and that's all right. I'll always be here if you need me, no matter what."

I had no idea what to say, so I didn't say anything. I walked into my room and shut the door.

CHAPTER SIXTEEN
Dale

THE NEXT DAY, COVINGTON, IRENE, Mabel, and Tina came over to John's apartment to start planning. Some of the Thrones joined us, too, including my favorite blond bitch Rebekah—and a short, muscular woman named Mae who wore cargo pants and a tank top despite the fact that it was a whooping thirteen degrees outside. Mae seemed like a bullshit-free type, and I really wanted to like her, but she kept glaring at me. Whether it was the fact that I was a demon, or the fact that I was their Typhoid Mary, I had no idea. But it's really hard to befriend someone who looks at you like you're a particularly nasty case of athlete's foot.

I ordered pizza, because any meeting where you discuss how to annihilate your enemies is better with some sweet, sweet 'za, and we sat on John's floor eating off of these china plates that probably worth more than what I made in a year at Griddles n' Grits. Seriously, he couldn't just eat his pizza off of paper plates like a normal person? Isn't there some kind of rule that antique china should never be covered in pepperoni grease?

Covington picked at his slice for a few minutes before he spoke up. "It sounds like you got some valuable intelligence from the human yesterday. I just wish you would have consulted me first."

I could almost feel the air in the room thicken with tension. "It all happened very quickly," Irene said finally. "We didn't want to disturb you."

"I was Amara's valet and personal assistant for over seventy-five years," he snapped. "I may be mortal, but I'm not incompetent."

Another awkward silence. When it didn't look like anyone else would say anything, I reached across the table and clasped Covington's hand. "You're right. I'm sorry. I was distracted because Nik was my friend, and I trusted her. But I should have called you. You worked with my mother for a long time, and you have knowledge that could be invaluable to us. Everyone here knows that."

The others chimed in with their agreement. Covington nodded, but there was still a frown on his face.

John stood up, shifting into leadership mode. "As Covington said, we did gather some valuable intelligence from Nik yesterday. But unfortunately, we still don't know the location of the Zetas' headquarters."

I furrowed my eyebrows. "I thought she said 'outside of DC.'"

"Have you ever *been* to DC.?" I shook my head. "The metropolitan area is huge. Anything between Baltimore and Richmond could be considered 'outside of DC.'"

I didn't really know what to say to that. Mabel pulled out a laptop and began typing rapidly. "I'll work on it. I can devise a search algorithm to run through some map programs. Something the size of the Zetas' headquarters has to have a footprint."

"Good," John said. "Use all the computer algorithms. We're counting on you. You did such a great job running down the locations of the other facilities for us. I don't think we'd be where we are without you."

Mabel grinned and thanked him. Meanwhile, Tina said under her breath, "Did he just say 'all the computer algorithms'? He does understand how computers work, right?"

"Undoubtedly he's thinking of a 'computer' as someone with scratch paper and an abacus," Covington replied.

John rolled his eyes, ignoring the comments. "We have another problem. As the human told us yesterday, if we take out Zetas' HQ without taking out the other field stations at the same time, our attack will be useless. They'll know we're on to them, and the field stations will simply pick up where the headquarters left off."

"So we take them all out." Tina twirled a six-inch knife between her fingers like a baton, seemingly oblivious to the fact that a blade that looked like something out of an old war movie danced dangerously close to her wrist and fingers.

"Once they know we're coming, they'll increase their defensive measures and the number of personnel protecting each field station. I'm afraid our first attack is going to be our only chance."

"So we take them all out *at once*." Never once did Tina's knife waver.

"Except we don't have enough people to do that."

I raised my eyebrows. "Even with the Thrones on board?" I asked.

John shook his head. "At last count, we have a roster of five thousand seven hundred and thirty-one active Thrones in the United States. I may be able to double that number if I start pulling in resources internationally. According to the intelligence we've gathered, the Zetas have one-point-one million. Now, not all of them are going to be combat-capable, nor will all of them be stationed at headquarters or the field stations…but even with that in mind, the numbers just don't add up."

"Are you serious? There's really less than six thousand of you?"

"Angels never procreated as much as demons did, Dale. For them, it was solely a means to an end—our part-blood children made great, disposable soldiers. And when Gabriel was in charge, he ousted anyone he thought was 'too human.' You remember what happened to Isaac."

Isaac, John's friend—and mine too, maybe in spite of himself—had been kicked out of the Thrones when he developed a brain tumor. He was mixed blood, but unlike John or me, his supernatural DNA wasn't enough to give him immortality. Even so, he was one of the most powerful angels I'd ever met, with the ability to create a mirage so real that you could actually touch it. If Gabriel was throwing those kinds of abilities away, who knew how many other angels were wandering out there with immense powers and no ties to their people.

John must have intuited what I was thinking. "I'm working on it, Little Demon. If I'd had a little more time, maybe…"

But I could do the math. John had taken over leadership of the Thrones after he'd killed Amara and Gabriel—and shortly thereafter, the Zetas' nanovirus had started manifesting in the supernatural population. He'd probably spent most of the last eighteen months doing damage control.

"All right, so we have to get the demons involved, obviously. That's why we're here. So do we have any idea how many demons we can pull in for this?"

I looked over at Covington for an answer. He sighed. "I'm afraid it's not good news. While Amara held nominal leadership of demonkind, she hadn't used that power in centuries. Demons do have a much larger population than angels, but as we stand now, we are…separate. Dispersed. With no way to reach out to our brethren, we can't assemble the numbers we need to mount such an attack."

"Mabel and I may be able to help with that," Irene said.

She nodded to Mabel, who typed something into her laptop before she set it on the coffee table. Mabel had pulled up a sleekly designed website with the words "The Amara Connection" in the heading. "For years, I've been wanting to find a way to reach out to and connect the demon world—not just for medical stuff, but for everything. When I met Mabel and realized how computer savvy she was, I asked her to help me."

Mabel picked up where Irene left off. "We started with a mailing list of just Irene's patients, and we only accepted new subscribers by referral. But then it grew, so I decided to put together a website. It's a darknet site, heavily encrypted and password protected. I've been working toward integrating biometric authentication into the site, maybe even use AziziCorp hardware to ensure the user actually has supernatural blood, but it's proved logistically unfeasible so far. Most people simply don't have access to that kind of equipment, and getting it to all the—"

BETH WOODWARD

"Mabel, focus," Irene said. "How many subscribers do we have now?"

Mabel grinned. "About seventy-five thousand."

I looked down at my feet, trying not to let the disappointment show on my face. Covington, however, was not so discrete. "It's still not enough," he said.

"It's seventy-five thousand more potential fighters than we had a few minutes ago," Mabel replied. "I'm sure once they realize what's at stake, they'll be happy to help."

Covington shook his head. "It's not that easy. The demons may have won the War of Purity, but angels won the war of information." With this, he glared at John pointedly. "Our entire history is filled with people trying to kill us once they realize who and what we are."

"But…people are dying," Mabel said.

"Only five percent. Many of the rest will choose to take their chances." Covington looked at Irene. "You've been around longer than I have. You've worked with our people and treated our people for more than a century now. You know it's true."

Everyone turned back to Irene. She sat down and braced her forehead on her hands. "I'm not as pessimistic as Covington, but…he's right. It could be a problem. Most demons don't see themselves as part of a 'community.' They're just trying to protect their own."

A tense silence filled the room. Finally I spoke, my voice tentative. "What if I spoke to them?" Every head in the room swiveled toward me. I took a breath. "Amara was the leader of the demons, for whatever that was worth. I mean, I don't think it's a coincidence that you called your website 'The Amara Connection'—she was the only person who ever unified us all together. She's gone now, but I'm here. I could make a video, send out some kind of message…"

"I don't know…" Covington said.

I turned to him. "Isn't this why you wanted me here, why you wanted me to be a part of this? So demons could have someone to rally behind?"

Covington met my eyes. "But no matter how secure this darknet site is, there's always a risk that the wrong person will access it, correct?" Mabel's tight nod confirmed Covington's statement. "Dale, the Zetas still want you dead. Not to mention the fact that you are uniquely vulnerable *because* you're Amara's daughter. Killing you would be a devastating blow to us demons, and our enemies know it."

With this, Covington glared pointedly at John, but John shook his head. "My people will not come after her," he said.

"I think we both know that you and your people are not always in accord," Covington said before turning to me. "Dale, when you came back into Amara's life…I don't think you know how much that meant to her, how much *you* meant to her. And I swore to her that I would keep you safe."

"That's not your job," I replied. "I'm not the baby Amara left behind, and I haven't been in a long time." I stood up, turning to face Mabel and Irene. "I'm in. Let's make a movie."

———— ◇ ————

WE DECIDED TO FILM THE video the next morning, to give Mabel time to get all the right equipment. In the meantime, I went to the drugstore to pick up a box of hair dye. Unfortunately, without John footing the bill, I couldn't afford to have my hair professionally done again, but hell if I was going to broadcast myself to thousands of demons with chunky highlights. Oh, 2002 called, and it wanted its hairstyle back.

I was deciding between "Autumn Sunset" and "Raspberry Beret" when my cell phone rang. It was a prepaid phone that John had insisted I start carrying with me in case of emergencies. He was the only one who had the number. But when I picked up, I was surprised to hear another voice on the other end: Chaz. I hadn't seen him since I'd left him with Nik in the Cow Tunnels the night before. "Where are you?" he asked.

"I'm at Duane Reade. How did you even get this number?"

"Which one?"

"Corner of Forty-Seventh and Lex. Chaz, are you all right? I'm so sorry about everything that happened with—"

He cut me off. "There's a Starbucks about half a block away from you. Meet me there in twenty minutes."

"Chaz, what are you—"

But before I could finish my question, Chaz had hung up.

I went to the Starbucks twenty minutes later, ordered a chai latte, and sat down to wait. Chaz was nowhere to be found

A few minutes later, an older woman, maybe about seventy but with a colorful way of dressing that put most women half her age to shame, approached me. "Are you waiting for someone?" she asked.

New Yorkers vacillated between perpetually disinterested and chronically nosy, and I was never sure how to respond to these types of inquires without risking setting off a crazy person. "Don't worry, I'm fine. Just waiting for a friend. He'll be here in a few minutes."

"It's just that a young man said you'd be waiting for him, and he asked me to give you this note." She handed me a folded slip of paper. "He said he was sorry, but he had to go home and help his mother right away. It was an emergency, he said."

"Of course, yeah. His mom has trouble getting around sometimes." Chaz's mother lived in California, and as far as I knew she was perfectly healthy.

The woman walked away, and I read the note: *ABC Diner, East 2nd and Avenue B. 5pm. Come alone.*

THE ABC DINER WAS LOCATED inside of a nondescript building in Alphabet City. Inside, everything was weirdly schoolhouse themed, from the primary-colored walls to the block-printed alphabet strip lining the ceiling. A chalkboard announced that the special of the day was the "Steak Thesaurus." I wasn't sure whether to expect a reference guide or a dinosaur.

Chaz sat in a booth in the back corner, wearing sunglasses, the hood of his sweatshirt pulled up around his face. I sat down across from him. "What's with the cloak and dagger stuff?"

"Did you tell anyone you were coming here?"

"No, I was too busy trying to figure out how the hell to get to Alphabet City. I had to switch over to the F train, and the closest stop is still four avenues over. What's going on, Chaz? What's so secretive that we couldn't have just talked at the Starbucks?"

Chaz took off his sunglasses. His eyes were red-rimmed and puffy. "They're going to kill Nik."

A chill ran through my body. "What?"

"I heard some of them talking when they thought I was asleep. They're planning to execute her."

I shook my head. "Chaz, I'm sure you misheard. I mean, they can't let her go right now, but after the Zetas are defeated—"

"That's when they're planning to do it: after you've attacked the Zetas and they're sure they don't need any more information from her."

The waitress came over to our table. Chaz ordered black coffee, and I ordered a Coke—and I worried even that would be too much for my now-turbulent stomach. When she walked away, Chaz reached across the table and grabbed my hand. "You have to save her."

"Chaz, I don't know what you expect me to do."

"Talk to them! You're supposed to be someone important, right? So tell them not to do it!" Chaz was so loud that several other diners turned to stare at him. He slumped down in his seat and lowered his voice. "It's my fault, you know. I was in a dark place after you left, Dale. I stopped working, I couldn't sleep…I barely ate for months. I'd lost twenty-five pounds by the end of last year."

Chaz was already thin. With twenty-five pounds off his frame, he must have looked like a skeleton. "I'm sorry."

"Nik was just trying to help. I know that she screwed up, and I know that she betrayed you, but she was only doing it for me." He wiped tears away from his face. "Sometimes the people who love you and the people who are related to you are not the same. Nik's not just my best friend; she's my family. And I—I can't lose her."

I moved to the other side of the booth, and I wrapped Chaz in my arms as he sobbed. The waitress came back with our drinks, but we ignored them. By the time we broke apart, Chaz's coffee had long-since stopped steaming and the condensation from my Coke had soaked through the napkin beneath it. "I'll talk to them," I said. "I'll do everything I can to save her."

He swallowed some tepid coffee before he spoke again.

"That's all I can ask."

CHAPTER SEVENTEEN
Dale

I ARRIVED AT THE COW TUNNELS—WHERE we had decided to film the video—at nine-fifteen the next morning. Mabel and Tina were waiting for me, setting up video equipment in what was probably supposed to be a closet. Afterward, Mabel planned on filming the sick—an "appeal to their empathy," she called it. Seemed pretty morbid to me, but who was I to judge?

At any rate, I had bigger fish to fry. Mabel and Tina must have realized something was going on as soon as I walked into the room, because they both froze. "You're here early," Mabel said tentatively.

"I need to talk to everyone. Covington, Irene, John, and whoever else is responsible for making decisions around here, and I need to do it before I film this video. Can you get them here?"

Mabel was texting furiously before I'd even finished my statement. "Dale...is everything okay?"

"I don't know."

Tina, meanwhile, positioned herself in a ready-to-fight stance. It was so casual that I wouldn't have even noticed it if I'd hadn't been looking, but she had angled herself between Mabel and me and positioned her arms in such a way that she'd be ready to draw her concealed sidearms at any moment. I felt myself snap to attention.

Mabel rolled her eyes without looking up from her phone. "Tina, I'm sure that's not necessary. Dale's not going to hurt anyone. Are you, Dale?"

"I wasn't planning on it," I said. But this answer did not mollify Tina. She pulled her hands away from her holsters while still keeping herself between Mabel and me, glaring furiously. Okay, I couldn't blame her for that. I wouldn't trust me, either.

Irene arrived a few minutes later. Her hair was disheveled, her clothes rumpled, and I guessed she spent the night in the Cow Tunnels. When she spotted me, she rolled her eyes. "Are you serious? Do you know how much I have to do? Three more people died last night. I can't afford to be—"

"It won't take long. We just have to wait for John and Covington to get here.

Covington arrived a few minutes later, dressed in a neon jogging suit that had eighties flashback written all over it. He looked like he was about to complain the way Irene had, but he took one look at me and sat down next to Mabel without another word.

John was the last to arrive. He hadn't been home when I'd come back the previous evening, so I retreated to my bedroom and locked the door. I dyed my hair in the en suite bathroom, and then I turned off all the lights and got into bed. By the time John came home, I was engaged in a reasonable facsimile of sleep. Ignoring the tension in the room, he zeroed in on my hair. "I always liked you better as a redhead, Little Demon."

The dye had managed to turn my hair back to a brownish-auburn shade; unfortunately, the chunks in my chunky highlights had turned out lighter than the rest, giving me a bit of a striped look. Still, it was better than it had been before. "Blondes might have more fun, but redheads get shit done." I wasn't trying to be cute, but John grinned at me anyway.

Irene cleared her throat. "All right, if you two are done flirting with one another, could someone please explain why we're here with Nik."

"I'd be glad to," I replied. "I need to know what you plan on doing."

Nobody said a word, and when I looked around the room they wouldn't meet my eyes. "All right, let me make this a little clearer. I won't put together your recruitment video until you promise not to execute Nik."

———◇———

For a long time, nobody spoke. Not surprisingly, it was Irene who broke the silence. "Are you serious right now?"

"As a funeral—hopefully not Nik's."

You would risk sacrificing all those lives—all of *our* lives—for one human who betrayed us all?"

"See, that's the problem." I paced the width of the room, feeling like a schoolteacher lecturing her students. "All you see is 'one human.' But what makes her life worth any less than ours? You can't measure the value of life like weight on a scale—supernatural is greater than human, thousands of lives is greater than one. It doesn't work that way. And who the fuck made you judge, jury, and executioner?" I directed my last question at Irene, who—to her credit—didn't flinch.

John jumped in before I could speak again. "Don't blame Dr. Kordova. We all decided. Covington, Mabel, Tina, Dr. Kordova, a few of the Thrones from my leadership council, and me. We voted. It was unanimous."

"*I* didn't vote."

"You're not objective about this, Dale."

"That's exactly why I should have been asked!" I shouted. We were at an impasse. I took a breath, trying to calm myself down. "Look, I know Nik screwed up. Big time. But it never would have happened if not for me. Her life, and Chaz's, got completely messed up because of me. Chaz has had PTSD symptoms ever since he got kidnapped by *your* people," I looked pointedly at John, "and Nik was worried about him. I had disappeared, and Nik was just looking for someone—anyone—who could help."

"Nik made her own choices," John said.

"Yeah, but there were mitigating circumstances!" I turned toward the rest of the group. "Look, I know Nik, and I know she would never want to hurt anyone. Keep her locked up, do what you need to do. Just...don't kill her. Please."

Nobody said anything for a long time. Finally, John stood up. "You're right. We should have allowed you to have a voice in this decision." Irene scoffed, but John silenced her with a stern look. "We also should not have withheld this information from you. Nik was—is—your friend, and you deserved to know."

"Thank you. I appreciate that."

John took a breath. "I'm willing to keep her locked up in a Thrones facility indefinitely."

Chaos erupted. Irene and Covington were up immediately, shouting at John. Tina pursed her lips and pulled a switchblade out of her pocket, twirling it in between her fingers in a way that told me she was fighting the urge to stab John in the neck. Even Mabel looked perturbed, reinforcing Irene and Covington's shouts with her own "yeahs" and "that's rights."

Meanwhile John just stood there silently, enduring their barrage for a minute or so before he put his hand up to silence them. "Since the Thrones will be holding her, it's my decision to make."

The tension in the room was thick enough to taste. Irene was the first one to leave the room. She stepped into my personal space on her way out. "Just because you're Amara's daughter doesn't make you a leader. A leader stays with her people. A leader fights. A leader doesn't run away just because shit hits the fan. I see what you're doing, but you don't fool me. You're not a leader. You're just a scared child." She walked away before I could respond. Covington followed her out.

Mabel swallowed hard. "Well, that was...something. If you don't mind, I'd like to take a few minutes to freshen up before we start shooting." Mabel grabbed Tina's arm and headed for the door, but before they walked out she hesitated. "I understand why you fought for your friend. I would have done the same thing, if it had been someone I cared about. But *you*," she glared at John, "...you bungled this. We made a decision, all of us, and you had no right to override that. That's not okay."

EMBRACING THE DEMON   195

Mabel and Tina walked out of the room, leaving John and me alone. An awkward silence fell between us. "So, uh, how about them Yankees? Shit, it's not even baseball season, is it?" I scrubbed my face with my palms. "Thank you for doing that, John. I didn't...I mean...I never meant to cause tension between all of you."

"Of course you did. Otherwise you never would have called us all in here and blackmailed us into doing what you wanted."

I sighed. "Yeah, I guess I did. But I didn't like it."

John's gaze was fixed at some far-off point, like he was staring through the wall. "Being a leader means trying to make the right decisions, even when they're not the easy ones."

"I understand." That had been what I was trying to do with Nik.

"I'm not sure that you do." He turned and gave me a sad smile. "But you will."

CHAPTER EIGHTEEN
Dale

THE NEXT FEW DAYS PASSED quickly. After I filmed the video and it went out on the Amara Connection site, we started receiving volunteers quickly. The nanovirus had infected demons worldwide, and without access to a supernatural-friendly doctor like Irene, many people were being forced to go to human hospitals. Unbeknownst to us, the phenomenon was so unusual that it had been written about in several newspapers and science blogs—the mysterious, rabies-like illness killing people with no rhyme or reason to it. It wasn't widespread enough to be front-page news—not yet, anyway—but the humans were starting to notice. And the last thing most supernaturals wanted was to be noticed by humans.

"We have more volunteers than I hoped for," Tina said about three days after the message went out, "but still not as many as we need. We're still greatly outnumbered, and they have the advantage of familiar territory."

"So what are we going to do?" I asked. We were all in apartment: Tina and Covington, John and his lieutenants, and me. Irene and Mabel were back at the Cow Tunnels, tending to the sick. Six more people had died in the past twenty-four hours, and Irene got anxious if she was away from the patients for more than a few minutes at a time—even though there wasn't a damn thing she could do about it.

The rest of us were all having a strategy session to plan our attack on the Zetas. Well…everyone else was having a strategy session. I was expending most of my energy just to keep my eyes open. I hadn't slept well for the past several nights, the weight of Nik's imprisonment and our impending strike against the Zetas bearing heavily on me. Not to mention that kiss. I was trying very hard not to think about the kiss.

"John and I have been working on it," Tina said. "We've been talking about a 'distract and divert' strategy. The first wave of the attack would be outside the building, luring the Zetas away from their posts and leaving security inside the building at a minimum. While the Zetas are busy fighting the battle outside, the second wave would go inside the building—where all the head honchos will likely be. We know we can't get everyone, so the most important thing we can do is get the people who matter—the brains of the operation."

I snorted. I couldn't help myself. Blame it on the lack of sleep. When everyone turned to stare at me, I defended myself. "Seriously? *That's* your plan? Blow stuff up *outside*, hope to hell they *come* outside, then run *inside* to mindfreak the brass? Who wrote this, Bert and Ernie?"

Tina glared at me. I'd been on thin ice with her since I'd issued my ultimatum about Nik, and I probably should have known better than to antagonize a woman who probably had a dozen weapons hidden on her—and that was her version of "lightly armed." I decided discretion was the better part of *not getting knifed* and shut the hell up.

"It sounds risky," Covington said.

"It is risky. There's a good chance it won't work. Even if all our volunteers show up, we're still outnumbered, and we have to divide our resources between the headquarters and the satellite offices. We'll have to make it seem like we have a bigger force than we do."

"How?" I asked.

It was John who answered this time. "Smoke and mirrors, basically. A lot of pyrotechnics, fireworks, that sort of thing. We're going to make a lot of noise, and then we're going to take out as many of them as we can using long-range weapons."

"I know someone who can get us a lot of C-four," Tina added.

"Why does that not surprise me," I mumbled. Honestly, I wouldn't have been too surprised if Tina knew someone who could get us the nuclear football. "But something's bothering me. Once they realize our force is smaller than they anticipated, what's to stop them from just slaughtering everybody?" And then it dawned on me. "Oh. I guess that's my role in all this. You want me to control the Zetas while we invade. Got it. I don't think my range is strong enough to reach all the Zetas on the compound, but I can at least manage…"

I stopped mid-sentence, realizing the room had descending into awkward silence before. It was Tina who finally spoke. "Dale…you're not going to be using your powers. At all."

"What? Why?"

"We'll need your ability to interrogate the Zetas' leadership. We can't risk that the Zetas will use their serum on you—or worse—and you'll be out of commission."

"But that's stupid. We'll be outnumbered, and on their home turf. We'll be slaughtered."

"Probably."

"Probably?" The casual way she spoke about such loss of life curdled my stomach. Memories of the night Amara died swam through my head. She'd known something was coming—the advantage of having a boyfriend with precognition. Her people had still been massacred. I still had nightmares about that night. Dreams warped it into something out of a horror movie, with blood running down the walls and glassy-eyed corpses begging me to save them.

"What do you want me to say, Dale? Yes, we're going to lose a lot of lives that day, but without the information you can get, we're facing the extinction of our entire species."

I looked at John. "What about an illusionist like Isaac? Or maybe… maybe there's someone with the power to clone themselves. That's got to be a thing, right? "

It was Tina who answered, her voice firm. "We're reviewing the skill sets and abilities of all of the volunteers. We'll use them to our best advantage. But the reality is, it doesn't change the fact that we're severely outnumbered and battling an enemy who will have home field advantage."

"So we just take these people who volunteered to help us and lead them to their deaths like damn lemmings? That's fucked up, Tina, and you know it."

"No. You don't speak to me that way. These are the kinds of decisions you have to make in a war, and like it or not, that's what we're fighting. And if it had been up to me, you wouldn't even be going into this battle at all."

John spoke up quietly. "Dale is an asset with or without her powers."

"She's an asset who screwed up the last two missions," Tina said bluntly.

There was a long beat of silence. I was the one who finally broke it. "I just don't know if it's worth it."

I looked around the room, but no one would meet my eyes. Not surprisingly, it was John who finally spoke. "Tina's right. We don't have any other choice."

———————◇———————

I HEADED BACK TO THE Cow Tunnels after that. The rest of the group remained at John's to strategize, talking tactics and weaponry and other things I didn't understand. They had wanted me to be a part of things because I was Amara's daughter and the presumed "leader of the demons," whatever that meant. But when it came to battle planning, I was completely clueless. It left me wishing that Amara had a beloved dog or something that could have stepped into the role of the demons' mascot.

Plus, I needed to remember what we were fighting for. Sacrificing some to save the rest still seemed like a horrible thing to do, and no matter what John or Tina said, I still couldn't justify it. But maybe if I saw the sick again, saw them struggling to survive against impossible odds. Maybe if I saw

BETH WOODWARD

their families cramped into the dark corners of the Cow Tunnels. Maybe then it would all make sense, and I wouldn't feel like I was part of leading lambs to their slaughter.

I found Mabel at the bedside of a man, wiping his face with a wet washcloth. He thrashed back and forth every time she touched him, but it was no use since he was strapped to the bed. He was so emaciated I doubted his own mother would be able to recognize him. "I'm here to relieve you," I told her. "Tina and the others are over at John's place planning out how to best kill the most people, and I thought you might like to join them."

Mabel handed me the washcloth, along with a bucket filled with ice water. Her eyes were bloodshot, her skin pale. "No. I think I'll just go take a nap or something. Tina's always been better with the death and dismemberment. Although I guess I've been dealing with it more recently."

"Anything I need to know?" I gestured toward the patients.

"Fitzpatrick over there in bed seventeen bites, so watch out for that. Sylvia in bed thirty-two is close to the end, I think, so you might want to check on her more frequently. I don't think she really knows that we're here, but…" Her voice trailed off as her eyes filled with tears. "There's really not much else we can do. Irene's been synthesizing your blood to come up with a cure. She thinks she's making progress, but it's years' worth of work. These people don't have years. They don't have *days*."

She sniffled, and I reached over and squeezed Mabel's hand. "Get some rest. I'll take care of things here."

Once Mabel was gone, I started my rounds with the patients. Mabel was right about Mr. Fitzpatrick in bed seventeen; he would have taken a chunk out of my forearm if I'd been a little slower.

Mr. Mertz in bed twenty-one had soiled himself, and I had to grab an orderly and a pair of heavy-duty latex gloves to clean him up safely.

Ms. Salvatore screamed whenever I touched her with the water, as if I was burning her with acid. But she was so feverish that I felt like I needed to cool her down.

Mr. Braun in bed twenty-eight was strapped down by his wrists and ankles, but he'd still managed to claw himself bloody with his own fingernails. I spent twenty minutes trying to cut them down so he couldn't hurt himself anymore. For a man who had been in a sick bed for weeks he was surprisingly strong, and he fought me every step of the way, rending bloody gorges into my skin.

And Sylvia—no one even knew her last name—in bed thirty-two spasmed violently as I was finishing up with Mr. Braun. I ran over to her bed and took her hand just as she opened her eyes. A clear, gray gaze met mine. "Maggie? Maggie, is that you?"

She exhaled once more, a long, shuddering sound, and then she breathed no more.

I held her hand for a long time after that, until I heard someone clear their throat behind me. Irene stood there, her eyes shadowed with fatigue. "Did you know her?" she asked.

"No. But it didn't seem right that she should die alone."

Irene gestured to a couple of orderlies. They lifted Sylvia's body, along with the bedsheets, and carried her toward the tunnel exit. "Where are you taking the bodies?"

"We made an arrangement with a cemetery out in Queens. We pay them, and they bury the bodies quietly. It's fine for now, but one day when they decide to build high-rise condos on that site, they're going to find dozens more bodies than they expected." She sighed. "But that's a problem for another day."

I felt queasy. The smell of urine and vomit and death overwhelmed me. I jumped up and ran toward the the tunnel exit. The daylight nearly blinded me after so much time underground, so I retreated back into the shadows of the buildings. But the cold air helped me feel a little more grounded again.

The back exit led to sort of a hidden alleyway, blocked from the eyes of onlookers by buildings on both sides.

I spotted the two orderlies loading their bundle—which, if I didn't know better, could have been just been laundry—into the back of a van. They shut the doors and then leaned against the back of the van. One of them got out a pack of cigarettes, offered one to his companion, and took one for himself. "Shit, man, I'm not looking forward to going back in there. What is that, the fourth one today?"

"Fifth." The second orderly lit up his cigarette.

"Fuck." He blew smoke into the air. "Well, hopefully it'll all be over soon. Shit's going down with the Zetas next week. Maybe Doc will find some kind of a cure at the headquarters, and then we can just fix them and send them all home."

"Yeah, but what about the human traitor? They'll still need someone to guard her in whatever prison they decide to keep her in, and why do I have the feeling that you and I will end up pulling the short straw again?"

"Don't worry about it. I overheard John talking to the old guy yesterday, and they're going to execute the human traitor. Apparently Amara's daughter was a friend of the human's, and she flipped her shit when she found out they were planning to execute her. So they told her what she needed to hear. Regardless, the human dies on Monday." The orderly stomped out his cigarette. "Guess we'd better head back inside. Another day, another dead body."

As they approached the tunnel entrance, I backed deeper into the corner, not wanting to give myself away. Fortunately, they didn't even glance my way as they headed back into the tunnels. I only dared to breathe again once I was sure they were gone.

CHAPTER NINETEEN
Dale

JOHN, COVINGTON, AND I SPENT the next several days continuing to interrogate Nik about the Zetas. Even though it became very clear, very quickly that Nik didn't know any more than she'd already told us, I continued to push for more sessions—ostensibly because I thought that asking more questions or going at something a different way might get us more information. It was true—I wanted information, all right. But not from Nik.

What I learned was that everyone—regardless of whether they were human or supernatural—needs sleep. And supernaturals, despite what every horror movie and paranormal romance novel would have you believe, were not naturally nocturnal. The Cow Tunnels began to settle down around ten p.m. as they scaled down to a skeleton crew. The screams of the sick were often the only sounds in the tunnels, but even the sick followed a roughly diurnal schedule: by midnight, they tended to settle into fitful sleep that would last until near sunrise.

I was most worried about Irene, whose dedication to her patients was incredibly inspiring—and incredibly inconvenient, given what I was planning. She was more unpredictable than the rest of the crew, but I noticed she usually shut herself in her office—where she had a small couch and a heavy quilt—by two each morning, not to emerge again until around six—unless there was some commotion from one of the patients, in which case she was up and out immediately. I think she only took that time away from her patients because Mabel threatened to wall her in if she didn't, and I half suspected she was actually awake doing research or spinning my blood samples around in a centrifuge yet again. It didn't really matter for my purposes. If I could time this right, Irene shouldn't be an issue. I'd just have to keep things really quiet.

I headed into the Cow Tunnels around three Sunday morning, dressed in a black hoodie, dark jeans, and a pair of gloves, carrying one of those reusable shoulder bags that you get at the more eco-friendly grocery stores. The guard at the television repair shop entrance—who had been on duty the last several nights when we'd questioned Nik—stood up when I arrived. His name was Henry and two nights before he'd told me about the old motorcycle he was restoring with his daughter, who was eight. He'd shown me her picture, all knobby knees and gap-toothed smile. He brightened when he saw me. "Dale, I didn't expect to see you so late. Are you—"

"You didn't see me. I was never here," I said.

His eyes glazed over in that way I'd seen on so many people I'd whammied, and a surge of guilt washed through me. But I wasn't hurting him, not really. He wouldn't remember any of this, and his life would go on as usual. But using my power always felt like I was burning a hole in someone's brain. For a few seconds as I looked at Henry, I wondered if I'd gone too far, if I'd accidentally lobotomized him and he'd never return home to his daughter or his antique motorcycle. But Henry sat back down in his chair, seemingly unharmed, and began flipping through his magazine again. But when I waved my hands in front of him, he ignored me. (Or didn't see me at all; I wasn't quite sure the logistics of how my power worked.) I crushed my guilt down into a small corner of my brain and walked past him into the Cow Tunnels.

As I suspected, the lights were dim, and only one nurse was in sight, sitting with his back to the wall, his eyes drooping. Perfect. I tiptoed past the patients toward Nik's room without the nurse even seeing me. But when I rounded the corner, I almost bumped into another nurse. Damn. "What are you doing here?" she asked.

"I'm not here. You didn't see me."

"I don't see you..." her voice faded as she walked right by me. I didn't even know her name.

Getting into Nik's room was going to be the most difficult part. It was guarded by two people at all times. I could Obi-Wan them, too, but in the long run that would make my role in Nik's escape even more obvious. *Our prisoner got out of her room mysteriously in the middle of the night, right under our noses, but we don't remember anything.* Yeah, right. Unfortunately for me, the ability to mind-control people into saying or doing or remembering pretty much anything you want was rare in the supernatural world. The only other person I knew of who had it was my mother, and she was inconveniently dead. At evidence of any mental manipulation, all signs would point to me.

So I had to be smart.

Guarding Nik's door was mind-numbingly dull work. Nik was considered dangerous by the angels and demons, but being badly wounded meant she wasn't doing a whole lot. She'd been catheterized up until two nights ago, and now she was doing her business by way of a bedpan stowed underneath her bed until necessary. She was secured to the bed by her hands and feet, and even if she wasn't, I didn't know that she could actually get anywhere without assistance. So basically, guarding Nik's door involved standing there, looking intimidating, while doing a whole lot of nothing. Not surprisingly, the guards had to take breaks from time to time.

I didn't know the names of the two overnight guards, so I started calling them Lenny and Squiggy. They started their shifts at ten each night, so I'd had a lot of opportunity to watch them over the past few days. Lenny, as it so happened, was a chain-smoker—a habit I was beginning to realize was quite common among the supernaturals. (I guess when you're immortal, you don't have to worry about pesky things like lung cancer or emphysema.)

No less than once an hour, Lenny would excuse himself to go smoke a cigarette. This worked in my favor. I hid in the shadows for several minutes until Lenny, predictably, excused himself. This was my time. I tiptoed over to Nik's door until I practically bumped into Squiggy. "What are you doing here?" he demanded.

"I'm not here."

"You're not here…" His eyes settled into that glassy vacantness I'd become used to seeing after I used my powers, and I entered Nik's room.

Unlike a normal hospital room, this one was lit only with a single light bulb dangling from the ceiling—which was on, in spite of the late hour—and the walls looked more like they belonged in a cave than a sterile hospital. I guess that was the risk of setting up shop in a 150-year-old tunnel.

Nik was still pale, the shadows on her face deep, the metal cuffs on her wrists glimmering in the dim light. An IV bag hung from a metal stand next to her bed, the plastic tubing leading into her hand and secured with medical tape. Shit. I hoped Nik was done with whatever course of antibiotics Irene had put her on, because the IV was going to have to stay here. I couldn't understand why Irene would bother healing her when they were just going to kill her, anyway. Maybe it was some kind of doctor thing. But to me, it was even more torturous—giving someone false hope that they might make it while plotting their execution.

Nik didn't speak when I entered the room.

Not surprisingly, Chaz was there too, fast asleep in the plastic chair he'd dragged in from somewhere else in the tunnels. I nudged him awake. He squinted up at me. "Dale?"

"I need you to leave," I told him.

He sat up, suddenly awake. "Are you going to hurt her?"

"I don't need to hurt her. I can wait twenty-four hours, and the others will just kill her."

He jumped out of his chair. "What the hell, Dale?"

I shushed him, looking around frantically to make sure no one had heard. "We don't have a lot of time. Say goodbye, and then leave out the front entrance. Don't say anything, and if anyone speaks to you just ignore them. Grab a taxi back to wherever you're staying, and pay cash." I handed three twenty-dollar bills to him.

Chaz looked back and forth between Nik and me, trying to decide if I was being sincere. Finally, he hugged Nik tightly. I could hear him sniffling as they both mumbled words I couldn't hear.

In the meantime, I was digging through the drawers, trying to find supplies: gauze, cotton balls, medical tape, antibiotic wipes, Band-Aids. I shoved them into a plastic bag I'd been carrying in the pocket of my hoodie.

Chaz and Nik broke apart. Chaz wiped his eyes. "Thank you," he said before he slipped out of the room silently.

I grabbed the chair Chaz had vacated and moved it closer to Nik's bed. She remained silent, staring at me with the resentful glare I'd become so used to seeing during the interrogation sessions. I grabbed her arm, removed the medical tape, and pulled out the IV cannula. There was more blood than there probably should have been, so I slammed several pieces of folded-up gauze to the wound and taped them down quickly. Nik swore under her breath.

Getting her loose was going to be the trickiest part; both her arms and legs were secured to the bed with handcuffs with extra-long chains between the cuffs, which gave her enough play to move her arms and legs into more comfortable positions, but not enough to get out of the bed.

But I hadn't advertised another set of skills I'd picked up through the years. I took a bobby pin out of my pocket, removed the protective coating from the tips, and bent it into an L shape. Then I slipped the tip of the bobby pin into the keyhole. After a little bit of jimmying, I popped the ratchet and the handcuffs sprang open. They hadn't even double-locked them. Supernatural superiority complex, I guessed. How could a measly human manage to escape a bunch of all-powerful supernaturals? Little did they know that I'd learned to pop handcuffs years ago, from a guy who had gotten into some trouble with the law when he was young and stupid. His name was Cody. By the time I'd met him, he'd grown out of his youthful rebelliousness, and he'd turned his ability to pick locks into an escape artist act that he performed for free at nursing homes and hospitals throughout the area. He was far too good for me, and I still wondered about him from time to time. He was just a mere human, and he could still manage to best a pair of handcuffs without breaking a sweat.

I popped the handcuff on Nik's other wrist. She looked up at me, confusion on her face. "Dale, what are you doing?"

"What does it look like I'm doing?" The third cuff popped almost as soon as I stuck the bobby pin inside. Seriously, if people knew how ridiculously easy these were to break out of, they'd be getting arrested all the time. I opened the fourth cuff. "Are you able to stand?"

"I'm not sure."

I plopped the shoulder bag onto her lap. "Get sure, and get dressed. We don't have a lot of time."

I turned around as Nik changed into the clothes I'd brought her. At the same time, I tried to search for Lenny's mind. I'd never tried to manipulate someone I hadn't been looking directly at, but as I practiced more and more with my powers I realized it should work…in theory. My ability wasn't a physical one, where I had to touch someone, nor did it require eye contact. Finding someone's mind was a totally different sense, and when I'd first discovered it, it was like trying to use a long inactive muscle. But now that I had it, I couldn't help but sense all the minds within my vicinity— and I knew my mental senses went well beyond what I could see or hear or touch. I closed my eyes and reached with my mind, finding the mind that "felt" like Lenny. I couldn't read his thoughts—that power, for better or worse, was not part of my skill set—but he seemed to be closer than he would have been if he were still smoking outside. I nudged him to head into the bathroom and have another cigarette—not that he needed much convincing on the latter part. I felt Lenny turn around and move away.

Nik cleared her throat. I turned around to find her fully dressed in jeans, a long-sleeved T-shirt, and a coat. Although they were all her own clothes—I'd finagled my way into the apartment she'd shared with Chaz by mind-controlling a maintenance guy—they hung too loosely on her. Had she lost that much weight over the past few days she'd been here, or had she been withering away for a while?

Whatever it was, I didn't have time to psychoanalyze it. She seemed steady enough on her feet, though, which was good, because carrying her out of here wasn't part of my plan. "Are you ready?" I asked. She nodded. "Be ready to run."

I opened the door to find Squiggy standing there. When he saw Nik, he reached for his gun. I slammed him against the wall before he could get to it.

This was going to be the hardest part.

I gazed into Squiggy's eyes. "The prisoner escaped. You're not sure how. She caught you by surprise. She slammed you into the wall when she broke out, and you lost consciousness. You didn't expect her to be so strong. There was no one else with her."

At the same time I was altering Squiggy's mind, I was reaching out to the other minds around me, as well, telling them to keep doing whatever they were doing and mind their own business. They wouldn't see Nik escape. More importantly, they wouldn't see me helping her. Their minds were largely unshielded, probably because they were so fuzzy with exhaustion and because they felt safe among their allies. John would have never made that mistake. But John made his priorities clear when he'd lied to me again.

Squiggy's eyes glazed over. That was my chance. I slammed his head into the wall. He crumpled and fell to the ground. I didn't know whether I'd hit Squiggy hard enough to cause him to lose consciousness, or if it was my mind control doing it. But whatever. Squiggy was out, and Nik and I ran thorough the Cow Tunnels, trying to keep as quiet as possible.

Nik had trouble keeping up with me. I slowed my pace down, but I pushed her hard. When I saw someone coming down the hallway, I pushed her back behind a corner. "I thought you already fucked their minds," she hissed.

I clenched my teeth. It was one thing to have those thoughts, to think those words, in my own mind, but another to hear someone else describe what I could do in that way, to make it sound so *violating*. "That's no reason to be stupid. The more they see, the more conflict they may have in their minds." Not to mention the fact that I wasn't exactly sure my gamble would work. No need to mention that part to Nik.

When the person had passed, I grabbed Nik's arm and started leading her down the tunnel again toward the back exit.

The supernaturals did not have anyone guarding that back exit. It was always locked, and you had to pass a biometric scan—courtesy of AziziCorp's supernatural-detection technology—in order to get inside, otherwise the security system would neutralize you immediately and every supernatural in the place would be on you within seconds. They were not worried about people getting out. They were worried about people getting *in*.

This was to our benefit.

We sprinted the last hundred feet or so to the door, although Nik was more than a little winded when we got there. I opened it, the lights of New York shining in, and found…

Lenny.

He had, in the few minutes since I'd ordered him to get another smoke, redirected himself to the back door for yet *another* cigarette. "I know you've got supernatural healing, but how the *hell* do you not end up with black lung? Seriously?"

Lenny turned toward us, the cigarette still dangling out of his mouth, and removed something from his side. It looked almost like a paintball gun, with a long, round barrel and a canister of some kind attached to the back. I raised my hands in a gesture of surrender. "I can explain…"

But before I could say anything else, he fired at me.

———◇———

SOME KIND OF AEROSOLIZED SPRAY hit me, splattering the front of my hoodie. Immediately, the clothing began to dissolve, pinprick-sized holes that grew bigger and bigger within seconds. But then the substance hit my skin, and it bubbled and blistered like it was being cooked from the inside. "Fuck me."

"No, thank you. But you will tell me what the *hell* you're doing with this prisoner."

I didn't respond. I wasn't sure I was capable of speech at the moment. Searing pain coursed through my body. My knees crumpled, and I fell to the ground.

"No answer? Maybe I'll just shoot her, then." He pointed the gun at Nik.

Angels and demons are hard to kill. Silver poisoning can do it, but it's slow, and you can counteract it if you catch it in time. Short of chopping off our heads or crushing us with a steamroller, there's not much that will spell insta-death to a supernatural, which is why so many of our weapons are designed to incapacitate rather than kill. It's much easier to decapitate someone who's already on the ground.

But the weapons were designed to incapacitate *supernaturals*. If I'd been human, I would have already been unconscious or in shock—and judging by the speed at which these burns were spreading on my body, death would follow not long after. If Lenny shot Nik, she'd be dead.

I pushed myself up and grabbed onto his mind with everything I could. "You were on a cigarette break when the prisoner escaped through the back door. She was alone. You fired your weapon, but you missed. You chased her, but she jumped into a cab and got away. She was heading north."

Lenny's jaw slackened, and the still-burning cigarette fell out of his mouth onto the ground. He nodded.

"You're going to go back inside. In three minutes, you're going to sound an alert that the prisoner is missing. You didn't see me here tonight."

"I didn't see you," he said. He scanned his retina and entered the tunnels without another word.

I looked at Nik. "We don't have much time."

We limped our way to the street, and Nik flagged down a taxi. She got inside, and then looked at me expectantly. "Aren't you coming?"

I shook my head. "I belong here."

"But you just helped me escape—"

"Because it was the right thing to do. That doesn't change the fact that I'm a demon, and these people are dying. They're dying, and you helped." I took a ragged breath. There was one more thing I had to do, and she wasn't going to like it. I grabbed hold of her mind. She fought me, her mind pushing back against mine—and given the state I was in, it might have worked if it had been anything less at stake. But finally, I broke through, sinking my claws into her. "You will never talk about what happened here. You will never talk about anyone you met, anything you heard, or anything you've learned. You will never speak to anyone about angels and demons ever again."

Nik's eyes glazed over. When she blinked, there were tears in them. "I'll never speak about them," she said.

I shut the taxi door and let it drive away. Then I flagged down the next taxi I saw, crossing my arms over myself to conceal the holes in my clothes—and the still-spreading burns underneath. I should have known better than to worry. New Yorkers might have noticed the craziness around them, but nobody gave a damn about it. "Where to?" the driver asked.

I couldn't go back to John's, not like this, and I needed someplace where I could rest and try to heal myself in peace. "I need a hotel. Someplace that accepts cash and won't ask questions."

CHAPTER TWENTY
Dale

THE DRIVER TOOK ME TO a seedy-looking motel just a few blocks south, the likes of which I hadn't imagined were in Manhattan. The clerk sat behind bulletproof glass, and there was a vending machine full of condoms and lubricant right off the lobby. A suspicious-looking man eyed me as I walked in. I didn't know whether he was a pimp, a john, or a cop, and I didn't really care. I got the key to my room and made my way to the elevator, using the wall to steady me.

I ignored the mirrored ceiling and the smell of stale cigarettes as I filled the bathtub with cold water. I stumbled back down the hallway twice to fill my ice bucket, which I then poured into the tub. I wanted to get more, but I didn't think I could make it again. I stripped my clothes off, carefully peeling the fabric from my damaged skin, and got into the tub. I swore as I hit the icy water, but I figured frostbite was better than cooked skin, and neither one was likely to kill me—much as I might have wanted it to.

I covered my still-blistering skin with the water. As it warmed, I drained some out and filled it up again. Slowly, my pain started to fade into numbness, and I drifted off to sleep.

By the time I woke up, daylight was creeping in from the windows, and the water had turned tepid. I shivered as I climbed out of the water. The burns hadn't spread any further—probably a good sign—but my stomach and chest were still covered with a white, scaly crust that was sensitive to touch. I got out of the tub and dried myself as carefully as I could manage. The towel felt like sandpaper on my skin. Then I stepped out of the bathroom, naked, and found John sitting on the bed. "Are you all right?" His voice was sharp, harder than I'd ever heard it before. I nodded. "You should have Dr. Kordova look at those chemical burns."

"Then she'd know that I—" I stopped before I could say anything too incriminating.

"Hmmm." He tossed me a pair of sweatpants and a hoodie. "Put these on," he ordered.

I don't know why I retreated back into the bathroom; it wasn't like John hadn't seen me naked before. I guess I wanted to preserve the last bit of my dignity...or avoid the daggers and laser beams shooting out of his eyes.

However mad John might have been, he was still considerate. Both the sweatpants and the hoodie were several sizes too big for me, which meant less skin-to-clothing contact. I had to roll up the sweatpants and cinch the drawstring as tight as it could go. A bra was out of the question at the moment, but the world would just have to deal. A few minutes later, I emerged from the bathroom. I looked like a hobo, but I wasn't going to get arrested.

John met my eyes, a blank expression on his face. "Nik's gone."

"Oh, no. How—"

"Don't." He took a tablet computer out of his bag. "I'm not one for technology, normally," he said. "But I am an assassin. And if there's one thing an assassin has to do well, it's surveillance." He tapped the screen, and a silent video began playing.

The back exit of the Cow Tunnels. There was Lenny, smoking his cigarette, as Nik and I emerged. Lenny shot me. I hit the ground. Lenny aimed his gun at Nik, but I pushed myself up before he could fire. Even in the poor-quality video, I saw Lenny's body slacken as my powers grip him.

EMBRACING THE DEMON

Then Lenny went back inside the tunnels, and Nik and stumbled out of camera range.

The video stopped, and I clung to the tablet like it was about to explode. "Why, Dale?" he asked me.

I didn't answer. I didn't think there was an answer that I could give him that would satisfy him. He picked up the water glass that had been sitting on the dresser and threw it across the room, smashing it against the wall. When I still didn't answer, he took the second glass and threw that one, as well.

"She was my friend," I said quietly, "and the only reason she was involved with the Zetas at all was because of me."

"She aided an organization that killed hundreds of supernaturals, that could kill thousands more before this is over. Her actions almost got *you* killed more than once."

"I mind-controlled her to make sure she wouldn't talk to anyone about angels or demons ever again."

"Hell, Dale. Do you really think her life is worth more than every supernatural on Earth?"

"No, but I don't think it's worth less, either!"

He ran his hands through his hair—both of them. He looked like he'd stuck his finger into an electrical socket.

I sat down next to him on the bed. "Nik was my friend. She was the first friend I had in a really long time. And I failed her when she needed me. She and Chaz had their worlds completely smashed because of me—"

"What happened to them wasn't your fault," he said.

"No, but it only happened because I was a part of their lives. And when the shit hit the fan, I ran away. That's what I'm best at, after all." I sighed. "I should have been here to help them through it, to show them that supernaturals aren't all evil or terrifying. Instead, I left, and they were left behind to draw their own conclusions. Everything that happened is because of me."

"You can't take responsibility for everything. Nik's an adult. She made her own decisions. And decisions have consequences."

"The consequences were *wrong*." John gave me a hard look, but I just gave it right back to him. "The Zetas injected me with the nanovirus two years ago—and who knows how long it was being developed before that. They've been plotting this thing for *years*. Nik only got involved with them a year or so ago. You didn't want justice. You wanted retribution. And you were getting retribution on the wrong person."

John stood up. I could hear him gritting his teeth from where I was sitting. "When you agreed to help us, I thought you were all in."

"I *am* all in, but on *my* terms. What kind of person would I be if I let you execute my friend? If I'd never met Nik, she might have never known about this world. I'm not going to let you kill her just because you've got a vendetta against the Zetas." I paused. "She's not immortal, she's not strong, and she doesn't have superpowers. That doesn't mean she's less than us, that her life means less."

John sat back down on the bed. I could hear the sound of his slow, steady breathing next to me, but I didn't dare look. Then, he took the tablet out of my hands and pushed a button at the corner of the touch screen. The video vanished, and a message popped onto the screen: "The file 'Hospital surveillance Dec 17' has been deleted."

"For the record, it wasn't just about retribution," he said. "It was pragmatism. The effects of your mind control will weaken over time. Nik is our enemy's asset, and has information that could seriously harm us."

"If that happens, we can—"

"But you're right." He paused. "I've spent too many years among immortals…too many years being an assassin. Nik's life is not worth less because she's mortal. Hell, maybe it's worth more because it is so short. We may regret it later."

I shrugged. "I'd rather be good than right."

CHAPTER TWENTY-ONE
Dale

I'D NEVER BEEN IN A war. The battles I'd fought had been quick, and sudden, defensive rather than offensive. But if I had, I imagine that the night before a big battle would feel very much like the night before we attacked the Zetas.

We had to keep ourselves as inconspicuous as possible—which was hard to do, when thousands of us were descending upon a small town in Virginia best known for being the site of some Civil War battle or another. So some of us were staying with friends or relatives nearby. Others were camping at a nearby state park. The rest of us were staying at various hotels and motels. Mabel had worked feverishly trying to find each of us accommodations, making reservations at every place she could find within a twenty-mile stretch along I-95 and cramming four or six people to a room. I had no idea how she did it, or how many—probably fraudulent—credit cards she had to use to make the bookings appear as if they were coming from different people. But Mabel was nothing if not efficient: she even had a "sleeping chart" made up by the end of it.

After we checked into the motel, Tina did video conference with the other teams staying at different motels and campsites around the area. Those of us at this motel—Irene, Mabel, Covington…and John—gathered around the laptop to listen. I didn't know why John had chosen to stay with us instead of with some of the other Thrones, but I didn't have time to contemplate that now. "Advance Teams Alpha, Bravo, and Charlie are going to move in first and detonate a series of explosions on the far side of the compound," Tina said. She pulled a map up on the screen and marked several locations with a stylus. "The goal is to get as many of the Zetas as possible chasing down the source of the explosions while we infiltrate the building on the other side. You'll need to arrive on-site early to set the charges. Stay out of sight. Naveen, since Alpha Team will be closer to the compound, you'll be going with them for cover."

Naveen, who was at one of the campsites, popped onto the screen. "Yes, ma'am. I'll be Alpha Team's personal cloak of invisibility."

Just to break up the tension in the room, I went ahead and made the obvious joke. "Yer a wizard, Alpha Team," I said in the most gravely British accent I could manage. There were a few chuckles, and more than a few blank stares. Sometimes I forgot that I was dealing with people who counted their age in millennia. John, who sat across the room from me, was one of the blank stares. If we made it through this, I'd have to bring him up to speed on popular culture of the twenty-first century. *Harry Potter. Lord of the Rings.* Maybe I'd toss in *Twilight* and *Fifty Shades of Grey* just to irritate him. He hated when his anachronisms betrayed him, so worked harder than most to blend in with the human world. But if he went around saying *Harry Potter* was a sequel to *Star Wars*, he might get some funny looks.

But I still wasn't sure I wanted to help him. We'd gone from being enemies to something else. Reluctant allies? Temporary partners-in-crime? I wasn't sure. But it wasn't friendship. I didn't think the miasma of emotions I had for John could ever evolve into anything as simple as friendship.

Tina's voice snapped me back to reality. "Our intelligence indicates that there's a small section on the opposite side of the compound that's relatively unguarded, but it's blocked off by a fence. The rest of us will need to get through the fence and approach the side entrance, located here." She circled another location on the map, along the side of the building. "We'll have two scouts branch out to locate the guards and incapacitate them. Then, when they give us the all-clear, we'll scale the fence.

"Once we get to the door, we're going to encounter a fingerprint scanner. Since Rebekah's power doesn't replicate fingerprints, we'll need Mike to teleport inside and open the door for us."

Mike's face appeared on the laptop screen. "One of the risks with this is that I won't be able to see where to land—which means I could come out inside of a wall or another object. What will you do if I'm unable to let you in?"

"We'll break down the door. Not my preferred method, because it'll set off alarms and alert Zetas to our presence right away, but it'll get us inside. Once we're in, we're going to split off into our respective teams and work your way through the building. Each of you has been given your team assignments, a list of your teammates, and the direction you're going to be searching. Remember that no matter what direction you're looking, you need to work your way up and out." Those of us in the room nodded, and no one on the video conference objected. "Think of yourselves as cockroaches scattering in the light. The Zetas may be able to kill some of us, but by scattering we can crawl into walls and evade them."

We all looked at each other, puzzled. It was Mabel who spoke. "Tina, honey, we're going to need to work on your metaphors."

Tina rolled her eyes. "The point is, protect your teammates, but not at the expense of the mission. Keep pushing through, even if someone falls, and don't worry about the other teams."

Tina paused. "We've got fifteen hundred people going in. According to our estimates, they've got *thirty thousand*. But we're fighting on behalf of every single angel and demon on earth. Anyone with even a drop of supernatural blood is vulnerable to this nanovirus. The odds are stacked against us. But if we can stop the Zetas and cut the head off of this monster, then it'll be worth it."

With that, Tina ended the teleconference.

BETH WOODWARD

Mabel, Tina, Irene, and I were sharing a room—which was super awesome, because it meant that Irene and I got to share a bed. Hopefully she wouldn't inject me with poison during the night. As afternoon crept into evening, we ordered dinner from a local pizza place. But before it arrived, Mabel and Tina had locked themselves into the bathroom.

"You can't do this!" I heard Mabel say.

"You knew the kind of person I was when we got together! You know I have to fight. You always said you were fine with it!"

"Thirty thousand Zetas? It's suicide! Especially since—"

A pause. "Especially since what? Since I don't have superpowers like you? This is bullshit, Mabel!"

Irene picked up the remote control between us and turned up the volume on the television. It succeeded in muffling their words, but not in tuning them out entirely. "Do you think the people next door can hear?" I asked.

"The rooms on both sides are our people. I think that's why Mabel picked it." A crash from the bathroom, the sound of glass hitting the floor and shattering. Then there was more shouting.

Irene reached into her bag and pulled out a metal flask. She took a large swallow and then offered the flask to me. I shook my head. "I thought alcohol was bad for supernaturals."

"So are battles you can't win." She took another drink.

Another crash. "Thirty thousand people!" Mabel shouted.

Twenty minutes later, Irene pushed herself up and announced that she was getting some sodas. She looked pale, but she managed to make it out the door without stumbling or puking all over everything, so I considered that a win. Getting some liquid into her that wasn't one hundred proof would probably be good for her.

A few minutes after Irene left, Tina stormed out of the bathroom, exited the motel room, and slammed the door behind her. Mabel came out of the bathroom shortly thereafter. She looked awful, her eyes bloodshot and puffy, her nose running, and tear tracks streaked down her face. I handed her a box of tissues. "I just want to keep her safe, you know?" she said as she wiped her face.

"I understand."

Mabel sniffled. "She's mortal, you know. Only a third demon. When we first got together, she was young enough…I had hoped that…but Irene did all the tests. She's aging, slowly, but she's aging." A fresh set of tears filled her eyes. "But I'm not. I get forever. But how can I face forever without her?"

Thoughts of John spun through my mind. "I don't know." I said.

"I always worried about her when she was in the Army. Every time she went on deployment, I'd barely be able to sleep through the night. But then she retired, and I thought it would get better. But this is even worse. She's just so little and powerless."

"Well, she's definitely little, but I'd hardly call her powerless." Mabel gave me an inquisitive look. "I mean, she's mortal, right? And she's got to be pushing fifty. But she looks younger than I do. I gotta ask, does she have an aging picture stowed away somewhere? Because that's probably a bad sign."

Mabel's lips turned up. I continued. "Also, there's the fact that she's more heavily armed than the average battalion—and she knows how to use them. I mean…I *did* hear she called Annie Oakley a poser on Instagram. But that could just be an ugly rumor."

Mabel chuckled. I handed her another tissue, and she wiped off her face and blew her nose. "You're right. And so is she. I knew who she was when I started dating her. I just…didn't think it would be this hard."

"I know. But it's not like any of the rest of us are in better shape tomorrow. Remember what Irene always says."

"Immortal is not unkillable."

"Exactly. None of us is guaranteed forever." I sighed. "Our chances tomorrow…they're not good. We're going into their territory, and they outnumber us twenty to one. There's a good chance none of us will make it out alive."

"So what do I do?"

"Go find your wife, and enjoy her while you can."

BETH WOODWARD

Mabel thought about it for a second. Then she stood up and wiped off her face again. "Thank you, Dale." Then she left the room.

A few minutes later, Irene stumbled back with a bottle of Coke in one hand and a bucket of ice in the other. She lay down on the bed and took approximately three sips before she fell asleep, snoring heavily. I put the remaining Coke in the ice bucket, grabbed the key card, and left.

The temperature had dropped several degrees since we'd checked in, and I was glad for the puffy coat I wore as I strolled through the parking lot. Christmas lights hung from the motel's entrance. A sign dangled from the door, reminding us that it was only three more days until Santa's annual good-cheer crime spree.

John's door was on the other side of the motel. I knocked on it and held my breath.

John was dressed in sweatpants and a white T-shirt that was tight across his muscular chest. He'd long since washed out the dark dye he'd used as Aaron Hill, and his hair was standing up every-which-way. It reminded me of other times…of better times. "You should be sleeping."

"I don't think I could sleep if I wanted to. Some guy with a jackhammer next door asked Irene if she could turn down her snoring, and I strongly suspect Mabel and Tina are going to come back to the room soon and have the loudest, most athletic sex possible by human or immortal standards."

He raised his eyebrows. "We all have our pre-battle rituals."

I took a breath. "Do you…I mean…would you like to hang out for a while? I just…really don't want to be alone right now."

John nodded. He put on his coat and shoes, and we walked out into the parking lot. There were no benches, and nowhere to walk to, so John sat down on the curb and patted the space next to him. I sat down, reveling in the feel of his body next to mine.

We sat in silence for a while, our breath forming clouds in front of us. "Do you ever think about Isaac?" I asked.

"Every day."

"I wish he were here. He could really help with this. He could scare the Zetas to death by making dragons or explosions appear."

"Or exploding dragons."

I chuckled. "I shudder to think how realistic that carnage would have been."

"Isaac always did pride himself on authenticity."

I picked up a pebble from the ground and used it to draw patterns in the dirt. It was better than meeting John's eyes. "It's my fault that he's dead." The Thrones—back when they were under Gabriel's leadership—had tracked us down at Isaac's amusement park in Vermont because I'd called Nik to let her know that the Thrones might be after her and Chaz. It was too late: the Thrones had already gotten to them. But my call had alerted them to our presence in Vermont, and Isaac had been murdered in the confrontation with them. "And it's my fault that our last missions failed. I couldn't control my powers well enough at the Grave, and six people died. And I completely lost control at the Obelisk. I still don't remember what happened that day. I might have hurt some of our own people, for all I know." I sighed. "Maybe I shouldn't go at all tomorrow. I break everything I touch."

"Dale, we asked you to do the impossible when we went into the Grave that night. It was a Hail Mary plan, and we probably should have thought better of it to begin with, but we were desperate. And I remember everything from the Obelisk. The Rage did change you, reverted you to something…more instinctual, more primal, but you were never out of control. You didn't hurt anyone who wasn't trying to hurt us. And Isaac…" John ran his fingers through his hair, the gesture so familiar it was painful. "If anything, Isaac's death was my fault. He was my best friend…maybe my only friend. I should have realized Gabriel would zero in on him." He paused. "You've never broken anything. Hell, you might be the one person who could fix me. I just wish I'd realized it before it was too late…before I did things that can never be undone."

He pushed up his coat sleeve and scratched his arm, so violently that I was afraid he might break the skin. "Are you all right?"

"Yeah, it was just a tag or something on my coat."

He pulled down his sleeve and sat there for a minute, his feet tapping the ground anxiously. When he turned back to me, there was a desperate gleam in his eyes. "What I'm trying to say is…you're amazing, Dale."

BETH WOODWARD

I furrowed my eyebrows. "Uh, thank you?"

"You have so much…when you fight…in the Rage…" He scratched at his skin again. "Dammit, not yet!"

"John, are you sure you're—"

Before I could finish the sentence, John collapsed to the ground and began convulsing.

CHAPTER TWENTY-TWO
Dale

BEFORE I COULD EVEN THINK about it, I threw John over my shoulder and ran back to his room. If anyone had seen us, they probably would have wondered how a woman could carry a man easily sixty pounds heavier than her, but I wasn't thinking about that at the moment. I fished his key card out of his pocket, opened the door, and set him on the bed. He was still convulsing, a thick, white froth coming out of his mouth.

I ran across the parking lot, back to the room I shared with Irene, Mabel, and Tina. Irene was alone, still fast asleep on the bed. I shook her awake. "John's sick. I think it's the nanovirus."

"Shit."

Irene grabbed her medical bag and we went back over to John's room. John was still convulsing on the bed, screaming things I couldn't understand. Irene took a syringe out of her bag and filled it with a clear liquid from a vial. Then, she rolled down John's sweatpants and jammed the syringe into his thigh. John tensed up for a second, but then slumped back down on the bed, every muscle in his body relaxing. "There's a blue duffel bag over in the corner. There should be restraints in there."

I opened the bag and pulled out two sets of padded restraints—one for his wrists, and one for his ankles. I'd seen them many times at the hospital, knew they were made of a special material that even supernaturals in the throws of delirium couldn't break. I handed them to Irene. "Lift the mattress," she ordered.

I did, being careful not to jostle John too much. She strung the restraints between the mattress and the box spring before attaching them to John's arms and legs. Essentially, John's own body weight was holding him in place. "Why did John have restraints in his duffel bag?" I wondered out loud. Irene paused for just a second too long. "And how the hell did you know he had restraints in his duffel bag? You knew he was sick, didn't you?"

She closed her eyes and took a deep breath. "Yes, I knew."

"And you didn't think this was information you should share with the rest of the class?"

"It wasn't my place. He asked me not to, and I couldn't violate our doctor/patient confidentiality."

"Oh, bullshit. We're not *human*, Irene. It's not like the government is going to come after you for HIPAA violations!"

She'd been shining a bright light into his eyes. She shut it off with a snap before she turned back to me, her voice like ice. "Just because I'm not a human doctor doesn't mean I don't have ethics. John is my patient, and I did what I had to do to mitigate any damage he might cause once his virus progressed to the later stages. I knew his virus could go active at any time. After we came back from Nebraska, I advised him to limit his activity and stick close to home so he could get to the hospital when necessary. He didn't. Why do you suppose that is, Dale?"

She put her medical supplies back into her medical bag and shut it so aggressively that I thought the zipper might pop off. "Looks like I'll be spending the night here. Keep an eye on him for a few minutes while I shower and change into something more comfortable."

I shook my head. "No, you go to bed. I'll stay here with him."

"Dale, you're an integral part of the battle tomorrow. You need to get your sleep."

I shook my head again. "I'll sleep here. I'll call you if we need anything."

"Dammit, Dale!" She slammed her hand on the door. "You're so selfish sometimes, you know that? There are people counting on you, people who look to you as their inspiration. You're the reason they're here. And if you show up on that battlefield tomorrow and get slaughtered because you didn't get enough sleep…"

"Who are we kidding, Irene? None of us are going to sleep much tonight, anyway, not unless we all get shitfaced like you." John made a noise from the bed, a barely audible moan. I reached over and took his hand. The zing of his power was almost gone. I'd only ever felt him this weak after he'd been shot by fractal bullets and almost died. "I can't let him be here alone."

Irene's voice softened. "He won't be alone. I'll be with him."

I squeezed his hand in mine. He didn't squeeze back, didn't even seem to feel it. It didn't matter. "I can't let him be here without me."

———————◇———————

John remained unconscious most of the night, strapped down with soft cuffs wrapped around his wrists and ankles. When he started to sweat, I went into the bathroom and wet a washcloth with cold water. That seemed to help a little, but he still writhed in his sleep, so I cracked the motel room door open using the deadbolt as a stopper. When he started to shiver, I closed the motel room door again and covered him with blankets off of the second bed. And when he started to moan and cry again, I took one of the syringes Irene had left on the nightstand and injected him in the thigh again.

I tried to sleep, but I couldn't get more than a few minutes at a time before I was jerking awake, terrified that he had left me in my moments of stolen sleep.

During one of these wake-ups around four a.m., I heard John making soft, moaning noises, like he was crying. I was tempted to give him another dose of Irene's tranquilizer, but he wasn't due for another two hours. Instead, I went over to him and stroked his hair, brushing a lock away from his forehead. When I touched his skin, he took a deep breath and relaxed. As soon as I took my hand away, he tensed and started moaning again. So I kept stroking his cheek, his skin warm and stubbly against my palm. His power didn't zing me at all now, which told me more than I wanted to know about how sick he was. So it was just John and me, and I touched him like a lover would. "I'll probably regret this later." I didn't say that it might be the last time I ever got to touch him, or speak to him, again. I didn't know how much he could hear, but I wouldn't risk saying anything that might stop him from fighting.

"I'm still mad at you, you know," I said. "But you were also my best friend. I think that's what makes me the angriest. You were the only person who knew all my secrets, the only person I trusted…the only person I ever loved."

I waited for a response. But of course, there was nothing.

John was finally breathing in a calm, steady rhythm, my voice and my touch enough to lull him into a more restful sleep. I stopped stroking him and got up to go back to my bed, but as soon as I did he started to moan again. So I sat back down and started to stroke him again and talk in a soothing voice. "There's a good chance I'm going to die today. Wouldn't that be ironic? You're the one that's sick, and I'll be the one that's dead before the end of the day."

There was no response, of course, but I thought I felt his grip tightening on my hand. "Yeah, yeah, I know what you'd say. That I shouldn't make jokes like that. Or maybe you'd go the motivational route, and say that I'm strong and well prepared and you *know* that I can win this battle. It's funny: you make these ridiculous statements, but you say them with such confidence and authority that part of me figures, 'Well, if he believes it, it *must* be true.' Maybe it's some kind of latent angel superpower you never knew about. I'm just lucky you never tried to convince me I could fly."

John's grip on my hand relaxed, and I felt, absurdly, like he was slipping away from me. "Don't go," I said, an unexpected edge of desperation in my voice. But as soon as the words came out, I knew I meant them with every cell in my body. "Don't go." Tears had started rolling down my face, and I hadn't even noticed. "Maybe I should take a cue from you, and give you a motivational speech. You're strong, and you're healthy, and I know you can beat this. There. Okay?"

I was on the verge of full-blown sobs. "But that's stupid, because I don't do motivational speeches, and I don't believe in fairy tales. So how about this? You need to live, because if I come out of this alive today, I don't know how to live in a world without you in it."

I rocked back and forth, my breath coming out in convulsive pants. "I tried to pretend you didn't matter. I tried, so hard. I went away, and I didn't talk about you, and I tried not to think about you at all. But I was lying to myself. You matter. You will always matter. I'm still so mad at you. I don't know how to forgive you for what you did. But it doesn't make a difference. You. Fucking. Matter."

I exhaled. My tears landed with a *plop-plop* on his chest. "You matter to me."

John seemed to be sleeping more peacefully now, and when I let go of his hand he didn't stir this time. Suddenly the room felt stifling, too small and too stuffy. I grabbed John's key card, put on my coat, and went outside.

I didn't get more than three steps from the door. I found I wasn't willing to go farther than that, even though the proximity to John was making my heart clench in my chest. Still, I took the time to wipe off my face and nose and breathe in the cold, dead air.

A few minutes later I heard footsteps beside me. I turned and saw Covington approaching me. "Irene asked me to check on you. You should be sleeping," he said.

"Couldn't."

"Is it the battle, or is it him?"

I shrugged. "Both, probably."

He nodded, and we sat there in silence for a while. "Your mother would be very proud of you," he said finally.

I snorted. "What, for going into a suicidal battle, or for holding vigil at the bedside of the man who murdered her?"

"Both, probably."

I leaned my head against the wall. "Covington, I'm tired, I'm stressed out, and there's a good chance I'm going to die in a few hours. You don't need to placate me. This relationship I have with John is all sorts of fucked up, I know that."

"Your mother loved Gabriel for millennia, even after he turned against her and was killing her own people. I think Amara would understand more than anyone."

I rolled my eyes. "I guess I came out on the 'nature' side of that 'nature versus nurture' argument."

"Things are not always black or white, Dale. You care about John—"

"For all the good it's done me."

"It's never wrong to care about people." He took a step closer to me, put his hand on my shoulder. "That was Amara's failing. Through the years, she cared less and less until there was very little left for her…and very little left *of* her. I guess when you lose so many people you care about, you start to build barriers around yourself." He paused. "For the record, I think John cares about you, too. Deeply. Perhaps more than he realizes."

I didn't reply, looking out into the motel parking lot instead. Someone had turned the Christmas lights off, giving the motel a ghostly vibe it hadn't had earlier. Suddenly, I had a strange feeling, like I wasn't supposed to be here. I was a trespasser on a sleeping world, one that never belonged to me at all. "I should get back inside," I said.

Covington nodded. But before he left, he spoke. "Caring about people isn't a weakness, Dale. Your mother never learned that lesson. Don't make her mistakes."

CHAPTER TWENTY-THREE
Dale

IT WAS COLD AND OVERCAST that morning. Fat snowflakes fell from the sky. By seven a.m., it had already coated the grass and was starting to accumulate in the road. I had the Weather Channel playing in the background as we got ready. "It looks like it's going to get worse."

"That might work to our advantage," Tina said with an assurance I didn't feel—had never felt, if I was being honest about it. "People in lower-level positions may take the day off because of the weather. Fewer people to fight, and fewer civilian casualties."

"And what if their head honchos decides to take the day off, too?"

Tina grabbed me by the shoulders and looked down on me—not an easy feat, considering she was about five inches shorter than I was, but somehow she managed it. "Stop. You're overthinking, and it'll get you killed—and you might take the rest of us with you."

It was hard not to compare what John would have said to Tina's blunt, matter-of-fact words: how he would have explained that, from all the intelligence we'd gathered, the members of the leadership coalition were driven, workaholic types. That a well-funded organization with former military ties wouldn't let the work stop because of a little bit of snow, and would probably have special vehicles set up to take the VIPs to work if necessary. That we were running a multi-pronged attack to take out the Zetas throughout the country, not just in Virginia. And that even if we failed to end the Zetas entirely, we may be able to retrieve the information that would lead to the cure for the nanovirus and damage them enough to prevent them from hurting anyone else for a while.

But I knew all this. I didn't need John to tell me. Still, it was demoralizing to know that he—the person I counted on more than anyone else here—was strapped to his bed, drugged into unconsciousness, while I was getting ready to fight a battle we were certain to lose. Crap. That was not the way to think about this. "You're right, Tina. I'm sorry. I'm just freaking out."

Covington, Tina, Mabel, Irene, and I took a Range Rover to the parking area of the state park adjacent to the Zetas' complex. We were dressed in full body armor, with masks covering our faces. The masks were more for me than anyone else; Tina wanted to ensure that they couldn't isolate me from the rest of the group.

When we got to our meeting place, dawn was just breaking over the horizon, but that hadn't stopped the other two dozen or so members of our team from meeting us there. I exhaled in relief; my first worry that morning had been that no one would show up. Tina got out of the driver's seat, immediately snapping into general mode. "All right, everyone. Advance Team Alpha and Bravo should already be on site. We should be hearing something from them right about now."

As if on cue, explosions rang out in the distance, rumbling through the sky like thunder. Tina pulled out her phone and stared at the screen. "Excellent. The Zetas are already rushing the detonation point. Team Bravo should be activating shortly. Secure your earpieces."

Sure enough, about two minutes later, another round of explosions echoed. Mabel, who had been hugging the side of the Range Rover as if she wanted to melt into the door, shivered. "It reminds me of London during the Blitz. Demon, angel, human…didn't matter. Those German bombs took everything in their path. There were nights when I was certain

I wouldn't make it out alive…" A faint English accent had slipped into her words as she spoke.

Tina turned to her, her whole demeanor softening. "Are you going to be all right with this?"

Mabel snapped back to the present and nodded. "I'm good."

"Are you sure? Because you don't have to—"

"If you're in, I'm in." Mabel grasped Tina's hand. "We do this together."

Tina squeezed Mabel's hand, looking deep into her eyes. "Together."

And then another round of explosions went off. "That's Team Charlie. It's time."

We crept through the woods, Tina leading the way. Our plan of attack was simple. The advance teams were a diversion to lure the strongest members of the Zetas' guard away from their posts.

We wore green-and-brown-tinted camouflage to make us more difficult to spot in the woods, but that wasn't going to do us any good once we made it to the Zetas' compound. We would have to move fast.

Our intelligence had indicated that there was a small section on the side of the compound that was relatively unguarded, since there were no entry or exit points nearby. It was, however, blocked by an electrified fence that stood about ten feet high. As the fence came into view, Tina motioned for all of us to get close to the ground and keep out of sight.

Tina waved the scouts forward. There were two of them—a man who looked old enough to be my grandfather, and a girl who barely looked old enough to drive a car. They sprinted off at inhumanly fast speeds—but then again, they weren't human. A few seconds later, a female voice came over our earpieces. "I got the guard coming from the east."

An older, male voice came on a few seconds later. "The west guard shot me. But I got the bastard!" Even over the ear piece, I could hear the pain in the old man's voice, the wheezing for air. Tina closed her eyes for just a second, an anguished look on her face, before she tapped her ear piece. "Paolo, get medics to sector fourteen. The rest of you, let's go."

We approached the fence until Tina held her hand up, silently ordering us to stop and drop to the ground. Tina tapped her ear piece to call the female scout. "Bianca, there's another guard in front of us, eight o'clock. You see him?"

Her reply came instantly. "Yes, I see him. But I'm out of juice. I won't be able to sprint again for at least another hour, and he's too far for me to shoot him from here."

"All right. I'll take care of it," Tina replied as she aimed her rifle.

I took a pair of binoculars out of my pack and looked. The guard was still some distance from us now, but he was coming closer. I didn't have to activate my power anymore to seek out minds; they were just there, a dim awareness in the back of my consciousness that I usually ignored. This man's mind was spongy and soft—and right there. "Tina, you don't have to do this. I can just—"

"No, Dale. We can't risk it."

I sighed.

The guard ascended the hill, coming into sight. Tina waited, let him get closer, and then fired without hesitation. Her rifle had a silencer on it, but it still sounded loud to me. The guard fell, dark blood pouring out of a wound in his head. Tina waved us forward.

When we got to the fence, we stopped. It was a row of vertical metal bars. Irene lifted her hands up, and one by one the vertical bars bent back and to the side until we were left with a gap, about three feet wide at the top but only inches apart at the bottom. It looked like Wile E. Coyote had left a "surprise" package for the Road Runner by the fence. "The bars are buried deep in the ground," Irene said, sweat dripping down her face. "This is the best I can do."

"It'll have to do." Tina went through first, slipping through easily. Of course, Tina was only five feet tall and maybe weighed 95 pounds on a bad day. I had to contort myself into an unnatural position, my feet going one way and my torso going another, in order to squeeze through.

And that's when I saw Zeta Headquarters for the first time.

If M.C. Escher had decided to design a government building, it would have looked like Zeta HQ. It was the same dull tan color that adorned municipal buildings and post offices across the country, but that was the only ordinary thing about it. The building looked like a Tetris game gone wrong, with cubes stacked on top of and beside one another with no particular rhyme or reason to them. The only way to get between the cubes seemed to be walkways that zig-zagged between them. The good news was that the walkways had walls along the side, which would prevent us from falling off. The bad news was that they had no roofs—and the snow had passed my ankles and was still falling.

The side door was not guarded, but it was blocked by a fingerprint scanner—which was a problem. Rebekah could transform herself to look like anyone. What she couldn't do was match their fingerprints. A forty-ish, nervous-looking man stepped forward. "I can't see through the door," he said. "I don't know where to land. I might end up in a wall or something."

Tina shrugged. "If you get stuck, we'll try to pull you out."

Tina had really missed her calling as a motivational speaker.

He gave a tense nod, and then he took a breath. A few seconds later, the door opened from the inside. Our jumper held it open with a big grin on his face. Behind him was an ordinary-looking hallway with tile floors and florescent lights, closed doors lining it on each side.

We walked in—and alarms started blaring.

Strobe lights flashed up and down the hallway, and an automated announcement started playing over the loudspeaker: "We've been infiltrated. Prepare to attack."

The doors along the hallway opened. Zetas poured out, dressed in their black uniforms and armed to the teeth. Tina's warning ran through my head: don't use your powers. The Zetas started firing.

Irene waved her arms, disarming several of them. I took that moment to charge them. I still wasn't great with weapons, and I was trying to keep my powers under wraps. But all the sparring sessions with John the previous year had paid off: I was good at hand-to-hand combat.

I tackled one of the Zetas and slammed him into unconsciousness. Another grabbed me from behind, wrapping his arms around my shoulders while I was still crouched over his comrade's body. I bent my knees and shifted all my weight forward, throwing him over my shoulders, body-slamming him into the ground.

Something that felt like a hot poker hit my side and sent me tumbling into the wall. A Zeta was charging me, a large rifle in his hands, extra ammo strapped to his chest, Rambo-style. Okay, that whole "keep your powers under wraps" in the middle of a war? Stupid idea. I reached out, preparing to grab his mind with mine.

And the rifle vanished. A small woman stood nearby, looking at me expectantly. "Don't just stand there, disappear all their weapons!" I yelled.

"I can only do one at a time," she said.

"So do it!"

She turned away from me. Other Zeta weapons began disappearing—one at a time, and much too slow. It was better than nothing.

I pushed myself to my feet. Blood covered my hand. I must have been hit by an armor-piercing round. Fantastic. The spreading burn in my side told me it was a fractal bullet, and silver shards were rushing their way to my heart right now.

But I didn't have time to worry about that at the moment. Another Zeta charged me. I grabbed the gun from my side holster. It was called the IntelliTarget. It had been modified with software that, once you aimed, would automatically position your arm in the best spot for a kill shot—which was good, because otherwise I could only hit the broadside of a barn one time in ten…if I was lucky. The software was still in beta, and it had been known to mistake other nearby objects for your target—a car, a tree, your neighbor's dog—particularly if your aim was very skewed. But when the choice was "gun with flaky targeting mechanism" or "certain death," suddenly it didn't seem so bad.

I pointed the gun. It yanked my arm upward about three inches, and I fired.

The shot hit right between the Zeta's eyes, and he went down. Someone else charged me from behind. I turned, getting ready to fire…

And found myself face-to-face with a middle-aged woman in a reindeer sweater with flashing lights on it.

She looked like the kind of woman you'd see working at a craft store or running a holiday bake sale, and she was shaking like a leaf. She had armed herself with a heavy-duty stapler in one hand and a pair of scissors in the other. It was a ridiculous sight, a woman closer to sixty than fifty, the light on Rudolph's nose flashing, ready to battle with office supplies. But she glared at me with such hatred, such violence. She'd never met me, but she wouldn't hesitate to stab me through the throat with her scissors or brain me with her stapler. I should have killed her. She was ready to kill me.

I just couldn't do it.

I shoved her away from me. "Civilians!" I yelled.

The woman charged me again, her scissors aimed for my throat. I whipped her upside the head with my gun, knocking her unconscious.

Tina's voice came over my ear piece. "Split up! With your teams!"

Irene, Mabel, Covington, and I were on Echo Team with Tina. When Tina had drawn up the original plans, there were ten people on Echo Team. Only eight followed us now, the other two on the floor in pools of their own blood. Irene took a shaky breath beside me. "I should help them."

"No," Tina said firmly. "We need Irene the telekinetic, not Irene the doctor."

Irene folded her arms across her chest, but she didn't say anything more.

We went through the back door and found ourselves surrounded by staircases, one on our left, one on our right, and one in the middle. We climbed the middle staircase, gripping the railing tightly so we didn't slip in the ice and snow, and found ourselves on top of another pod.

From this angle, it was easier to see that the building was arranged in sort of a zigzag pattern. In order to get to the top pod, we'd have to climb across all the others, running to the staircases that connected the roofs. The entrance to each pod was on the roof of the pod underneath it, like the whole thing was constructed out of Lincoln Logs. Even from here, we could hear the blaring of the alarm alerting the Zetas to our presence.

Tina took a breath. "All right, let's start clearing the pods." She gripped her rifle and headed to the door in front of us.

"Wait," I said. I pointed to one of the pods above us. It was the highest one. Unlike the other pods—which had two staircases leading to them on each side—it looked like there was only one staircase leading up to it from the pod below. "If I were trying to keep my leadership council safe, that's where I'd put them."

Tina studied it. "If you're wrong, the Zetas will be able to come up behind us and trap us there."

At that moment, a group of Zetas ran up the staircase toward us. Mabel raised her hands, and they froze. She looked at Tina. "That won't hold for long."

"This will help." Irene pushed her way over and raised her hands. The roof of the pod shook and buckled as a solid wall sprung up between us and the Zetas. She turned to Tina. "They'll break their way out soon enough, though."

"So make it thicker."

Irene shook her head. "The roof is already unstable. If I take any more material it'll collapse."

"Tina, the Zetas already know we're here, and there are way too many of them for us to fight," I said. "We're not going to have time to clear all these pods. It's a risk, but I think it's our best option."

Tina studied the top pod for what seemed like a long time—but in reality was probably only a few seconds. Then she nodded. "All right. We'll head in that direction. I'll tell the other team leads to head that way."

Snow and ice covered the stairs, up to my knees now. We gripped the railings hard as climbed the pods, ran across the roofs, and climbed to the next pods. We ran into a few Zetas as we climbed, whom we got rid of easily. Mabel froze one of them before pushing him off the roof. Irene walled off two more and tossed a chunk of concrete at a third. "We're almost there!" Mabel cheered as we climbed to the top of the last pod.

We should have known it would never be that easy.

When we reached the roof of the last pod, Zetas, dressed in black combat uniforms and armed to the teeth, poured out the door. Others climbed up the single staircase behind us. Still more descended from the sky, using some kind of belt that looked like it could have come out of *The Jetsons*. There were at least a hundred of them, more than I ever thought could fit onto that roof.

We were surrounded. There were only two ways off the roof: through the door into the pod, or back down the single set of stairs. The Zetas blocked them both.

Shots echoed through the air. I grabbed the gun from my holster and returned fire, taking out two of the Zetas. A shot hit me in the arm, hard enough to sting but not hard enough to pierce my body armor. I fired again, hitting the man who shot me.

My IntelliTarget ran out of bullets. I ducked behind the corner and reloaded. The IntelliTarget only held ten rounds, so I had to be careful. I fired at one of the flying Zetas. He slumped in his harness, bobbing in the air like a balloon. Then I hit another Zeta who was charging at the girl who'd disappeared his weapon.

To my right, Mabel fell to the ground when a large Zeta fired at her. On my left, another Zeta pushed Tina back to the edge of the pod, where she fell off the roof. I gasped and ran to the edge where she had fallen. She had landed on the pod beneath, her arm bent at an awkward angle.

In front of me, Irene had been cornered by two Zetas. They'd already lost their guns, but that apparently didn't matter to them. As she lifted her arms to toss them in the air, one of them grabbed a knife and slashed her throat.

And then there was Covington. A Zeta fired at one of our people, the young girl who had been disappearing all their weapons. Covington pushed her out of the way. The bullet hit him in the head, blood and ichor splattering on the wall of the pod behind him as he fell to the ground.

The red haze of a Rage bled across my eyes.

Control it, control it, control it.

My breath came in unsteady pants.

I'm a fuck up.

Everyone is dying, and it's all my fault.

I can't help them.

I can't do anything.

I break everything I touch.

But then another voice came into my head: John's.

You've never broken anything, Dale.

BETH   WOODWARD

"You're wrong," I whispered.

You might be the one person who could fix me. I just wish I'd realized it before it was too late...

And if we didn't come back, it would be too late for John—that infuriating, beautiful asshole of a man who never failed to get under my skin. And it would be too late for Irene and Mabel and Tina and all those people lying on cots in the Cow Tunnels. And it would be too late for me, because even if I survived the day, I could never live with myself knowing that I'd been right there and done nothing.

Nothing else mattered. I channeled my anger, my fear, my sadness, my fury, and pushed them into the Rage.

The world bled red again.

I plowed through the crowd, firing at Zetas. When one got too close, I stabbed him with the knife hidden in my belt. Another grabbed me around the waist. I head-butted him. Then I dug my fingers into his eyes.

I reached out again with my power. Their minds were blocked; the Zetas must have taken the serum. But in the Rage, everything seemed simpler. My ability was will-based. No serum should change that. I was the biggest, baddest thing here.

They can't stop me.

I pushed harder. When I felt the weak flickering of their minds, I reached out and grabbed them as tightly as I could, throwing everything I had into the command: kill yourselves.

The Zetas froze for a moment. Then one of them dove off the roof, on the side where there was nothing to stop him but the ground hundreds of feet below. Several others turned their own weapons on themselves. The few remaining Zetas just collapsed.

Tina had made her way back up the steps, cradling her damaged arm to her chest. She put her fingers to the throat of one of the fallen Zetas. "They're dead," she said.

"Yes."

"You're bleeding."

"Probably." Couldn't feel it. I kicked in the door of the pod.

Twelve people sat around a rectangular table. "Who's in charge?"
No one answered. "Tell me who's in charge."

A man at the end of the table stood up. The Chairman. Even through
the haze of the Rage, it struck me how normal he seemed. Middle-aged,
balding, paunchy. Was I expecting a Bond villain with metal teeth and an
eye patch? Instead, I was facing an ordinary-looking middle-aged man and
his minions in a conference room with a world clock on the wall and one of
those motivational posters with a picture of a flying eagle on the wall. "Tell
me about the nanovirus."

His mind fought against me, and I still had to push against the effects
of the serum. But finally, I felt his mind crack, and words spilled out of his
mouth: about its creation, about the scientists who worked on the project,
about how I was the perfect vector to spread the infection.

Irene stumbled in as he was speaking. Blood covered her shirt, and there
was a barely healed slash across her neck, but she was alive. Supernatural
healing had its perks.

As the Rage receded, my injures began to hurt badly. I felt like someone
was crushing my head with a vise. The last wisps of my power clung to the
Chairman. "Do you have what you need?" I asked Irene.

"I think so," she said.

"Good." And then I collapsed.

CHAPTER TWENTY-FOUR
Dale

I WOKE UP BACK IN THE Cow Tunnels.

The muddy-looking brick walls hadn't changed, nor had the bare bulbs hanging overhead. But for the first time in the time I'd been there, the place felt…clean. There were no medical supplies scattered around the room, nor did it smell like pee and vomit. A fan stood in the corner of the room, circulating the stagnant air. It looked like it came from the Sharper Image catalog…as opposed to Soviet Russia. An improvement, to say the least.

Every bone in my body weighed a ton. An IV bag dripped into my arms, and several machines monitored my heart rate, my blood pressure, and other things I couldn't make sense of. I managed to roll my head and look over the side of the bed. A bag filled with urine hung from a hook there, in plain sight of anyone who walked into the room. Ew. Guess I was not having a good day.

The door opened, and Irene walked in. Guess that shouldn't have surprised me. "We've got to stop meeting like this."

She froze, unable to hide the shock on her face. "You're awake."

"Seems like it. How long have I been out?"

She hesitated. "Two and a half months."

———————◆———————

MY BRAIN HAD IMPLODED. AT least, that's what Irene told me, and since she wasn't exactly known for her sense of humor, I had the terrible feeling that she wasn't exaggerating. Forget Christmas. I'd missed New Year's and Valentine's Day, and now the orderlies were betting on which holiday I'd wake up for.

"Which one did you pick?" I asked Irene. "Easter? Mother's Day?"

"Honestly...I wasn't sure you'd wake up at all."

But my actions had turned the tide that day, and somehow, miraculously, we had won the fight. The Chairman and the rest of the leadership council had been executed, and our computer techs had managed to extract additional information from their computer files. Between the Zetas' data and my on-demand DNA, it had been enough: Irene had managed to synthesize a compound that neutralized the effects of the nanovirus. She'd been able to treat the afflicted patients, and they'd all gone home.

Tina had come through the battle with just a broken arm, but Mabel had been in bad shape. At first, it wasn't clear who was in *worse* shape when we returned, Mabel or me. But Mabel had woken up just a few days after our return to New York, exhausted and sore but otherwise no worse for wear. Tina had been so overjoyed when she awoke that she promised Mabel she'd never fight again. "I don't think she'll be able to keep that promise," Irene told me. "That woman was meant to lead armies. It's in her soul. Tina shouldn't deny that part of herself."

"Mabel just worries about her," I said.

"Yeah, but it wasn't Tina who had to be dragged away from the Zetas' headquarters unconscious." She sighed. "Immortal isn't unkillable. I think sometimes we take life for granted, those of us who have immortality. It's easy to forget how quickly it can be taken away."

Covington hadn't survived. I was hoping I'd imagined that part, but nope; he'd been killed by a Zeta's rifle while saving one of our people. He was too old, and too frail, and too Goddamn *mortal*, and he never should have been involved in the battle at all…but he'd died a hero. Or maybe he'd died because he cared enough to sacrifice his life to save a girl he'd never met before, who probably had no business being there, either. He'd said it was never wrong to care about people, but I had to wonder whether it was worth it. Isaac had died trying to be a hero, too, because he'd cared. But even as I wondered, I knew it was way too late. I'd almost killed myself controlling the minds of those Zetas, because I'd cared, and I'd do it again if necessary. I'd never wanted to be a hero, but I couldn't just sit around and do nothing when doing *something* was an option. But when I thought about what it cost, what I'd lost…it pretty much sucked.

As for John…when I finally got the courage to ask about him, I found out he'd recovered shortly after the treatment was administered. He hadn't been sick as long as many of the others, so he'd bounced back faster. Once the patients started to get better, the truce between the angels and demons started to break down almost immediately, and the angels returned to wherever the angels went when we weren't working together anymore. "So why haven't you moved hospitals?" I asked.

"Because I don't care about some millennia-long grudge between angels and demons. I'm a doctor—the only doctor, that I know of, that specializes in supernaturals and their genetics. And the genetics don't differentiate: angels and demons are exactly the same. I don't care whether they think otherwise."

So John was gone. I don't know what I expected—that he would hold a vigil at my bedside the way I had at his. Please. I'd almost let myself forget for a minute, but I'd known how it really was since the night he killed my mother. He'd chosen taking control of the Thrones over me. He'd chosen his revenge over me. He'd chosen everything except me.

When I woke up, I was so weak that I couldn't even get out of bed on my own. Supernaturals, I found out, were not immune to muscle atrophy. My mind-control powers were MIA. The massive amounts of energy I'd used at

Zeta HQ had fried me so badly that I didn't even have enough mojo left for a game of Simon Says. Irene assured me that my powers would return, in time. My brain had been focused on healing the critical injuries first, and after the battle it had been bleeding so badly that my first MRI had looked like wonton soup. After a few months of healing—and the placement of a catheter in my skull that allowed the excess blood to drain out and left me with a shaved patch on the back of my head—my brain had ceased to look like food products, which was good news. Everything else would get back to normal in time.

I hoped.

It took three days to convince Irene that I would be better off recovering at home than stuck underground. Even then, I couldn't make it across the room without assistance, so Irene made me use a walker that I'd previously only seen little old ladies using, the ones that usually had tennis balls stuck to the legs.

I sought out Irene before I left. I found her in her makeshift office, a small room overcrowded with medical texts and manila folders stuffed with paper. It had the same dull stone walls and the same overhead lights as the rest of the Cow Tunnels, but Irene had warmed it up a bit by putting a Marvin the Martian lamp on her desk. It was almost…homey. "I wouldn't have taken you for a Looney Tunes fan."

"What…oh." She brushed some dust off the lampshade, a soft smile on her face. "My husband was. I bought this for him years ago as an anniversary present. He could do a dead-on imitation of Marvin. It always made me laugh."

I could hear the affection bleeding through her every word. "I'm so sorry about what happened to him."

"I just keep thinking that if I'd been faster, if I'd worked harder."

I pulled up a chair next to Irene's desk and patted her on the shoulder. "You can't blame yourself. Without you, all those people would have died. You saved everybody."

"Did I? I'm not sure about that." She pulled the elastic band out of her hair and unleased her curls. She looked like she'd been riding around with the window down. On an airplane. "I was able to cure the symptoms, but the nanovirus is still in people's systems—it's just dormant right now. And I still can't get past the fact that only five percent of the infected got sick. If the purpose was to sicken us, why release a virus that's so ineffective?"

I shrugged. "Maybe it just didn't do its job very well."

"Technology like that would have cost millions, maybe billions, in research and development. But they couldn't manage something that would give the other ninety-five percent of us so much as the sniffles?"

I sighed. "All right, so maybe all the rest of us will end up developing shingles or something. But that's a problem for another day. Go home. We won. You did good."

For the first time, Irene smiled at me. "So did you. You are…more than I gave you credit for."

I bit my lip, hesitating. "So, uh…I wanted to tell you that the website you and Mabel put together to connect demons was a really good idea. I mean, there's no way we would have won the fight without it."

Irene nodded. "I've been wanting to make the demon community more interconnected for a long time, but it was Mabel who came up with the means. Those of us born before the twentieth century sometimes have difficulty keeping up with the new technology, and honestly, if it's not medical-related I don't even bother trying."

"Well I was just going to say that I think it's a good idea to keep it going…even when, you know, we're not all in danger of dying. And I'd really like to be part of that effort. If it would be helpful, that is."

I couldn't read Irene's expression. "Were you planning to stay in New York for a while?"

"I can."

Irene tapped her pen against the desk. "So Mabel and I plan to meet next week to discuss the way ahead with the site and how to get more of the demon world connected. You could come."

After two months in a coma, even my facial muscles were stiff with disuse. But in spite of that, for the first time since I woke up, I grinned. "I would like that."

I TOOK A TAXI BACK to Chaz's apartment in Hoboken. I wasn't sure what my reception would be, but to be honest…I wasn't sure where else to go.

When Chaz opened the door, he was wearing lounge pants and a threadbare T-shirt, and his face was smudged with dirt. When I shuffled into the apartment, walker in tow, I found myself surrounded by boxes. "Are you moving?"

"Nik paid three-quarters of the rent—must be nice having rich parents—and I can't afford this place without her. I would have left months ago, but after I came back I found out that an 'anonymous benefactor' had paid the next three months of rent."

"Nik." Damn. I should have told her not to connect with her old life in any way. Irene had mentioned that the supernatural community was still hunting her. The more she interfered here, the more she risked getting caught.

"Yeah, of course it was Nik. It was the least she could do after conspiring to kill you and breaking the lease. But now my ninety days are almost up, and I need to find a new place." He sighed. "I've been looking on Craigslist. There's a room in the Bronx available for seven hundred dollars a month. According to the ad, the outside door is triple-bolted and made out of the same material used to construct military tanks. Just what a boy always dreams of!"

I sat down on a clear section of the couch, pushing the walker to the side. "So, uh…maybe you don't have to move."

Chaz frowned. "What do you mean?"

"Covington settled my mother's estate when I was gone last year. I'm the sole heir. Turns out, you can become pretty loaded when you invest wisely for a few millenia."

He cocked an eyebrow. "How loaded?"

To be honest, I hadn't been able to process the implications of the money. All I knew was that I'd never seen a number with so many commas in my life. "Loaded enough to afford three-quarters of the rent on an apartment in Hoboken…or all of it, if you want."

Chaz moved a box filled with anime DVDs and sat down on the couch. When he didn't say anything, I sat down next to him. "I'm going to be sticking around New York to help Irene and Mabel with their demon darknet site. And if you don't want me here, I'll find my own apartment, no big deal. But the truth is, I don't want to be alone. And I don't think you do, either."

He looked down at the floor. "They don't know about what you did for Nik."

"No, they don't."

"But you're working with them?"

"My mom really dropped the ball on uniting the demon world, and the Zetas almost decimated us because of it. But this battle proved that we're more powerful than we realized. We have to keep building on that, otherwise the next threat may take us out completely."

A puzzled expression came over his face.

"Chaz, you saw what happened with Nik, the damage she caused, and that was just one person. If humans find out we exist, it would cause panic. There'd be fighting, and a lot of weapons. We might have powers, but there are more of them than there are of us. And then there's the Thrones… demons might have the numbers, but the Thrones have the training, the weapons, and the money. And if I know John, he's working on bringing more angels into their fold now. We have to be ready, and in order to do that we have to be united. And I can help with that."

Chaz studied me intently. "So what are you, then? Are you Team Human or Team Demon?"

I hesitated, but only for a second. "Why can't I be both?"

———————◇———————

I'D BEEN AT CHAZ'S FOR two weeks when John showed up at the door.

He wore jeans and a Henley top, no jacket in spite of the early spring chill, and he was carrying some kind of potted tree with a bow tied around the trunk. I was alone in the apartment; Chaz had gone to a bar in Manhattan to celebrate St. Patrick's Day with some friends. Seeing as how I didn't drink, and I'd only just been able to make it across the apartment without using the walker in the last few days, I decided to pass.

I thought I'd never see him again. In my astonishment, I said the stupidest thing I could have: "You're here."

"I am." He gave me that tight smile…and damn it all to hell, it still made my knees melt. "Can I come in?"

I let him inside and led him over to the couch. He set the tree down on the floor and sat down. "I heard you decided to stay in New York for a while."

"Yeah, I thought I might." Chaz and I had gone down to the office the week before and updated his lease. We removed Nik's name and added mine. No longer did I have to crash in shitholes that accepted cash and didn't ask questions. I'd dusted off the identity documents Covington had given to me after my mom died. Dale Highland was a real person now, with a checking account and a driver's license and a Social Security Number.

"You'll be working with Dr. Kordova?"

"Yeah, if we don't kill each other first." I'd already met with Irene and Mabel, plus a few other people they'd assembled to work with us. It had been…interesting. Irene had ideas, and I had ideas, and we both liked to express them. Loudly. In spite of everything, I was amazed at how intelligent she was, and not just about medical stuff. The sheer volume of knowledge she had about demons and the supernatural world astounded me. She was a walking, talking supernatural Google. Now that I was getting to know her better, I actually kind of liked her sometimes. The rest of the time, I kind of wanted to beat her senseless, but it seemed to be working for us. The darknet's site user reach had already expanded 15 percent since the battle, and we'd started releasing new content weekly to keep people updated on any news or information important to the demon world.

"I'm sure you'll make it work." He shifted in his seat, betraying a nervousness that I rarely saw in him. "I got you something. Sort of a housewarming present." He gestured to the tree beside him. "It's a ficus. It's, uh, it's pretty easy to take care of. Just keep it away from drafts and direct sunlight, and make sure you water it when the soil gets dry."

"You got me a ficus."

"Well, I thought, since you'd be staying in one place for a while, you might want something to make it feel more...homey."

He doesn't come to see me when I'm in a coma, and now he has the nerve to show up with a houseplant? I resisted the urge to throw his damn ficus across the room, because the poor plant didn't have anything to do with John being a gigantic ass. Instead, I picked it up and took it into my bedroom, the room that Nik had formerly occupied. Over the past few weeks, Chaz and I had packed up all of her stuff and taken it to a self-storage place in Jersey City. Chaz didn't have the heart to throw anything away. For Nik's sake, I hoped she never returned to claim any of it, but for Chaz's sake, I hoped he always believed that she might.

But it left me with a room that was decidedly minimalistic at the moment: nothing but a bed, a dresser, and a bookcase that only had four books in it. When Chaz had offered to take me shopping to get some things to make the room more personal, I'd told him I was tired. But the truth was, I felt overwhelmed by the idea of personalizing the space. Things like wall decorations and throw rugs were impractical expenses when you might have to go on the run again at any moment, and I spent so many years pretending to be someone else that I wasn't even sure what I liked anymore.

I set the ficus on the floor next to the bookcase. Already, just that little splash of color seemed to warm the room up, make it feel a little more homey.

I decided I liked it.

John dug his hands into his pockets and relaxed his shoulders a little. Had that deceptively casual pose of his ever fooled anyone? It had never fooled me. "It's a nice room. It's big. You could probably fit a desk or a chair over there, if you wanted. And maybe you could get some paintings, or a few more—"

"What do you want, John?" I was tired, and I was starting to get a headache—a more common occurrence since I'd woken from the coma.

"I just…I wanted to see that you were all right."

I sat down on the bed and rested my head against the wall. "You had two months to see whether I was all right! You didn't bother."

"Wait, Kordova didn't…" He closed his eyes and sighed. "It's complicated, Dale."

"It always is with us, isn't it?" I shook my head. "Are you okay? The last I saw you, you were delirious and strapped to a hotel bed."

He smiled softly. "Yes, I'm all right. Between the information retrieved during the battle and the DNA you'd already provided, Kordova was able to develop a treatment pretty quickly. It took about two weeks to work its way through my system, but there don't seem to be any lingering effects from the illness. Everyone recovered."

"Everyone who hadn't died already." I couldn't hide the bitterness in my voice.

"That's on the Zetas. And I'd say they've paid for their crimes." I didn't respond. "I heard about what you did during the battle. You were a hero that day."

"I made a lot of people die. Doesn't feel very heroic to me."

"I know. But you saved a lot of people. You can feel good about that. Sometimes the right thing to do is also the hardest."

I closed my eyes. "John, I'm awfully tired. I think you should go now."

"All right. But there's one more thing I want to tell you."

When I opened my eyes, I found him crouched down next to me, looking deeply into my eyes. He kissed my cheek, just the slightest of brushes against my skin. "You have always mattered to me."

EPILOGUE
Dale

IT WAS A SUNNY SATURDAY afternoon when it happened.

Chaz and I had just gotten off the subway in Times Square when all the cell phones in the area made that screeching noise to indicate some kind of emergency. Thinking it was a weather warning or one of those missing kid alerts, I pulled the phone out of my purse to check it. But the screen was black, and no amount of button-pushing could convince it to come back on again. I heard Chaz curse. "Stupid thing. Not again. C'mon, Verizon, what am I paying you for?" I looked around. One glance confirmed that dozens of other people in the street were simultaneously fiddling with their cell phones, identical frustrated looks on their faces.

Then the video screens in Times Square went black.

I had no idea that thousands of people could go silent at the same time, but that's what seemed to happen as we all stared up at the blank screen.

And then a face appeared. A face I recognized.

Nik.

She'd dressed conservatively, in a button-down blouse and black jacket, and her tattoos were all covered with makeup or cinematic magic. She stood behind a podium, a blue curtain behind her. It looked like a room where the president would give a news conference or something—except minus the US seal behind her. But it was the kind of serious, professional setting that would get everyone to snap to attention—and it was now streaming over every video screen and television and cell phone in Times Square.

"Good afternoon," she said. "My name is Nicole Cohen. Until recently I, like most of you, thought we were alone in the world. But then I discovered how wrong I was."

"I thought you said you Obi-Waned her so she couldn't talk about you," Chaz hissed into my ear.

"I thought I had," I replied.

Nik continued. "I belong to an organization called the Zeta Coalition. Our goal is to ensure that humanity maintains its rightful position as the rulers of Earth, and that the creatures among us—the supernaturals—don't overtake us."

People around us started to chuckle. They probably thought this was some weird bit of performance art. Oh thank God, maybe we'd get out of this unscathed yet.

"Unfortunately, the supernaturals recently attacked us and killed most of our leadership. But those of us who remain will continue to fight to ensure that these supernaturals are exposed for what they really are."

I processed through what Nik was saying, and something clicked. "Shit," I whispered to Chaz. "I told her not to talk about angels and demons. I never told her not to talk about *supernaturals.*"

All the power in the world couldn't account for simple human ingenuity. She'd gotten around my mind control on a technicality. I picked up my phone to call John, to call Irene, to call *anyone*, but I couldn't get the call screen to come up. I couldn't even get the damn thing to turn off. Nik's video overtook everything.

"These supernaturals are stronger than us, immortal, and they have powers that no person should have. Some can move things with their minds. Some can change their appearance on a whim. Some can start fires or freeze oceans. Some can even control minds."

I swear, it felt like Nik looked straight at me when she said that.

"You probably don't believe me. And that's understandable. But I can prove it to you. Years ago, the Zetas developed a nanovirus that only infects supernaturals. The supernaturals believe they've cured it. But they're wrong."

"Oh, shit." This couldn't be good.

Nik pushed a button.

Pain ripped through my head as my power flared out in a way it never had before. I could feel *everyone*. Every mind in Times Square…in the city…maybe in the entire country. Millions of them, billions, all crushing against mine.

Distantly, I heard Chaz's voice. "Dale? Dale, are you all right?" Maybe he put his hand on my shoulder, but I couldn't tell. I wanted to tell him to go away, to run as fast as he could, but one word from me and the entire city would be on its knees. I closed my eyes and covered my ears—as if that would do anything to keep the minds away—tears streaming down my face. I think I screamed.

I don't know how long it lasted. Probably just a few minutes, but it felt like hours. Then the pressure let up suddenly, and my mind cleared.

I wasn't the only one who looked dazed.

Not far from me, several cars burned in front of the stoplight, and a man gazed down at his hands as if he'd never seen them before. A woman dressed in a Statue of Liberty costume floated off of the ground, before she finally drifted down in front of a stunned crowd. A child, who couldn't have been more than about five, sobbed. Every fire hydrant within 50-foot radius of her had burst open, flooding the streets.

On the video screens, footage played. In front of the Eiffel Tower, a man sprouted wings and flew to the top. In London, a woman shot electrical bolts out of her hands, causing power outages throughout the city. In China, a man caused an earthquake so powerful it produced cracks in the Great Wall.

The footage continued to play, angels and demons in every corner of the Earth, their powers suddenly activating beyond their control, creating damage and chaos wherever they were.

I heard Nik's voice again. "There they are, ladies and gentlemen. They're all over the world, in every country on every continent. They've been right in front of us all along. *This* is what we're up against."

————◇————

ACKNOWLEDGMENTS

I CAN'T BELIEVE I'M DONE WITH the second book in the Dale Highland series. It seems like just yesterday I was banging out the original draft of *The Demon Within* on my laptop, but it's been almost eight years since then! So many things have happened, so many things have changed, and yet Dale and John live on.

This was the first book I ever wrote knowing ahead of time that it would be published. So many people helped me get to this point.

First of all, I have to thank my editor, **Robert J. Peterson**. Thank you for always pushing me to be my best self, and the best writer I can be. I am continually amazed at how much better *The Demon Within* became—and how much better *Embracing the Demon* began as—because of your feedback, and because of your devotion to this series.

Carolyn Crane, Jenn Bennett, Joe Alfano, and Jodi Scaife were my very first blurbers/reviewers for The Demon Within, and I didn't get a chance to thank them in my last acknowledgements. Thank you for lending your support to my very first book. Some of you have also already blurbed or reviewed Embracing the Demon, as well, so I'd like to thank you for continuing to support this series.

To **Kristine Chester**: Thank you for your valuable insights and thoughts, and for sharing some of your own experiences with me. I am really grateful that you opened up to me, and you have no idea how much you helped me in the development and revision of the book.

To my brother, **C.J. Woodward**—one of the few things I'm thankful for, after our mom's death, is that we've developed a closer relationship. We don't have much in common, but I know you always have my back. Thank you for being an early reader and supporter of my work, even when the subject matter got a little bit…awkward. (Along those lines, maybe you should just go ahead and skip to the end of chapter one. You're welcome.)

I'm so lucky that, when I got married, I gained the coolest in-laws ever—many of whom have been among my biggest early supporters and fans. (Seriously: who else has a father-in-law who recites the ISBN number of their book in his wedding toast?) You guys are awesome. Thank you for welcoming me into your families.

And last but not least, to my husband, **Jason**: thank you for being my cheerleader, my confidant, and my inspiration. Thank you for letting me gripe when I was frustrated with the process, and thank you for encouraging me when I needed it. Also thank you for lending so much of your crazy brain to the storming process that I still kinda sorta think you deserve a co-writer credit! But mostly, just thank you for being you.

ABOUT THE AUTHOR

BETH WOODWARD has always had a love for the dark, the mysterious, and all things macabre. At twelve, she discovered the wonders of science fiction and fantasy when she read *A Wrinkle in Time,* which remains the most influential book of her life. Growing up, she was Meg Murray with a dash of Oscar the Grouch. She's been writing fiction since she was six years old; as a cantankerous kid whose family moved often, the fictional characters she created became her friends. As an adult, she's slightly more well adjusted, but she still withdraws into her head more often than is probably healthy.

When she's not writing, Beth enjoys traveling, going to sci-fi and fantasy conventions, watching movies, and reading voraciously. She is a rabid *Doctor Who* fan and spends a lot of time with the two cats whose household she shares. She currently lives in the Washington, D.C. area.